W9-CMP-007

The Tidal Poole

Karen Harper

The Tidal Poole

WHEELER
PUBLISHING, INC.
ROCKLAND, MA

★ AN AMERICAN COMPANY ★

Published in Large Print by arrangement with Delacorte Press, a division
of Random House, Inc., in the United States and Canada.

Wheeler Large Print Book Series.

Set in 16 pt Plantin.

Library of Congress Cataloging-in-Publication Data

Harper, Karen (Karen S.)
    The tidal poole: an Elizabeth I mystery / Karen Harper.
        p. (large print) cm.(Wheeler large print book series)
    ISBN 1-56895-894-3 (hardcover)
    1. Elizabeth I, Queen of England, 1533-1603—Fiction. 2. Great
Britain—History—Elizabeth, 1558-1603—Fiction. 3. Queens—Fiction.
4. Large type books. I. Title. II. Series

[PS3558.A624792 T54   2000b]
813'.54—dc21

00-039865
CIP

I want to give special thanks for research or resources to

Dorothy Auchter, the Ohio State University Library

Dr. Geoffrey Smith, Rare Books and Manuscripts, the Ohio State University Library

Kathy Lynn Emerson, author and researcher extraordinaire.

Thanks to Tracy Devine for the wonderful support, fresh ideas to enrich the era, and for loving Elizabeth too.

Much gratitude to Sara Narins for her hard work and enthusiasm to help launch this series.

As always, love to Don for the jaunts to and walks through England.

1533 Henry VIII marries Anne Boleyn,
January 25.
Elizabeth born, September 7.

1536 Anne Boleyn executed.
Elizabeth disinherited from
crown.
Henry weds Jane Seymour.

1537 Prince Edward born.
Queen Jane dies of childbed fever.

1538 John Dudley suggests a marriage
between Thomas Seymour
and Mary Sidney, widow of
Henry VIII's illegitimate son,
Henry, Duke of Richmond;
rumors that she is Thomas's
mistress.

1543 Henry VIII weds sixth wife,
Katherine Parr, who brings
Elizabeth to court.

1544 Act of succession and Henry
VIII's will establish Mary and
Elizabeth in line of succession.

1546 John Dudley, Duke of
Northumberland, again fails
to have Thomas Seymour wed
Mary, Duchess of Richmond.

1547 Henry VIII dies.

Edward VI crowned; Edward
Seymour, Duke of Somerset,
his uncle, becomes his pro-
tector.
Thomes Seymour, King
Edward's younger uncle, weds
Henry's widow, Queen
Dowager Katherine Parr, in
secret.
John Harington enters Thomas
Seymour's service.
Seymour tries to seduce Elizabeth
in Parr's household; when
Katherine Parr catches them
kissing, Elizabeth is sent
away.

1548 Katherine Parr dies in childbirth.
Thomas Seymour makes over-
tures to Elizabeth, who
rebuffs him.
Thomas Seymour tries to court
Jane Grey.
Thomas Seymour's attempted
coup fails to gain control of
King Edward.

1549 Thomas Seymour arrested for
treason.
John Harington accompanies
Seymour to Tower.
Elizabeth, questioned about
complicity in Seymour plot,
denies it.

$\mathcal{T}$HE $\mathcal{B}$EGINNING

Thomas Seymour beheaded; Harington released.

Edward Seymour ousted from power as Lord Protector by John Dudley, Duke of Northumberland, father of Robert Dudley.

1550 Robert Dudley, age seventeen, weds Amy Robsart.

1552 Edward Seymour executed.

1553 Lady Jane Grey forced to wed Guildford Dudley.

King Edward dies.

Mary Tudor overthrows Northumberland's attempt to put Protestant Queen Jane Grey and her husband, Guildford Dudley, Northumberland's son, on throne.

Robert Dudley sent to Tower for his part in rebellion.

Queen Mary I crowned.

Northumberland executed.

Queen Mary weds Prince Philip of Spain by proxy; he arrives in England in 1554.

Queen Mary begins to force England back to Catholicism.

1554 John Harington weds Elizabeth's Lady Isabella Markham.

Protestant Wyatt Rebellion fails, but Elizabeth implicated.

Jane Grey and Guildford Dudley beheaded.

Elizabeth sent to Tower for two months, accompanied by Kat Ashley, John and Isabella Harington.

Henry Grey, Duke of Suffolk ("Queen" Jane's father), executed for his part in Wyatt Rebellion, after being previously pardoned for his part in Jane Grey plot.

Two weeks after her husband's death, Frances Grey, Duchess of Suffolk, weds her horse master, Adrian Stokes.

1555- Elizabeth lives mostly in rural
1558 exile as queen sickens.

1558 Mary dies; Elizabeth succeeds to throne, November 17.

Elizabeth appoints William Cecil Secretary of state.

Robert Dudley made Master of the Queen's Horse.

1559 Elizabeth crowned in Westminster Abbey, January 15.

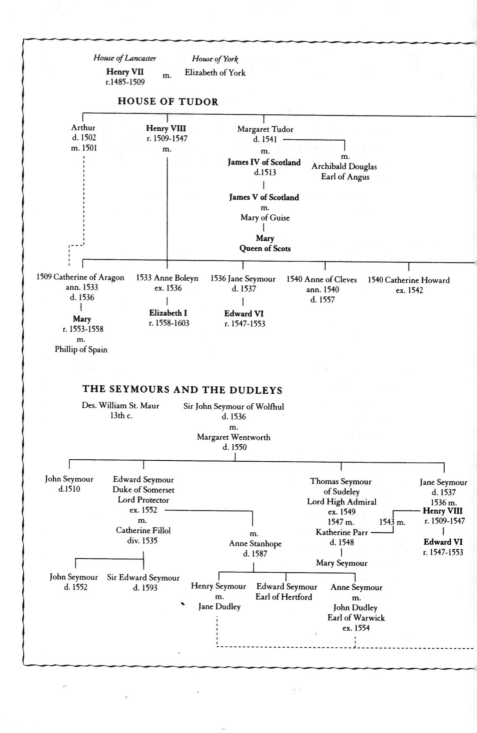

House of Lancaster   *House of York*
Henry VII   m.   Elizabeth of York
r.1485-1509

HOUSE OF TUDOR

Arthur   **Henry VIII**   Margaret Tudor
d. 1502   r. 1509-1547   d. 1541
m. 1501   m.   m.
                                              James IV of Scotland   m.
                                                      d.1513   Archibald Douglas
                                                                      Earl of Angus

                                              James V of Scotland
                                                      m.
                                              Mary of Guise

                                                  Mary
                                              Queen of Scots

1509 Catherine of Aragon   1533 Anne Boleyn   1536 Jane Seymour   1540 Anne of Cleves   1540 Catherine Howard
        ann. 1533   ex. 1536   d. 1537   ann. 1540   ex. 1542
        d. 1536   d. 1557

        Mary   **Elizabeth I**   **Edward VI**
    r. 1553-1558   r. 1558-1603   r. 1547-1553
        m.
Phillip of Spain

THE SEYMOURS AND THE DUDLEYS

Des. William St. Maur   Sir John Seymour of Wolfhul
        13th c.   d. 1536
                                      m.
                              Margaret Wentworth
                                  d. 1550

John Seymour   Edward Seymour   Thomas Seymour   Jane Seymour
    d.1510   Duke of Somerset   of Sudeley   d. 1537
                  Lord Protector   Lord High Admiral   1536 m.
                    ex. 1552   ex. 1549   **Henry VIII**
                        m.   1547 m.   1543 m.   r. 1509-1547
                  Catherine Fillol   m.   Katherine Parr
                    div. 1535   Anne Stanhope   d. 1548   **Edward VI**
                                              d. 1587   r. 1547-1553
                                                          Mary Seymour

John Seymour   Sir Edward Seymour   Henry Seymour   Edward Seymour   Anne Seymour
    d. 1552   d. 1593   m.   Earl of Hertford   m.
                                          Jane Dudley   John Dudley
                                                                            Earl of Warwick
                                                                              ex. 1554

Mary Tudor
d. 1533
m.

is XII of France
d. 1514

m.
Charles Brandon Duke of Suffolk
d. 1545

Frances Brandon
Duchess of Suffolk
d. 1559

m.
Adrian Stokes

m.
Henry Grey
Duke of Suffolk
ex. 1554

1543 Katherine Parr
d. 1548
m.
Thomas Seymour of Sudeley
Lord High Admiral

Jane Grey   Katherine Grey   Mary Grey
Queen 1553
ex. 1554
m.
Guildford Dudley
ex. 1554

Mary Seymour

John Dudley
Duke of Northumberland
Lord Protector
ex. 1553
m.
Jane Guildford

Ambrose Dudley   Guildford Dudley   Mary Dudley
Earl of Warwick   ex. 1554   m.
d. 1590   m.   Henry Sidney
                                Jane Grey
                                Queen1553
            Henry Dudley   ex. 1554   Robert Dudley   Catherine Dudley
                                                 Earl of Leicester
                                                        m.
                                                  Amy Robsart

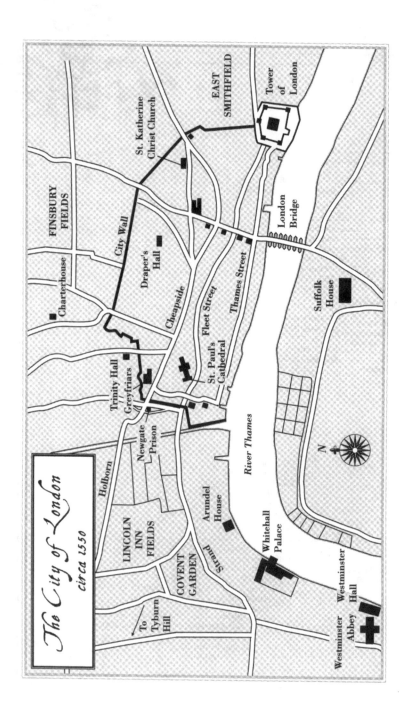

The City of London
circa 1550

FINSBURY FIELDS

EAST SMITHFIELD

Tower of London

St. Katherine Christ Church

City Wall

London Bridge

Charterhouse

Draper's Hall

Cheapside

Fleet Street

Thames Street

Suffolk House

Trinity Hall
Greyfriars

St. Paul's Cathedral

Newgate Prison

Holborn

River Thames

N

LINCOLN INN FIELDS

Arundel House

To Tyburn Hill

COVENT GARDEN

Strand

Whitehall Palace

Westminster Hall

Westminster Abbey

The Prologue

January 13, 1559

"I swear I can still hear cannon booming in my ears from our entry to London," the queen said when her presence chamber finally cleared of courtiers and Kat closed the door behind them. "And from tonight's chatter," she added, shaking her head with a smile. "Oh, Kat, send the guard on the door for Jenks. I am going out."

"Out?" the older woman repeated, surprise plain on her round face. "Out where? The Thames breeze bites cold this late, and Lord Cecil said it's spitting snow."

"Out for a breath, to clear my head. And simply because I can go where I will with no more wardens—even in this place."

Twenty-five-year-old Elizabeth Tudor had been queen scarcely two months and in that time had come to London in triumph from her life in rural exile. Queen Mary had been buried with pomp befitting her station, though most people hated her for burning Protestants and bankrupting the treasury with her Spanish husband's foreign wars. But Elizabeth was all English, a vibrant new beginning, and the whole country rang with her praise.

Kat bustled to fasten an ermine-edged cloak about the queen's slender shoulders and fetch her fur-lined gloves. Katherine Ashley, called affectionately Kat, was Elizabeth's longtime

1

companion, for she had been governess, lady-in-waiting, and the only mother the former princess could remember. Now First Lady of the Bedchamber, Kat was proud but even more protective.

"I shall accompany you," she declared with a decisive nod of her gray head.

"Not now. But for Jenks I go alone. He is the only one I know who will not talk, dearest Kat. I need some silence. Do not fret as I am but going to church in peace."

She kissed Kat's wrinkled cheek, then went to the door to send for Jenks herself. The excitement and so many new people had befuddled Kat of late, for she had worn herself out fearing her mistress would not live long enough to claim her kingdom.

"Send Stephen Jenks to me from Lord Robert Dudley's men," Elizabeth commanded the guard but did not shut the door. She preferred doors and windows open here, for this was the place she still dreaded most on earth.

The Tower. The Tower of London. Tradition decreed a new monarch spend a week here in the state apartments to be followed by triumphal procession to Westminster Palace on the morrow and the coronation in the Abbey the next day. So, she thought, she was yet a prisoner of privilege and power.

Jenks came running so fast he skidded into the room. Her young man, who had served her well in exile, had a sword at his side and a pistol stuck in his belt, for Elizabeth's Master of the Horse, Robert Dudley, was much enamored

2

of firepower. And, she thought, with a stiff-lipped smile, Robert—her dear Robin—seemed much enamored of the firepower that crackled between them with nary a weapon in sight.

"To me, Jenks," she said, and swept out past her red-and-gold-liveried sentinels.

"*Outside?*" Jenks asked, wheeling around to follow her. His blue eyes widened under his thick brown hair, low-cut across his broad forehead. Though he was tall and strong, he had to stretch his strides to match hers in the long hall. Jenks's wit was for horses, but his strong arm and devotion were entirely hers. "This late at night?" He demanded the obvious.

"And I told Kat you would obey without a word." She sighed and shook her head to rattle her pearls under her hood.

The queen set a fast pace with guards scrambling to unbolt and unlock doors before her. What a heady joy to go where one would after years of rural manor cages, she exulted. And yet the dear soul she was going to see was imprisoned within these gray stone walls eternally.

As she headed toward the small church across the inner ward, a crisp river breeze bucked against her and curled into her clothes. The Thames lay still unfrozen, murmuring in its reach into the moat and water landing called Traitor's Gate. Elizabeth felt chilled clear through.

Though torches and lanterns guttered and glimmered along the thick stone walls, she shuddered and wrapped her cloak closer, not against the air but her own thoughts. In flickering shadow loomed the Bell Tower, where her sister had shut her up during the Protestant Wyatt Rebellion. Along the walls stretched the parapet she'd walked for exercise and from which she had seen Robin wave forlornly from his prison window. Here on this brittle, frost-etched grass had stood the scaffold where royal prisoners, including her own mother, had been beheaded.

When Jenks saw where she was going, he ran to open the church door. St. Peter in Chains was a small, squat edifice of arched windows under a tower with a bell that tolled for deaths inside these walls.

It was warmer here, the dimness lit by thick altar candles and four large lanterns. "Wait outside. Let no one enter," she told Jenks, dropping her hood from her coiffed and jeweled head. "I will not be long."

She went straight down the center aisle toward the high altar. Her mother, Anne Boleyn, the former queen of England, had no tomb, for King Henry had ordered her severed head and body quickly interred but a few paces from the scaffold where she died. At the last minute—Elizabeth had later learned, for then she was but three—her mother's murderers had borrowed an elm box that had held arrows and put her in that and under these paving stones in the chancel. The site was yet unmarked but for the scars on her daughter's heart.

One hand on the altar, Elizabeth knelt,

4

then sat back on her heels, smashing her thick skirts. She would not bow nor curtsy to anyone again, but all this must be put away: the bitterness, the deep-buried anger at her father and her sister and those who had once declared her Anne Boleyn's bastard.

"Mother, 'tis I, Bess," she whispered in a wavering voice. "Your Bess grown and now queen in my own right with no husband to obey or please. I am taking your badge of white falcon on the tree stump for my own to let them know my pride in Boleyn heritage as well as Tudor."

Her words hardly echoed to the dark-beamed ceiling overhead. She heard some scraping sound. Had Jenks come inside?

She stared hard at the marble effigies of a knight and his lady wife in the nave, their carved faces staring straight up toward heaven. The sounds must have been her imagination. Shadows shifted and darted from the closest torch. She leaned forward to lay her palm on the dusty, cold paving stone.

"I am King Henry's daughter—they all say that when they see my red hair—but I am yours too with my dark eyes and oval face and long fingers...and your bravery. You died not to brand me bastard, so I swear I—"

Her head jerked around at another sound. A whisper?

"Who goes there?" she demanded, and stood. "Show yourself."

Two men rose like apparitions from behind an effigy of an armored knight. "Forgive us,

Your Majesty," the shorter and slighter of the two said, clearing his throat. "We came in to see the place afore you to visit my father's burial site and didn't want to disturb you, but—"

"I'll not be spied upon. Come here, both of you. Your names?"

She recognized the one who had spoken as he stepped out. Both men appeared slightly younger than she. They came closer and swept her deep bows, the thin speaker gracefully, the taller, sturdier man as if he were a stranger to court ways. Edward Seymour was the one she knew, nephew of Queen Jane, who had followed fast upon Anne Boleyn's death. Edward evidently spoke the truth about why they were here. His father, once Lord Protector of Elizabeth's half brother, the boy king Edward, had been executed in that short reign and lay buried between Queen Anne and Queen Catherine Howard.

Yet who was the other young man? She was certain she should know him, for his rugged face and bold eye glinting in torchlight seemed strangely familiar.

"Your Majesty," Edward was saying with another sweeping bow, "may I present to Your Most Gracious Majesty my cousin Jack St. Maur."

"Ah," she said loudly, as if someone had punched her in the belly. St. Maur was the Norman family from whom the Seymours had descended. "My dear friends John and Isabella Harington's foster lad," she said. "At least I thought you were a lad."

"I am near on twenty-one, Your Grace," Jack said, turning his plumed velvet cap in his big hands. "My own father lies not here with your mother and my uncle, Edward's sire, in the chancel, but back in the jumble of commoners under the floor of the nave."

She turned away to look where he pointed, into deep shadows. Tom Seymour, Lord Admiral of England, also Queen Jane's brother, had once been Elizabeth's protector—and nearly her doom.

She kept her face averted so these strong, young Seymour heirs would not see a queen blink back tears. And she cried because Jack made Tom seem alive again when she had come here to bury the past for good.

Not trusting her voice, she nodded to each, then walked past them. Edward stepped back properly so her cloak and skirts would not touch him. Jack, his muscular legs spread, stood his ground, and her hems brushed heavily against his big, booted feet.

Near the door she called out to them in a firm voice, "And where will you be on the morrow for my royal progress through the city, lads?"

"On the Strand, Your Grace," Edward answered. "Lord Arundel has invited quite a party to view it from his gatehouse windows."

"They call it Arundel House." Jack's deep voice rang out. "But it used to be Seymour House, my father's, my real father's."

Elizabeth turned to the double doors and rapped once for Jenks to open them. "Much used to be your father's," she muttered to herself.

She clasped her gloved hands hard together and pressed them to her breasts as she plunged back out into the cold.

Chapter The First

The main thoroughfare of London was awash with banners, pennants, and brocade bunting on the new queen's recognition day. Despite the cold, in a canopied, open litter borne by white mules, Elizabeth Tudor rode the adulation of her people through the swirls of their hurrahs. Down Fleet Street to where crowds poured into the Strand, she glittered in her gown and mantle of cloth of gold.

Like a great tide came her red-coated gentlemen pensioners with ceremonial battle-axes, then squires, footmen, and men mounted on a thousand prancing horses. Behind her rode Robert Dudley, her handsome Master of the Horse, mounted on a charger and leading her unmounted horse, which was covered with golden cloth. The members of her Privy Council, her governors, and her lieutenants seemed swept along in her broad wake.

The royal progress took all day, for the queen bade her cavalcade halt when someone in the crowd tendered an herbal nosegay or held up a baby. At certain sites proud citizens enacted play scenes, presented pageants and recitations, or sang madrigals. Despite the constant pealing of church bells, the Queen's Majesty stood to make impromptu speeches. The crowd would hush to hear, then blast the wintry air with roars louder than the river churning under London Bridge.

"Why did you bring me here, Meg?"

With all the noise Ned Topside had to put his mouth to Margaret Milligrew's ear so she could hear him. His warm breath made her shiver.

Looking for a good place to see their queen pass by for a third time, they had spent an hour elbowing their way ahead through crowds along the back entrances to the grand houses along the Strand. Part of Elizabeth's household, Meg and Ned had already seen her as she departed the Tower and again as she went by on Fleet Street.

"Don't exactly know why here," Meg shouted back. "But it seems a fine spot with that triumphal arch they built. She'll have to halt, we'll catch her eye, and she'll know we're with her all the way."

She saw Ned's green eyes narrow when he caught her darting glances overhead at a hanging apothecary sign of a painted Turk's head with a gilded pill on his extended tongue. She wasn't sure why that sign intrigued her so, but it did. She liked this area. Several people had smiled and greeted her, though most kept their eyes on the street.

"That apothecary's not going to be open today," Ned chided, shoving her along with a hand on her back, "so just forget dragging me in to see what herbs they sell." He took her elbow and pulled her along. "Since you've got me this far, we need to find a tree or windowsill to see in this stew of people. Ah, but what a fine crowd this would make for an audience if our queen would but let me make a speech and recite a scene along the way today."

Meg could barely hear his words when huzzahs swelled again. As ever, she felt Ned's mere touch, even an angry one, clear down in the pit of her belly. Of course, it could be caused by her melancholy since they all had to live in London now. Meg both mistrusted the place and felt its pull—just like with Ned Topside.

"Can't see someone called Queen's Fool putting on such airs," she scolded.

"That's the pot calling the kettle black. Your face lit like a yuletide candle when Her Grace said you are to have a stipend for being Strewing Herb Mistress of the Privy Chamber. Gads, you'd think she'd given you Cecil's lofty title."

"At least," she shouted back, "just like in the country, we're all still her Privy Plot Council. Her Grace promised."

Ned rolled his eyes. "You think a queen will have the time or cause to unravel plots or murder schemes like the one that almost got us poisoned? Besides, doesn't all this show she'll have smooth sailing?" he asked with a gesture so broad he knocked a blue-coated apprentice on the back of the head.

The burly lad turned, a grin on his broad face but fists up, evidently spoiling for a good fight. "Oh it's you, mistress," he blurted when he saw Meg.

"Oh, aye, it's her all right," Ned said,

playing along. "Come on, then," he ordered, yanking her after him, this time by the wrist, through the press of people. "I guess I've got to save you from that stale come-hither line 'Haven't we met before, my fine lady?' "

Suddenly Meg decided, as Her Grace always put it, to show her mettle. She jerked free from Ned's grasp and stood erect with her chin thrust out when he rounded on her again.

"Just stick with me, my man, and I'll get us a good place up front to see. Follow me, if you please.

"Stand aside, clear the way for the Lord Banbury," she called out in her best imitation of Elizabeth's crisp, clear, ringing voice, with tone and enunciation Ned had taught her. "You there, churl, Lord Banbury's coming through." Gaping, people parted for them as if they had the plague.

"Who in the deuce is Lord Banbury?" Ned asked out of the side of his mouth when they were finally settled on the inner edge of the crowd. They had a prime place just down from Lord Arundel's three-storied gatehouse, which overlooked the street, facing the Ring and Crown Tavern across from it.

"Lord Banbury? Don't have a notion," Meg admitted. "Like you in a pinch, I made him up."

"Look, there's the first of her parade coming!" Ned cried, and threw an arm around Meg's shoulders.

She leaned lightly against him, not daring more, because she still could not remember who she really was. But if she could, she'd probably still want Edward Thompson, alias the queen's new fool and principal player, Ned Topside.

The great lords' houses of the Tudor years stretched between the two main thoroughfares of the city: the Strand, the street that connected the city to Whitehall Palace out their workaday backs, and the busy river out their fine painted and façaded fronts. Barge landings and water stairs lined the river, for the nobles of the lands usually disdained street travel.

Within the deep acreages of the mansions lay stables, gardens, orchards, bowling greens, and lawns. Each property was backed by a tall brick wall with a gatehouse through which came and went carts, carriages, and horses. The gates were now closed against the press of the rabble in the mud-rutted but frozen Strand.

Though Lord Arundel rode in the procession as the queen's Lord Steward, those he'd invited enjoyed the hospitality of his city mansion. As crowd noise from the street swelled, guests strolled toward the gatehouse viewing site along paths lined by a collection of Greek and Roman statues in the frost-blighted gardens.

The older generation of guests was first to climb the stairs to the second story, from which to see the passing panoply. Awaiting them were brass foot warmers and trays with heated wine and plates of comfits.

"Oh, how kind of his lordship," Isabella Harington observed to Lady Frances, the Dowager Duchess of Suffolk. "Drink and sweets to toast our dear queen. And benches so we won't have to stand, for she'll no doubt give a speech after the play scene here, and you know she can speak long and loud, just like her sire."

"Mmph," Frances replied, settling her bulk on the center of the bench at the right window—always the seat of honor at tournaments—while Bella and her husband, John, took the left one. Their winter cloaks and her skirts took up such space that their foster son, Jack, and Bella's sister Penelope would have to stand behind when they arrived, Bella thought.

"Are you quite comfortable, dearest?" Adrian Stokes, Frances's ginger-haired husband, asked, hovering over her. His breath puffed out clouds in the chill when he talked. He was as pleasant-looking a man as Frances was formidable, Bella noted, and hardly deserving of the whispers behind his back, for she blamed that Tudor-blooded harridan Frances for all their troubles.

Adrian was sixteen years younger than Frances. Pregnant with his child, she had wed him but a week after her husband had been executed with their daughter Lady Jane Grey, the nine days' queen, for trying to usurp the crown from Queen Mary. Though Frances had been the wife and mother of traitors, her heritage as King Henry's niece had assured she was treated well. Especially, Bella noted again, by poor Adrian, however rudely she used him.

14

"Shall I fetch Katherine and Mary, my dear?" Adrian was asking, for Frances's two surviving daughters lived with them, and he fretted for their well-being. "They must be dawdling over the statues."

"Or cannot bear to rejoice after what befell their sister and father during the last queen's brief reign," Frances said with a sniff. "Then too, my Katherine is this queen's lawful heir and should be soon recognized as such and not be relegated to—to a gatehouse as if we were all a ragged band of lickspittles."

Frances stared Bella down as if to dare her to repeat that. Bella looked away. She knew Frances was proud, but not that she was foolhardy after she'd almost lost everything four years ago. Or did people not yet realize the power Elizabeth meant to wield and the strength with which she would therefore deal with any hint of a plot?

"Well then, go on," Frances commanded Adrian over the noise outside. "Go see what is keeping the silly chits."

"John," Bella said, plucking at her husband's sleeve, "if Jack and Edward miss this, I shall skin them alive."

"And what about pretty Penny?" John asked, rising so fast his sword clanked and his boots creaked.

His nickname for her younger sister annoyed her, especially in front of the duchess. Penelope was so fair and beguiling that she could pull the wool over any man's eyes.

"Penelope," Bella said, emphasizing each

syllable, "vowed she would be here, so don't bother beating the bushes for her."

John frowned, then followed Adrian down the stairs to gather the latecomers.

"Then wherever," Frances said, still fussing with her hair ribbons, which Bella thought looked entirely silly on a forty-three-year-old dowager, "did Penelope Whyte, Lady Maldon, disappear to—oh, a good half hour ago, while the rest of us finished our repast inside?"

"Did you not hear her say she felt indisposed, duchess," Bella replied, trying to sound pleasant, "and went to lie down?"

"Oh, yes, indeed, lie down," Frances intoned with a smirk to make Bella realize her sister's reputation as a light skirt must be even more far-reaching than she'd feared.

"And I believe you heard her remark," Bella said quickly, hoping to shift subjects, "she adores the idea of a young, fashionable queen, and I'm certain she will be here soon—Penelope, that is, as well as Her Majesty."

"Mmph," Frances snorted again, and slid slightly forward on the bench to peer down at the crowd. "We shall just see, shall we not?"

It was the third painted canvas-over-scaffolding triumphal arch of the day, this one all gilded with flying cherubs, but it pleased Elizabeth mightily. Despite a few snowflakes and a biting wind, she ordered her procession halted and her canopy moved away so that the crowd in the upper windows might see her. Each time she smiled, nodded, or waved, their voices roared to the skies.

She remained seated in her elevated litter, nodding during the short play scene given by adults and children. This crowd, she noted, was a brew of the common folk and their betters. It was obvious that the second and third floors of the taverns and gatehouses commanded the best views. They sprouted courtiers, especially women, for many of the men were in the procession.

Elizabeth smiled and nodded to Meg and Ned when she saw their eager, proud faces in the crowd again, right up in front. Where had she seen them last along the way? When she but closed her eyes, around her spun arches and more arches; the three-storied buildings and gatehouses slanted out over the street to make an arch of people waving pennants all around the triumphal arch. She was getting dizzy with exhaustion as well as exhilaration, and her face muscles ached from smiling. Her nose was starting to run too, but nothing would make her haste away this blessed day.

Then she realized exactly where she was. The wooden and canvas arch had been erected between the homes of the executed Seymour brothers, Edward and Tom. She sniffed hard and forced her mind back to the lengthy recitation of her womanly virtues two children were reciting. When it was over and the cheers swelled again, the queen rose to make a speech of thanks.

"Good people all," she called out.

It took a moment for the crowd to realize she would speak. Some began to shush or shout down others. Behind her someone signaled a trumpet fanfare to quiet everyone.

"Just as the stream of the Strand pours itself into the larger Thames"—her voice rang out as she turned and gestured to both sides of the street—"the stream of your loyalty and love flows now into my new life as queen." She stared out, suddenly awed, over the sea of heads, the men's uncovered, some folks with children on their shoulders. She found her voice again. "I vow to you that in the years to come, with one heart and mind, we shall make our England safe from invaders so we shall live in a new age of peace and profit to you all."

When she nodded and gave a stiff-armed wave, the noise exploded. God knows, she thought, but her people had suffered under Queen Mary. The currency had been devalued, the treasury bled dry, Catholic France and Spain were covetous of her crown and country, and the towns were full of vagrants and unpaid soldiers.

But now she heard trumpets, cheers, a dog barking, horses, and then a woman's shrill shrieks somewhere here in the crowd. One of her mules jerked, and she sat down hard and fast. Two horses ahead whinnied and reared. Suddenly Robert Dudley was at her side, still mounted, leaning toward her at eye level.

"We must push on," he told her. "Some disturbance in the crowd."

Her eyes darted wildly. More than one woman

18

was screaming now. Yet others still cheered and hurrahed as if nothing were amiss. "Robin, show no alarm. Go on but slowly."

He spurred his mount ahead to speak to the man holding the first white mule. Though shaken, Elizabeth sat stoically, still nodding and waving. Robin did not let them halt even when an old woman rushed forward with a nosegay of dried rosemary extended in her upraised hand. He put his horse between the woman and the queen and leaned down to snatch it himself. He laid it in Elizabeth's lap as he rode beside her.

Her thighs tingled where his hand had brushed and where the nosegay lay cradled. She gripped it as her canopy bearers rushed to catch up with her and the litter swayed on, past Arundel House. In the second-storied gatehouse window she glimpsed her dear friends Bella and John Harington, leaning out, smiling, waving wildly as if nothing in the world could ever be amiss again.

"So," Bella said to her husband, "Her Grace looked right at us and smiled. It's a good thing I went to fetch you and Jack, or you'd have missed that."

"You might know," John said, hardly listening, as he brushed again at the smudges and snags on his fine dove gray velvet doublet and hose, "I'd be chased by a rabid dog right through the rosebushes. Can you see Jack out there on the street? He stayed here but a moment before he wanted to be out in the excitement again. It's in his blood." He whispered the last words.

"Silly of the boy," Frances put in as if they had addressed her, "not to watch from here, where he would not be jostled by the rabble."

Frances's daughters, Katherine and Mary Grey, stood stiffly behind her now like ladies-in-waiting. Though she should have been long grown, Mary was a tiny girl, but four feet, almost a dwarf. Katherine was tall and fair of face, but, Bella thought, she might as well have been one of those icy marble statues on these grounds for all the warmth she showed.

And you'd think, Bella fumed silently, considering their dour expressions, the Suffolk party had just watched a funeral cortège. At least Mary had not held back her smile earlier, and Adrian, who'd missed most of the parade anyway, fetching cherry cordials for his ailing wife, had leaned forward to watch and hear the queen's speech avidly, but mayhap that's how he did everything.

"And," Frances said with a sniff, "'tis unforgivable for Penelope to miss this since she was rattling on so about the queen's pretty person, as if one's countenance or gowns have aught to do with being a good queen."

"I'm certain Penelope saw the whole thing from a better vantage point than we." Bella thought she'd best try to defend her sister again, though she was furious with her. "But I must say I'm going to see if she is still unwell. She's excitable and rather hard to bridle—"

"Indeed," Frances muttered, standing with her hands on both Adrian's and Katherine's arms as Edward Seymour walked in, quite out of breath. "I vow," she went on with a sly wink at Edward, "if I ever caught my Katherine dallying about with a young man the way Penel—"

"Enough, duchess," John insisted. "Bella and I are doing our best to counsel her to virtue and wisdom while she resides with us."

Bella nodded, flushed with anger, but her high color was naught next to the hue of boiled radish poor Edward Seymour had taken on. So, Bella thought, and tucked it away in her mind to tell the queen, mayhap young Seymour bore watching with the young woman who was by blood Elizabeth's heir, though Her Majesty would no doubt be loath ever to name her so.

On the stairs, following the Grey party down, John whispered to Bella, "The old raven's right about one thing. We can't leave if Penelope's lying down or gadding about, not with such a crowd outside. But I've no stomach for searching for her after that mad dog came in off the street and nearly bit me. I'd like to have run him through, but the cur went back out through the postern door that stood ajar. And if your sister has run off to some *liaison d'amour,* I'd like to run her through."

"Please, my lord," Bella protested, lifting her index finger to her lips. At least, she thought, only a serving girl edging her way up the stairs could have heard as the duchess's party was chatting among themselves.

"Excuse me, sir, madam," the wench said as she plastered herself against the wall to let her betters pass, "but I saw a fair-haired young lady going upstairs a bit ago."

"That can't be," Bella said. "She never came into the room."

"*Those* stairs," the girl said, pointing upward to the narrowed staircase that went to third-floor garret under the eaves.

"I suppose," John said, "it would be a loftier vantage point, but Arundel said it's full of my Lord Seymour's old boxes and such. I recall," he went on as the Duchess of Suffolk stopped below to look up and listen, "it's where he planned much of his..."

"His rebellion, his treason?" Frances put in, her voice cold as river wind. "Spit it out, man. We've all been touched by both and can only pray there will be none such in this new reign."

"Amen to that," Bella whispered.

John surprised her by tugging away and heading up the steps. Excusing herself, lifting her skirts, Bella hurried after him.

"Penelope, are you up here?" she heard John call.

Dim, dust-drenched, the chill room was gabled with a beamed roof and crowded with waist-high draped boxes covered with old brocade coverlets and velvet curtains. This upper room had broad windows on two sides, yet the shutters were closed but for a single shaft of light that stabbed itself into the floor-boards.

"No one's here or has been," she said, and sneezed. "Let's go look for her at the house."

"It's a damned lot colder up here than below," he said as if he weren't listening again. To her dismay, before she could snatch his arm, he clomped across the wooden floor to throw open a shutter. She sneezed again at the dust he had disturbed and some strange, acrid smell.

It was then Bella saw the familiar shoes peeking out from between two big chests. Satin shoes with legs in them, the buff-hued stockings wrinkled and uncharacteristically loose-gartered. As Bella gasped and leaned forward, bare, splayed thighs came into view. The left one above the knee bore the distinctive rose-shaped birthmark. Layers of petticoats and the green gown were twisted up about naked hips.

John jolted so hard when he saw he jerked back into the shutters to make a hollow bang. He began to retch. But that, like the remnants of crowd noise outside, was drowned by Bella's piercing scream.

Chapter The Second

Where, Elizabeth wondered, was Bella Har-ington? Surely, she dared not be late for this. Of the thirty-nine women lined up behind her, each pulling a sixteen-yard-long train of costly velvet, Bella was missing from her place. Worse, Kat was whispering to Elizabeth's Principal Secretary, William Cecil, who should have been long seated with her Privy Council in the Abbey just a short walk away.

Elizabeth stood bedecked in a cloth of gold and brocade gown. The ermine robes lay so heavy on her slender shoulders that they gave her pause. The Keeper of the Jewels had warned her that the crown would be heavy too, as well as the jewel-encrusted orb and scepter she would touch for the first time in the ceremony this morning.

Did they think because she was a young, slight woman, she could not bear up under all that was to come? As soon as she was crowned, she would set them all straight, and quickly too.

But where was Bella? Elizabeth raised her voice above the excited whispers and constant hum of crowd noise from the packed street outside. "Kat Ashley and Lord Cecil! To me!" Looking as if they'd been caught filching sweets, they came posthaste.

"I warrant *I* am the one who should be overwrought, not you," Elizabeth insisted when he dropped a swift, smooth bow and she a curtsy. "Your countenances could curdle milk. Is there some stir to compare with the mere crowning of the queen? And where is Bella Harington?"

They dared exchange quick looks without answering. Finally Cecil cleared his throat. "She is indisposed, Your Majesty."

"Sore ill? I saw her but yesterday along the route of my procession, looking hale and hearty, her lord too."

"Suddenly ill," Kat put in, gripping her hands along the broad expanse of her waistline. She shot another glance at Cecil. "After the ceremony we'll have time to talk of such."

As if that settled the matter, Kat began to fool with the gold-edged neck ruff Elizabeth wore. She ignored her fussing and stared Cecil down over Kat's bent head. "I have charged you, my lord, not to fail to tell your queen what she must know."

Wily lawyer or not, the man looked surprised. Aha, then, she had guessed something was afoot besides the entire populace of London waiting for her outside these palace doors.

"Your brilliance and perspicacity never cease to amaze me, Your Grace," Cecil said with a nod. "But we did not wish to have anything sully the beauty of this day for you. Bella's younger sister has died under circumstances we are trying yet to ferret out. The matter is in competent hands, and I shall have a complete report for you after the long morning in the Abbey, which must begin now."

"So Bella is not ill but shocked and grieved?"

"Sick at heart," Kat put in.

"I understand. John too, of course." The queen commiserated, realizing how much she had recently profited from her own sister's death.

Bella had also suffered a falling-out with her

sister, Elizabeth recalled, but hardly one as dire or momentous as that between the royal Tudor sisters. She shook her head, which taught her *not* to shake her head. Wearing her long red-gold hair loose to remind them all she was a maiden yet but with her father's blazing hair was all well and good, but her tresses kept snagging in her ruff and crimson cap.

"Kat," she said as her dear friend saw her plight and reached to free her hair, "is it not sad the Haringtons have come so far with me, seen me at my lowest ebb, and then must miss this crest of my life to—"

Her voice caught. The impact of it struck her as the crowd stirred restlessly outside. Her people and her realm awaited. In her heart this was not only a coronation but a marriage ceremony, whether solemn-faced Cecil and her nobles knew it or not. Now they awaited in the vast church, anxious for her to come and be blessed and wear her crown. Her father's crown...her weak, fond brother's...her cruel sister's...

Elizabeth turned away so Kat and Cecil would not see her eyes flood with tears. The wretched Catholic bishops, who feared the Protestant faith she would bring back after Catholic Mary's bloodbath, had refused to crown her, though Cecil had finally found the Bishop of Carlisle to do the deed. With God as her witness, the bishops and the peers of the realm had best learn to fear crossing or displeasing *her*, for she meant to rule for the people's good as well as her own.

She sniffed hard and blinked back womanish tears. With a flick of her wrist Elizabeth indicated she was ready. Kat fell back in place, and Cecil disappeared out a side exit. The massive double doors of the palace opened. The Duchess of Norfolk lifted the young queen's twenty-three-foot mantle of silver and gold so it would not drag. The Earls of Pembroke and Shrewsbury hurried forward to escort her. Elizabeth lifted her chin and squared her shoulders.

She began to walk, trying to bridle this sudden sweep of emotion. *Mother, you should see me today,* she thought as she blinked into the gray sky spitting snow. *Father, Great Henry, I shall care for your kingdom, for the power is now mine.*

She gave not another thought to Bella when the waves of cheers washed over her and the sky split to send a shaft of sun so she seemed to glitter. Despite the dismay of the crimson-coated guards who tried to keep the press of people behind the railings, it amused and moved her to see them cut and rip that blue carpet she had just trod to have a keepsake of their queen.

However solemn the coming ceremony, however twisted the paths that had brought her here, Elizabeth smiled. Even later, when the warm oil of consecration was poured on her head and smelled rancid and the clumsy bishop knocked the crown atilt when it first touched her head, Elizabeth smiled through her tears.

27

But the best was when the bishop turned to the congregation and intoned the traditional question: "Do you, good people of this realm of England, desire this royal person, Elizabeth Tudor, for your lawful, God-given king—ah, queen?"

As if from one throat, the hundreds shouted, "Aye! Aye!"

Drums began to beat, drowning the array of portable organs and fifes. Trumpets blared and bells clanged in the Abbey tower, then spread like wildfire to all city steeples. London rocked with roars.

Still holding her regalia, Elizabeth Tudor stood at the front entrance of the Abbey to show herself to her people. The crown and cape felt light, the orb and scepter mere baubles, the cold day warm. Nothing dire or frightening could ever assail her again, the new-crowned queen told herself, as she nodded and smiled. Absolutely nothing.

"I intend to keep you close and use you for England's service, my dear Harry," the queen told her cousin Henry Carey the next evening. She had just elevated him to the peerage today as Baron, Lord Hunsdon, but he would always be dear Harry. She sniffled and wiped her nose, but not from sentiment, for she had a wretched cold coming on.

Voices buzzed like the sound of the sea as hundreds supped to celebrate her coronation banquet in the great hall at old Westminster

Palace. Feeling everyone's eyes on her, seated in her jewel-encrusted gown in the center of the table on the raised dais, she lifted her goblet in salute to Harry. No more must she hide her affection for her Boleyn kin or anyone else she desired in her presence. She felt, finally, fully queen.

But her smile faded as she recalled her poor friend Bella Harington's sad plight again. As queen, Elizabeth would want Bella with her soon, but the poor woman would be in mourning. Elizabeth had told Cecil to report posthaste whatever he learned about Bella's younger sister's sudden death, but she hadn't seen him for a few hours. Mayhap he was busy about that very business.

But now Harry had brought his wife and two young children down the long table to thank their royal benefactress. Elizabeth liked his wife, Anne, and intended to also ask her to join her ladies at court. Harry beamed at Anne, who had lived in exile in Europe these past years of Bloody Mary's reign. The Carey family reunion had obviously been heartfelt and passionate. A sudden longing for a love of her own seeped into Elizabeth's soul, but she shoved it deeper down.

"You have ever had our loyalty, Your Grace," Harry said, "and now shall have our utmost efforts in your service. We are grateful for my creation to the lords and our place at Your Highness's table on this momentous day for all England."

She nodded graciously, and they shared a

swift smile. Harry was the son of Anne Boleyn's deceased sister Mary, though he looked auburn-haired and -bearded, ruddy Tudor through and through. She regretted that, especially what the gossipmongers whispered of him, but she shoved that fear away too. No more trepidation, she told herself, for she bestrode her own destiny now.

"As my Boleyn cousin," she declared loudly enough that the rest of the table heard, "you stand as close in blood and dear to me as any Tudor kin."

She glanced down the table to where her cousin Frances, Duchess of Suffolk, sat with her young husband, though the two Grey girls were seated at a table below. Frances bore watching. Right now the old shrew was the one watching with a frown crumpling her fierce features, no doubt furious her eldest daughter did not sit at the queen's table. 'S blood, Elizabeth thought, let her take the warning then.

She looked back at Harry and lowered her voice. "Your help to me during the poison plot that threatened us all will never be forgotten, Harry."

"Your Majesty does not intend," he said, leaning closer, "to privily pursue this murder of the Harington girl everyone is whispering about?"

Elizabeth startled before she managed to control her countenance again. "Murder?" she whispered. "Cecil told me only she had died."

Harry looked aghast. "He obviously could not bear to sully your day or burden you—and

I did not realize..." His voice trailed off, his face turned ashen.

"I know Cecil will serve me well," she hissed, more to herself than to him, "but he is not to coddle me, not as queen. You may tell the man that next time I am the last to know—even the second soul to know—he will be privy secretary to some obscure clerk and not his queen. No, never mind. I shall save all that and tell him myself, as he is probably about that very business so he can report all to me. But she was murdered?"

Harry nodded solemnly and she suddenly felt everyone was whispering of it and she hated that—not today. It seemed an evil omen: a young woman losing her life hard upon the heels of her own royal one finally being found—and crowned. Was that why the Duchess of Suffolk was smirking? Oh where was someone to cheer her again?

"Lord Cecil also said," Henry went on, apparently recovering his aplomb when he saw she would not explode at him, "that the constable and coroner both declare the murderer is unknown and so there is to be no report to the justice. They have inquired of the brace of witnesses who were about the grounds of the crime, including the Duchess of Suffolk, the Greys, and Seymours."

"Aha," she said, shooting a quick quelling look toward the duchess. "So that is to be that? No further inquiry?"

"I know not, Your Grace, but wondered if you will order the court into mourning so near this festive time."

31

"No, and I thank God I now have others to oversee such an investigation besides myself, cousin. Cecil has done well to hurry all this, and I shall await his report and not dabble one finger in it. After all, Mistress Penelope Whyte is—was—not truly of my court nor permanently residing here. She was wed to Lord Maldon of Blackwater," she went on, trying to convince herself not to get entangled. "Still…"

"Maldon, a name and man from the old days at your father's court," he put in.

"True. And Bella and Penelope's father, you recall, was long Sergeant at the Tower, though I fault him not for that. When he was my warden, he was but doing his duty," she said, blotting under her nose again. "God willing, we shall all do that."

"At least, this time, praise God," he said with a sigh, "this murder has naught to do with you."

She nodded, but she was deeply disturbed. She had no time nor real cause to deal with an investigation, yet she could not let it go. But now she was starting to sound as if she were in a barrel. All the meetings, the conferences, privy and public, Christmas revels, all this pomp—and now Penelope's vile death—had sapped her strength. And it was not so easy to take to her bed as it had once been.

"Still," she said to Harry, "I shall order tomorrow's joust postponed and the opening of Parliament set back for a period of mourning. I shall see that justice is done for poor Penelope, though not," she concluded in a whisper, "be directly involved."

32

She saw he would say more, but his young son began to clap and shout while Lord Arundel, as the new Lord Steward and master of this feast, rode his horse around the circumference of the huge hall. Several, including her Master of the Horse, Robin Dudley, had permission to do so. The arrangement of tables, the crunch of courtiers, army of servers, and vast displays of food on the groaning boards and sawhorses took the entire vast hall, so certain men must move about quickly to oversee and observe.

The Careys excused themselves, though Harry nearly had to pull his awestruck young son away when Robin dismounted near the wall and strode directly to the queen. She sat up straighter, hoping her nose was not red. Robin was the pinnacle of poise, both ahorse and afoot, his carriage and demeanor the most elegant yet most masculine of all. If anyone could lift her spirits, it was he.

"Robin, will you not join me for some powdered beef or sturgeon in lemon sauce?" she asked as he rose from his bow. "You have been working far too hard in my service this day."

"You may wear me out over the years, and I shall only ask for more," he said, and smiled. His teeth glinted in torchlight, and his dark, close-clipped beard gleamed like a frame for his strong jaw, straight nose, and velvet-brown eyes. Though his father's part in the Jane Grey rebellion—Robin's brother had wed the girl—had ruined his family financially, he looked entirely dashing in silver cloth doublet with hunter-green slashings and hose to emphasize his manly legs.

"I came, my queen," he went on when she could not find a voice for a fast rejoinder, "to tell you I have discovered what was the disturbance in the crowd along the Strand during the procession yesterday. You said I should inform you straightaway if I knew."

Well, she thought. At least she could rely on Robin to report things quickly, even if Cecil seemed to take his time. "Say on," she prompted him. "I intend to be aware of all eddies in the current, though I may not put my foot in them, dear Robin." There, she thought. That was what I should have answered him for his double entendre and impudence a moment ago. For all his sweet, hot looks and teases, the man was married.

"Ah, yes," he said, and smiled again, politely ignoring her next sneeze. "It was, I warrant, a rabid dog that attacked and bit a woman in leg and backside—the backside of the crowd," he added with a swift shrug as if he had made a jest. "She screamed, someone else screamed, and a man dispatched the raving thing to save the day."

"Then nothing to worry for. Nothing amiss there," she said, frowning again as she recalled poor Penelope's murder near the site.

"I shall make it my life's business that you have nothing amiss, nothing to worry for ever again, my queen. And as for your kind invitation to dine, I shall sit at your feet and take

34

morsels from your graceful hand anytime you bid."

"I did not bid, but asked. Nor shall you sit at my feet, at least this night," she said, gesturing for a chair. "And you are still the flatterer, Robin."

"Ever truth teller, my queen. Trust me for that."

He sat beside her on a chair a gentleman usher jumped to wedge in next to hers. Yes, she thought, she trusted Robin as much as she trusted Harry or William Cecil as much as she trusted any man.

Chapter the Third

At last, long after midnight, Elizabeth entered her state apartments in Westminster Palace. She had just come from a brief, privy meeting with William Cecil, who had apologized for not telling her all the news of Penelope's death before Harry or someone else blurted it out. But, he'd explained, he had waited for the coroner's report that the victim had been suffocated to death. And, he'd hinted darkly, there might be more sad news by morning.

"If I'm going to be ill of exhaustion and a cold, Kat, I'm not staying in this draughty old place," the queen declared, ignoring the fact that flames blazed high on the hearth and the room was warm. "Whitehall is ready for me, the river is not frozen, and I can bundle up and be rowed there in a trice. This old place is quite getting to me, so—"

Behind Kat, she saw Robin's sister, Mary Sidney, drop her a curtsy with several others of her ladies-in-waiting. Elizabeth was still not used to so many faces. And behind them, at the hearth, stood Isabella Harington, in tears. She went straight to her.

"Bella, they did not tell me you had come, or I would have left the banquet sooner. I am deeply grieved for you and your family at Lady Maldon's cruel loss."

"I was content to wait, Your Gracious Majesty, for I would speak with you—privily, if that is possible," she said with a quick glance as more ladies spilled into the room.

"Now all things are possible," Elizabeth declared, and made a quick motion to gesture them out. When no one budged, she rounded on the ninnies. "Out, out for now, all of you. Kat can put me to bed if I stay here. But be prepared to move to Whitehall on the morrow."

Looking at their pouting faces, listening to their whispers, Elizabeth realized they all had much to learn of pleasing their new queen. She had intentionally kept none of her sister's women intimately close, and soon enough these would learn her ways. But Bella was her friend from long ago.

"Kat is still my confidant, Bella, so she stays," she explained as the room emptied.

When Bella barely nodded, Elizabeth realized she must be taking her sister's death very badly, though someone had said today they did not get on. But sometimes, she thought, the guilt of that could put one on the rack of remorse.

"Some wine for Bella, Kat," she said as she sat her friend on a padded, pillowed bench before the marble hearth and perched beside her, their skirts touching. "Is not John with you, my dear?"

"He rode himself to inform Penelope's estranged husband in Essex. Though she insisted on calling herself Penelope Whyte, their surname, she should have gone by Lady Maldon of Blackwater."

"Ah," Elizabeth said, glimpsing much grief in so little said.

"I am so sorry, Your Grace, to have...lost c-control," Bella stammered between a new torrent of sniffs and sobs. Such a collapse was so unlike her, Elizabeth thought, even in tough times, as when she and John had been sent to prison.

"You always were the strong one, Your Grace, in those days I s-served you at Hatfield and in the Tower."

"You were the only one strong enough to beat me at bowls and archery—but never at riding." Elizabeth tried to lighten Bella's mood.

"No, never at r-riding," she admitted, dabbing at her eyes, then taking a slow swallow from the goblet Kat proffered. "Now that you are a crowned queen, I warrant I'd not dare beat you at the other two either."

Once they would have giggled at such banter, but Elizabeth now only grasped Bella's wrist. The woman's hands were big and square next to Elizabeth's long-fingered, slender ones. Isabella Markham Harington was a blond, blue-eyed, big-boned woman of bold features, strong and skilled at sports and games, but now she was trembling so hard the wine almost slopped out.

They sat in silence as Bella slowly calmed herself. A stray shred of music drifted from the great hall, for Elizabeth had bid them carry on with their dancing. The hearth flames crackled and spit sap. Bella's broad shoulders settled, and she blew her nose.

"Foul murder is a dreadful way to lose a sister," Elizabeth said, "especially a young, comely, healthy one."

Bella nodded. Their eyes met, Bella's red and moist, Elizabeth's bleary from sneezing and lack of sleep.

"I—I need to tell you the worst of it, Your Grace, though we do not want it noised about in general. But now mayhap all shall know."

"What? What could be worse than being murdered, to be smothered, as the coroner's report claimed, to have no breath left as if one were drowning?"

She shook her head to clear it. "Or do you mean that all of you are yet suspect? Surely my constable or justice has not charged or arrested anyone, for the preliminary ruling is that the crime is unsolved."

"True, but the Duchess of Norfolk is saying that the murderer must be our foster son, Jack, because Penelope was sporting with him at the table, then rebuffed him before she said she was indisposed and went to lie down. But she didn't lie down and must have gone outside, maybe to meet someone, and Jack was out on the grounds, but so were others. I swear he's innocent, Your Grace," she cried, gripping her goblet, "and I am begging you to help us clear his name. He's not of our blood, but you know how desperately we have wanted a son, how I have prayed for a son—"

"I know, I know. You and John deserve a son. And so that is the worst of it, that the duchess accuses Jack? I shall speak with her."

"I think she knows I disapprove of her Katherine as your heir. And forgive me, Your Grace, but she keeps saying that the apple falls not far from the tree."

Elizabeth sat up straighter. "Implying what?"

"That...since Jack's father was a—forgive me, Your Grace—because of what passed between you and my Lord Seymour years before..." She cleared her throat. "The duchess claims that since Tom Seymour was a skirt chaser, as she put it, Jack is too, and she says the boy lured Penelope to the attic and—"

"I've met Jack briefly. He is hardly a boy. Also like his father, I warrant"—Elizabeth's voice came clipped and cold—"young Seymour does not need to harm women to get them to—to want to plunge willy-nilly into the pool of his charm."

"Exactly!" Bella said, leaning over to put her goblet down on the hearth. "Your Majesty, I

39

am asking you to help me protect Jack from her unjust accusations. I am begging you to oversee someone you trust to find who really murdered my sister, so we don't lose Jack too, should the duchess's claims cause the Lord Justice to open this instance again."

Elizabeth leaned forward and laid her hand on her old friend's velvet-covered shoulder, watching tears plop on Bella's skirts. The queen closed her eyes a moment, mustering her strength and mastering her heart. Her head felt so stuffed up, but her mind too was stuffed with memories of the days Bella and John had gone loyally with her to the Tower, the times in that fearsome place when Bella had begged indulgences and favors for Elizabeth from her father, who was master sergeant there. The times Bella had tried to cheer her during the long years of rural exile from her family and her people until Elizabeth had given John permission to court and wed her and take her away...

"I will see to it, Bella," she vowed. "But is there anything else I should know, something that will help us discover who is the real murderer? I must know everything."

Tears gilding her eyes in firelight, Bella nodded. "As I said, the worst. John and I have kept it secret so far, though I think the duchess suspects something. Before she and her family ran in when I screamed, I put Penelope's skirts back down and pushed her legs together because it was too dreadful...."

Elizabeth stood, her arms stiff at her side.

Bella gaped up at her as if she were seeing her old friend for the first time as queen and it frightened her. She jumped to her feet. They stared eye to eye.

"I must admit, Your Grace, I tampered with the way we found Penelope. I regret to say, my sister was also ravished in that old garret where they say Jack's father once planned his rebellion."

Bella took a quick step back from the anguished look Elizabeth was not swift enough to hide. Across the room Kat Ashley gasped. Bella stepped back and sloshed blood red wine across the hearth until it sizzled.

By noon the next day word buzzed throughout the court and the city that the new queen had taken to her sickbed in Whitehall Palace just downriver from Westminster. It was true her head cold had hit her full force, but that was not stopping her from pursuing Bella's request.

She had called a hasty meeting of her Privy Plot Council from her days in exile. They had barely two weeks to solve this murder, she reckoned, since her first Parliament would now convene on January 25 by her own decree, and then she'd have no time for anything but governing in full view of England and all Europe.

Elizabeth sat in the bay window seat of her bedchamber, which overlooked the Thames. She was bundled in flannel wraps over a wool robe, her attire a far cry from that with which

41

she'd lately been bedecked. Kat fussed over plumping the down pillows between her back and the mullioned windowpanes, and Meg kept pressing her with a posset with chamomile and bergamot.

Finally Kat, Meg, Ned, and Jenks sat close around a long, narrow gaming table, which Jenks and Ned had pulled up to put the queen at the head of it. Their faces turned toward her, curious and proud. Now that she was queen, she had seen their once-easy camaraderie stiffening to formality.

"Though I did pray," Elizabeth began, "we would never be reassembled thusly when I was queen, it seems a particular unsolved murder comes hard upon the heels of my accession."

"That lady what's related to the Haringtons, Your Grace?" Jenks asked, frowning.

Elizabeth was surprised he had spoken but pleased her people were not cowed. Besides, as a lad Jenks had been a groom in Tom Seymour's service so had known John Harington, one of Tom's closest men.

"The same lady, Jenks, Penelope Whyte of Maldon in Essex. Their country seat is up on the Blackwater. Though I am relieved to say that this crime does not strike at the crown, I will not have some murderer and rapist—and that latter is not to be spread abroad—skulking about my court and kingdom."

"Meaning," Ned put in, "you believe a courtier is guilty?"

"Meaning some are saying the murderer is

descended from courtiers, and we shall start from that."

She explained what Bella had revealed and that the Duchess of Suffolk was making accusations against young Jack St. Maur.

"Heard he's living with the Haringtons but larking about with Master Edward Seymour now," Jenks piped up again. "Jack is the bastard son of my first lord, the Admiral Seymour," he explained to everyone with real pride, which touched Elizabeth's heart despite it all. At least there was such a thing as loyalty through fair and foul, and she could hope for no more from these simple, good people who would serve her over the coming years.

"But who is this Jack's mother then," Ned asked, "if Tom Seymour was never wed but to Queen Katherine Parr after your royal father died, Your Grace?"

Elizabeth's narrowed gaze locked with Kat's, and the older woman looked away. Kat knew how hard it was for her to resurrect the painful past when she finally had her foot on the bright future's threshold.

"His mother, as I recall," Elizabeth explained, "though it was denied and covered up by her family, was Mary Sidney, Duchess of Richmond, to whom the Lord Admiral Seymour was nearly betrothed twice before he wed my widowed stepmother, Queen Katherine. Mary is dead now, but she was the Duke of Norfolk's daughter and Surrey's sister."

"Quite a family tree for an alleged murderer," Ned said, drumming his fingers on the pearl-inlaid tabletop. "Traitors all at one time or the other: Norfolk, Seymour, Surrey."

"*Alleged* murderer is the key here, Ned," Elizabeth insisted. "We are out to find who really murdered Penelope Whyte so that we can bring one of my dead subjects the justice she deserves and clear Jack St. Maur's name." When everyone just stared at her, she hastily added, "Because his foster parents, the Haringtons, are dear and loyal to me as are all of you."

Several of them jumped when a knock sounded on the door. Their old furtive days being watched and retained were hard to put aside.

"That will be Lord Hunsdon and Lord Cecil," she informed them. "Jenks, we won't stand on ceremony, and Kat's worn out with unpacking for me. Go bid them enter."

While the others jumped up and shifted down the table to put Harry and Cecil on either side of her, the queen explained what they knew so far. She had realized Cecil would protest her involvement with another murder investigation, so she had written him a note to head that off. But she saw her other worry was valid. Her household staff looked at their social betters nervously and fidgeted. Both Cecil and Harry had helped them solve the poison plot, but from a safe distance.

"Do you recall King Arthur's roundtable?" she suddenly asked everyone. She plunged on quickly, wanting no one to be embarrassed when she called them together—from her chief adviser of the realm to her herb girl. "Though we do not have a round table," she explained, "all must contribute on equal ground when we have a crime to solve privily. Is that understood?"

Everyone acquiesced aloud or nodded, though Cecil looked wary and Harry surprised.

"And remember," she added, "when we are at such a meeting, I am simply Bess and not the queen."

Cecil shifted in his seat but nodded. Harry looked so nonplussed she wondered if he'd be of help here. But her sturdy band of servants had seen it all before and sat waiting for what came next.

"Also, I do this for my own safety, should anyone overhear you speak of me in relation to such doings, as there are many called Bess and but one called Your Majesty or Your Grace. Now, about this foul murder. As soon as possible I am going to question both my cousin Frances, Duchess of Suffolk, who is making the accusations, and Jack St. Maur."

After a discussion of why he hadn't been arrested—no hard evidence or witnesses, despite an investigation by the chief constable immediately following the discovery of the crime, she said—silence reigned. Was it, she wondered, because they knew of her past with Jack's father or because they did not? Most must, for once it had been England's scandal and her shame.

"And what may I do to help, Bess?" Cecil asked.

"Firstly, I want you to be certain Lord Arundel is not at home this evening at dusk; summon him to a meeting with you or some such. Others of us will go to look around the gatehouse where the body was discovered. By then I'll have it clear from the duchess where people were during my progress by the house—" She hesitated, frowning.

"What is it, Your Maj—Bess?" Harry asked.

"Nothing. I cannot see how a rabid dog in the crowd just outside Arundel's gatehouse could tie to a murdered woman within." She explained that there had been an altercation in the crowd there, but that Robert Dudley had solved it to her satisfaction. Again, she noted, Cecil squirmed.

"Meg, of course," she went on, "with Kat's help, you will temporarily impersonate me, staying supposedly sick in my bed while I take Ned and Jenks to look around Arundel House. Understood?"

"Your first chance to be queen," Ned said, and elbowed Meg. "You know, I used to do a long speech by Warwick the Kingmaker in an old play, but now I've become a queenmaker, teaching you, Meg Milligrew, to mimic Her Majesty, though now that she's queen you'll have a lot new to learn, my girl."

"Not all muffled up in a sickbed for a few hours, she won't," Kat put in. "And I doubt anyone will miss Meg in this mass of servants here, this early in the jumble of new duties, at least."

"Well, fine then," Elizabeth said. "My Lord Cecil—"

"Am I not just William or Will here, Your Grace?" he said as if to stick her own admonition to her. Cecil's narrowed eyes went from one to the other of them. Elizabeth could tell he was seething over something, but she could not read what. "Good. Yes, Will—and Harry," she said, with a glance at her solemn-looking cousin.

"But," Harry said, "it all sounds risky."

"Without bold tactics we'd never have found your mother's murderer," Elizabeth reminded him, "or exposed the one who would have been Meg's and mine."

"I want to help," Meg said, fiddling with a tiny nosegay of dried herbs in her hand, "but I don't fancy being left behind playing you all the time since I'm always stuck in bed. Ned's the player, and he gets to go gallivanting off with you and Jenks, so—"

"A bed sounds plenty good to me right now," Elizabeth interrupted. "And I meant to ask you, Meg, did the vast herbal beds of the privy garden here seem goodly space for you to grow my strewing and pomander herbs come spring?"

"Oh, yes, Your Grace, it looked like heaven on earth to me, that's sure."

"Good. Well, I meant not to veer off our path. Keep your eyes and ears open, all of you, even for rumors flying around about this murder. Someone—either Kat or mayhap Meg—will deliver messages to you later about our tactics or a new meeting."

She asked them if they had anything to

contribute now, but no one knew a whit that would help. As they bowed their way out, Bess became Elizabeth again to sigh and glance out her oriel window.

The state apartments at Whitehall were built above the water gate that protruded over the river, where she could go down privy stairs to enter the royal barge. Though the Thames was not frozen, now and then a chunk of ice bobbed past barges, horse ferries, and boats of every kind, ripped along by the current and strong tide. Tonight she was going to take that turbulent road back to see a place Tom Seymour had once loved.

She jumped when Cecil cleared his throat. "Oh, my lord, I did not know you were still here."

He bowed again. Cecil had been her bulwark, her legal adviser through perilous times, and she meant to rely on him fully as her principal aide in her Privy Council, the council that would advise her in running the kingdom, not in solving this crime. Cecil was nearly forty, a London-educated lawyer with a shovel-shaped beard and long, lined face that made him look older than his years. The weight of the world leaned on Cecil's thin shoulders.

"When you named me Principal Secretary," he began, shuffling two papers in his hands—Cecil's hands were always full of papers—"you bade me ever tell you the truth, to give you my best counsel."

"Yes, and that includes around this small

table as well as the large one in the council chamber, my lord."

"I must say," he went on, "whether you are blunt Bess Tudor or clever queen, you manage to control both tables with the same grace and wit...and iron charm."

"Iron charm, my lord?" She turned the still-warm silver tankard of posset in her hands. "If this is going somewhere, say on. This cold I have is real enough whether I am Bess or queen. Do you have news of this murder plot or some other subject? I am exhausted and sick but determined nothing shall stop me."

"And it never shall!" he said so fervently she startled.

"What then?"

"I want to warn you not to become...ah, overly protective of young St. Maur. I overheard Adrian Stokes say he is quite a charmer too."

"Too?" Her voice rang out. She sat up straighter, shoving the end of the table away from her to stand. "And you believe his appeal will warp my judgment, turn my head? Just spit it out, my lord, as it is not like you to mince words. The boy has naught but half his blood and his black hair in common with his father."

She knew the untruth of that even as she said it; the mere thought of how much Jack had reminded her of Tom panicked her. In the brief moments she had seen Jack St. Maur, his appearance and demeanor, his swagger... "I am sure of that, as he never knew his father," she finished lamely, "so how could he be like him?"

"Just as you have naught but half your blood and dark eyes in common with your mother because you never knew her?"

"Enough! I am not some green girl of fifteen now," she cried, standing and nearly tripping on the folds of flannel Kat had wrapped her with like some damned Egyptian mummy. "Well, what is it? I can see your next words struggling to get unstuck from your sharp brain and sharper tongue."

"I need not tell you that Adrian Stokes himself is the cause of gossip because he was the Duchess of Suffolk's Master of the Horse, Your Grace, her servant before they wed. It is not their age difference that is snickered over and certainly not that she was pregnant when she wed him."

"And..." she prompted, stepping out of her bonds to approach him in her night rail and bundling robe with her mules flopping on her feet. Behind him, across the long room, she saw Kat Ashley gesture to keep calm, but she ignored her.

"And I'll not have your enemies—yes, there are still enemies out that door, Your Majesty—snicker at you for favoring *your* Master of the Horse, so—"

She threw the posset at him just as Kat ran over. It bounced off his knee but flung its curds and herbs on Kat's hems before skidding along the Turkey carpet.

"Now, Your Grace—" Kat began in her most soothing voice.

"Cecil, I tell you what," Elizabeth declared as he stood his ground, glaring at her like a schoolmaster. "As soon as I've questioned Jack St. Maur, I shall put him into your household for the duration of our investigation, so you can keep an eye on him—and me—separately. And here I thought I was done with censurers. But I'll not abide any hint that I would ever wed my Master of the Horse, however dear Robin is to me."

"Not even if you raised him high?" Cecil dared. "You have no doubt thought of that."

"Of all the things I ask, and pay, for you to do, my lord, the merest mention of my marriage is not part nor parcel of your duties. Never bring it up to me again."

"But as your adviser, for the good of the state—"

"Leave me, Master Secretary!" she shouted, and began a fit of sneezes.

He bowed his way out, even dared to bid her good afternoon. Still sneezing, she shook Kat's fussing off. And kicked the empty posset tankard into the wall when she heard Cecil mutter to himself, "For good or ill, her sire's daughter."

Chapter The Fourth

Though she still felt rotten, Elizabeth insisted her women dress her formally for her audience the next morning with Frances, Dowager Duchess of Suffolk. When she saw her cousin lurching at her like a black-clad harbinger of doom, she was glad she had chosen the sunlit waterside gallery today, for naught was cozy or intimate about it. Here she could glance out over the river, enjoy the sun streaming through the bank of windows, and walk away if need be. She could recall an audience years ago when the woman had boxed her ears.

Yet it gave Elizabeth no joy when the older woman curtsied stiffly and her joints creaked. She almost swayed, so the queen reached to steady her shoulder as she rose. "I hear you are ailing, Your Majesty," Frances said, and thoroughly looked her over as if to check for a dirty face and hands.

"I hear you are too," she countered. "Does your stomach grieve you sore?"

"Cherry cordials and hippocras, that's what they say for stomach stones."

"I have a new herbalist I brought from the country," Elizabeth said as a sudden thought struck her. She would get Meg close to this woman for more than healing. "I shall send her to you with a good remedy."

"Ah, but no remedy for this murder," Frances declared.

Though Elizabeth had intended they should walk, she indicated two chairs angled close under a tapestry of a stag hunt.

"The only remedy," Elizabeth replied, keeping her voice calm, "will be to find the true murderer and see that he—or she—in turn finds queen's justice for killing a queen's subject. That will take proof and witnesses, of which

I believe there are neither, though I hear some are claiming suspects." She lifted her chin and leveled a long look at her cousin.

"Hmph. I have no doubt Isabella's run to you. Just that morning of the murder I saw Jack Seymour—I mean, St. Maur—and that girl have a spat."

"That girl... I assume you mean Penelope, for I understand that both of your daughters were there too."

"Of course I mean Penelope. Both she and Jack went their ways in a huff—as a matter of fact, Penelope tore from the table just after, claiming she felt ill. But I've no doubt that came to blows later in private."

"Blows? You are claiming Penelope was beaten to death?"

"Do not twist my words, Your Grace. Smothered evidently, and who knows what else?"

"Exactly. Who knows, and therefore, who should say at this point, for that would be simply spreading gossip."

"I see you intend to wear no mourning for her." The stony-faced woman shifted topics instead of rising to that bait.

"Penelope Whyte was not of our court, cousin, but that does not mean I do not intend to see justice done for her."

"She was a flibbertigibbet, I tell you. And yet I heard her praise you, your 'pretty person and clothes,' I believe she said."

"Really? She thought I was pretty? But where did she see me?"

"She could not wait for your recognition parade, she said. Before she left the midday table at Arundel House, she mentioned she saw you enter London as queen a week or so before. Running about here and there, she was a great burden to the Haringtons, who have struggled valiantly to restore their reputations from the old days—"

"We all know about striving to repair reputations, do we not, cousin?"

Ignoring her implication, Frances plunged on, "Penelope was estranged from her husband and was acting quite unbridled here. She hung on many men, including both Edward Seymour—"

"Whom you would rather have attentive to your Katherine?" Elizabeth inquired sweetly. She had seen them briefly together when she left the banquet last night—in the back corner of the vast room, where they evidently thought they could whisper unseen, at least by their new sovereign.

"Not at all, Your Grace. I would, however, have you realize how much Katherine admires you and is anxious to wait upon Your Majesty in any way she can."

"I am greatly pleased to hear that. So, were you implying that Jack St. Maur might have been angry with Penelope for using his friend Edward to make him jealous?"

"Hardly, as she'd hang on any man. You should have seen Bella's face in the barge on the way to Arundel House when Penelope pretended to be bounced into John Harington's lap. And she fussed over my Lord Adrian when she thought I wasn't looking."

"In other words, you too could be angry with her, not only Bella, as you are evidently meaning to imply."

That silenced Frances for a moment. She looked like a fish gaping for air. How, Elizabeth thought, this woman could have been bred by two of the handsomest people in all Christendom, her mother so fair she was called the Tudor Rose, was beyond her. Could it be that great disappointment of Frances's life— to be so plain and have it so remarked upon— had made her grim and bitter to anyone who was comely, including Bella and Penelope and herself?

"I was not angry with the chit, Penelope," Frances declared, "just sorry for Bella in more ways than one. Adrian is ever loyal to me, I'd bet my life on that."

" 'S blood, someone has bet his or her life in taking that of my fond subject Penelope Whyte," Elizabeth declared, standing.

The duchess was forced to rise too. Cursing her cold, Elizabeth turned aside to muffle a sneeze into her handkerchief.

"Pray tell me before you go, cousin," she said, sniffling, "exactly where everyone was standing in the gatehouse before and during the royal parade. I am just trying to picture the scene for myself. I glanced up to see the Haringtons in the window but cannot personally vouch for anyone else."

"I'll tell you my Katherine was there,

55

cheering you on, in an old, cold gatehouse barely above the rabble, and you did not notice her? I hope it will not be such between Your Royal Highness and my Katherine here at court."

"Do not presume or push. I shall interview her soon, though, I promise you."

Frances looked appeased, even pleased, at that morsel. Elizabeth did not tell her that she was going to find a way to question everyone who was in spitting distance of the gatehouse the day poor Penelope died.

The queen considered calling Katherine Grey to her but decided she would rest for an hour before facing Jack. Trailed by four of her women, she walked the short distance to her state apartments.

Within sprawling medieval Whitehall, rooms of royalty were arranged in an ever-narrowing hierarchy of people who were allowed access to them: The great hall was open to many; the great chamber to courtiers; the presence chamber to advisers and intimates; and the privy chamber, guarded by the sergeant at arms, just to the queen's closest women and servants. The bedchamber, the ultimate refuge, was only for Kat and those the queen bade enter and, of course, servants who were summoned.

When Elizabeth spotted Meg passing through the presence chamber with strewing herbs in a basket, she whispered, "Meg, to me." Acknowledging the round of curtsies when her other women saw her, the queen gestured

Meg over behind a frame stretched with needlework.

"I would like some herbs for my head cold," Elizabeth said loudly enough for others to hear.

"I already brought them—"

"Listen to me," she said, speaking quickly and quietly. "I want you to gather something that would be good for a stomach ailment and creaking joints—"

"Not for you, Your Grace?"

"For my cousin the Duchess of Suffolk. Something that must be prepared fresh so you need to visit her frequently. Against my better judgment, I've given her rooms here, though she has a fine house across the river too. I want you to try to discover certain things by listening and looking. But for now fetch the herbs, then come to me so we can plan. But do not interrupt me if I am speaking with someone."

"Oh, surely, Your Grace, I'll fetch comfrey root and lots more for your cold," Meg declared in a voice loud enough to carry to the queen's women, who seemed to be shifting curiously closer.

Meg curtsied and walked out, around the edge of the room as Kat had taught her. Elizabeth felt a jab of affection for the girl, who carried on so loyally despite her great burden. Meg had been kicked in the head by a horse, and it seemed only her keen knowledge of herbs had stayed with her. She had carried on cleverly in her other calling for the queen. By keeping her hair tucked up in kerchiefs and letting her freckles show, with her slouching walk and country talk, she was hiding her strong resemblance to her monarch.

Elizabeth was making for her bedchamber when a man called her name. She spun to see Harry.

"Your Grace," he said, going quickly down on one knee, "John Harington's ridden in from up by the Blackwater to see you. I take it," he added, lowering his voice as he rose, "before he rode back to his wife."

"I'll see him directly, Harry. Bring him 'round the back way to the barge landing. I'll be just inside the door."

"But it will be cold there. You'll catch your death—"

His face shifted from concern to embarrassment he'd used those words. "Harry, do as I bid," she whispered. "I don't want anyone here to know I am so involved in this."

In her bedchamber Elizabeth told Kat, "You may clear the room. I am going to rest now."

Nodding her approval, Kat swept them all out and closed the door. "And," the queen added, "I'll need my warmest plain cloak."

"You're not going out again?"

"I'm going to speak privily with John Harington, and I'll stay out of the wind until I actually get on a barge tonight, all muffled up. Do not fret, for Harry will be there too, down by the landing."

"But you know John Harington has kept Tom Seymour in his loyal affection all these years, just as Jenks has. And—"

"And some say I deserted the Lord Admiral Seymour at the last and wish me ill? He deserted me first. I had to protect myself, even if it meant his life. And John Harington, just like Jenks, is loyal to me, I know it."

She took the thick beeswax candle Kat offered and let Kat fuss overlong settling the cloak about her shoulder. She opened the small, squeaky door, nearly invisible in the dark wainscoted wall. It led to a narrow corridor that went to stairs and two turns down to a privy entrance at the barge landing. Before she closed the door, she turned back to Kat.

"I recall you once cared for Tom Seymour too and championed his wishes, my Kat. No woman was immune to his allure, just as no one is immune to—to catching a damned cold like this, which if not cured can do one in." She sneezed again as if to punctuate her words and, gathering her skirts close, hurried down the dim hall to the steps.

Years ago, when Whitehall Palace, then called York Place, had been taken by her father from Cardinal Wolsey, the king had greatly expanded it. One thing he built was this wing of the state apartments with back corridor, stairs, privy water gate, then beyond that the three-storied bridge protruding out over the river with a waterside gallery for walking and viewing up and down the Thames.

She went down to the ground level, stepped

to the barge door at the bottom of the stairs, and knocked. Two guards just outside opened it, astounded to see her unannounced and alone.

"I need some air," she said. "Open the door and tell no one."

One mumbled something, but they swept wide both doors. The candle gutted out and splattered wax on her gloves before she could put it down. The river wind and glare of sun almost staggered her, but she pulled her cloak tighter and stepped out. Harry and John waited between the two rocking barges moored here, buffeted by the wind. Harry stood his ground, but John came forward, his muddy cloak flapping, to go down on one knee and kiss her gloved hand.

"Rise, John. And come stand back in this corner and buffer me from the blasts," she said, perching on the ornately carved wooden bench where courtiers sometimes waited for the royal party's return.

He sat, leaning slightly toward her, blocking her in, each breath he took becoming a tiny cloud the wind ripped away.

"You are ill, I hear, Your Grace. I will make this brief."

"Say what you must. I have seen Bella."

"Ah," he said as a slight frown flitted across his broad forehead. "I told her I would ride direct to you once I had told Penelope's husband, but I can understand her haste. This is dreadful business, Your Grace, and to happen the very day your triumphal procession passed—"

"Exactly *when* did it happen, to the best of your reckoning?"

"Between the time—mayhap high noon—when Penelope felt indisposed and said she would leave us to lie down before the parade, but evidently never did. And then it must have been nigh on two when you had passed and a servant girl said she'd seen her go upstairs. Bella and I ran up to the garret and found her...that way."

She told herself she must have that unnamed servant girl questioned. Though she had promised Bella she would look into this, she did not want even the Haringtons to know how personally she meant to be involved.

John kept fiddling with his sword in its scabbard, making a clatter, though he seemed too distraught to notice. Ordinarily she might have wanted to protect him, but why had he not protected Penelope? Was the barge ride the day of her murder the first time the girl had bounced into his lap? He indeed loved Bella, but men were men, she'd seen that. Glaring at his sword hand hard enough to still it, she decided she must play inquisitor to see what would spring loose.

"I take it no one passed you on the stairs when you raced up to find Penelope. Perhaps it was not haste that made the man or woman who murdered her leave her shamefully displayed as well as dead like that."

"Man...or woman?" he stammered. "But she was overpowered, ravished, and suffocated somehow. It couldn't be a woman—"

61

"For now, John, we rule no one out. Either he or she was demented, or he or she wanted to humiliate Penelope even in death, or someone wanted it to be overly obvious a man had committed the rape and hence the murder."

"You cannot believe it could be a woman," he insisted again, leaning closer.

"Women were there, John, women with some anger at Penelope. Is this not true?"

"Ah, well, the Duchess of Suffolk thinks we are jostling parvenus, but Katherine Grey, who could be angry Edward admired Penelope, has ice in her veins, Mary Grey's too tiny, and— you don't mean Bella!"

Bella had been the last one she had in mind, but she recalled those rumors that the sisters did not get on. 'S blood, she hated rumors, yet they often had their filthy feet mired in fact.

"Of course not," she said. "Bella seems terribly distraught."

"The truth is, she feels guilty...only, I mean, that she and Penelope used to quarrel. Who could blame Bella, with Penelope the way she was and Bella the guardian of our new-won respectability? Then, too, Penny was dainty and pretty, things Bella thought she herself was not, however much I tried."

He hung his head a moment, frowning at his knees. Mayhap, Elizabeth thought, dear Bella and that damned Frances might have something in common. Mayhap both envied and resented someone so beautiful and brazen as Penelope—Penny, as John had called her.

But that was hardly a motive for murder. Besides, Frances did not look physically up to it, however much she'd like it noised about that Penelope had died a strumpet's death. And Bella, though strong, agile, perhaps even outraged, would never want the notoriety for her family. No, John's initial protests must be right: The murderer was a man.

"You know," he was saying, "Bella always fretted that I'd loved my first wife more because she gave me a child and mayhap Bella cannot...."

She was so exhausted she had let her mind wander, and she'd missed the shift to this topic. What had this agonizing to do with the problem at hand? John was shaking his head, and tears pooled in his brown, wide-set eyes. Though masculine and determined, he could be tender and fanciful. He wrote poetry, collected that of others, and wrote songs, some which her royal father had praised and sung.

"But I only came, Your Grace," he went on, "to tell you that Penelope's body will be sent home to her husband's country seat for burial after the northern roads clear a bit. Until then Lord North said she can lie in the crypt on his grounds here, for in this cold a body will—will keep without being embalmed. I came too," he went on, fussing with his sword hilt again, "to beg you to help us, if you will, to protect Jack, whom Bella clings to as our own and whom I promised the woman to whom Lord Seymour entrusted him as a babe that I would help bring to manhood."

"I hear Kate Willoughby, the Dowager Duchess of Suffolk's stepmother, reared Jack at first?"

"Aye, though the duchess always hated the fact Kate had kept Jack on their land at Grimsthorpe in Lincolnshire. The Seymours, like the Haringtons, were always upstarts to the duchess."

"So," she said, hitting her gloved fist on her knee, "the duchess would have reason to dislike Jack. You know, Kate never liked me anymore than the duchess did, for Kate's mother was one of Catherine of Aragon's women—"

"Whom your mother replaced. But you don't mean Kate turned Jack against you? He adores you, Your Grace!"

"Adores?" That was always what Tom had said to her: *I adore you, my Bess, my princess.*

"Don't you think that a lad my Bella and I had these last years would think as we do and be thankful you are now safely queen?"

She stood and moved to the carved railing, squinting downwind into the stiff wind. Was there such a thing as to be safely queen? she wondered, but she said only, "I have sent for Jack. I will speak to him, then—tell Bella I think it best—put him in my Lord Cecil's household for now. And," she added, turning to face him though the wind slapped her face, "I will do whatever I can, John, and will keep you both informed."

He bent to kiss her gloved hand. Mayhap he

was surprised to find her trembling, and she could only hope he believed it was from the cold.

Elizabeth bade Kat unlace her. She shed her heavy skirts, long, puff-shouldered sleeves, and starched small ruff to lie bundled on her bed for an hour, still in her bodice, stockings, and shift. The day loomed long with an interview with Jack and the night's covert trip to Arundel House. She meant to just lie here to reason through what Bella, Frances, and John had told her, but soon she swam in the warm sea of sleep.

Or rather, she was just waking, lying abed some sunny morn in Queen Katherine Parr's house in Chelsea, and Kat had stepped out of the chamber. Time to rise, but her limbs lay so heavy, the sunbeams drowsy that danced through the half-pulled bed-curtains....

She gasped awake when a big, square hand ripped back the heavy brocade. A deep laugh pierced her.

"Oh, my Lord Tom! What are you doing here?"

"Up, my beauteous flame-haired wench. Up before I get up seeing you all disheveled and sleepy like this in bed!" he commanded, and reached to tug her covers down.

"But you are already up, my lord."

"Ha! I am indeed!" he roared, and reached to tickle her. "But I adore you, adore you,"

he whispered now, his voice all thick and raspy.

Wide-eyed, she resisted. He put one bare knee—dear God in heaven, he was still in his nightshirt—on the mattress, and the weight of it rolled her toward him. He laughed again, his pirate's laugh as when he'd told her she was his booty and slung her over his shoulder to carry her to her chamber door last night while Kat and other servants and his wife protested his rough play.

Now he dared cup one huge hand around her hip, his fingers drumming on her bum as if he were gently spanking her. And when Kat rushed in squawking for him to get out, he patted, then pinched, then gave Elizabeth a smart smack there, though he blocked Kat with his broad back so she could not see.

Little sparks flew and burned the young Princess Elizabeth's breasts, even between her legs. He grinned down at her, his teeth flashing white, his single freebooter's earring dangling like a noose, for he had fought the pirates of the Scilly Isles when he was Lord High Admiral.

"Be gone, my lord," Kat shouted, and tried to tug him off. This time only his eyes, dark and devilish, raked Elizabeth as she half cowered, half reveled in his presence, leaning bold over her nearly naked body in her bed.

"I'll call your lady wife, the Queen's Grace," Kat cried, "and she'll put an end to this! Be gone, my lord."

"For now, but I'll be back, sweet Bess," he teased, and began to sing a bawdy song called "Mistress Mine," putting the name Sweet Bess in the lyrics

instead of Alice. "I'll be back for more, because I adore..."

Gasping, then coughing, Elizabeth sat bolt upright in bed, the coverlet clutched to her breasts. The bed curtains still stood ajar, but this was not the bed, not the place, and the face of a much older Kat appeared to offer her a drink of beer.

She downed it to halt the fit of coughing that made her eyes water. "A bad dream, lovey?" Kat soothed, rubbing her back in circles. "You were murmuring and thrashing in your sleep."

"I...meant not to sleep," she managed to say, and took another sip. "I must get dressed. I've sent for someone."

"Not Lord Robert. Not here."

" 'S blood, you sound like Cecil. Robin's just my friend. I must question Jack St. Maur. Well, take this," she ordered, thrusting the goblet back at her and scooting off the broad, high bed to the mounting stool before Kat could say aught about Jack. "And please fetch someone to help me don my skirts and sleeves."

"You think I cannot do it?" Kat said, arms folded across her ample breasts. "How many years have I done it when you were denied ladies, not to mention decent gowns to cover your royal backside?"

Elizabeth recalled the dream again, but she felt soothed by Kat's old-fashioned scolding. "All right, my Kat, but we must get used to all the titled women and highborn servers hereabouts. They will think we are snubbing them and court tradition too. But yes, help me if you will, since no one knows I'm all ungowned. And tell me what you recall about John Harington's first wife."

"Ah, are you sure 'tis the tale you want to hear?" She grunted as she stooped to arrange petticoats in a circle for her mistress to step into.

"Would I have asked if it were not? And it was a command."

"As you know, Your Majesty," Kat said as her hands bent to her work, "that woman went by three names, mayhap to cover her real identity, though everyone knew who she was well enough."

"I know John's first wife was one of my father's bastards, Ethelreda, if I remember aright."

"Or Audrey or Esther, and her mother was Joan Dyngley or some such. His Majesty, so I recall, had the child fostered out to his tailor John Malte, who claimed her thereafter as his natural daughter. The king endowed the child with some lands near Bath, which Malte controlled and then, of course, which went to John Harington. All that happened when the Seymours were in style and John was Tom's man. His Majesty, so I heard, asked Tom to find a husband for the girl, and John wed her, simple as that. Obviously Tom had his sights set on bigger fish in the pond."

Elizabeth ignored that. "Tell me of John and

Audrey's child," Elizabeth said as she wriggled into her skirts.

"Oh, aye, Hester, and she'd be near marriageable age now, so maybe John would want to bring her to court under Bella's wing to show her off a bit."

"I doubt it, as that would make dear, childless Bella's pain the worse," Elizabeth mused as Kat's hands pulled tight the lacings on her back, then plucked up her stuffed shoulder puffs.

"How's that then?" Kat muttered, pointing at the long looking glass as if she'd hardly been listening. Elizabeth glanced in it, then, fluffing her huge skirts, studied herself as she spoke.

"John had a child with his first wife, yet Bella does not conceive," Elizabeth explained. "So my old friend is doubly desperate to have me save Jack St. Maur, and yet he—and Hester— are constant reminders to them both that Bella cannot really give John the son he so desires."

"And all men want a son. Queens too."

"This queen wants you to stay with me when I speak with Jack in the empty apartments below where Lord Cecil is bringing him. Stay back so he'll speak free, my Kat, but do not leave me."

Elizabeth picked up the pomander Meg had stuffed with dried rose petals and gillyflowers, then went to the small jewel box by her bed. She jammed on rings, even at the knuckles so her long fingers looked speckled with them. Until she decided about this young

69

man who was Tom Seymour's son, she must go armored against his touch or tricks.

Chapter The Fifth

Directly beneath the state apartments the suite of rooms where Elizabeth's mother had once lived now stood empty but for a bench by the door and a table and two chairs before the bare hearth. Queen Mary had died at St. James's Palace, but Elizabeth had ordered every chamber in Whitehall scrubbed and aired before she moved in. Though she had held hopes for a new, clean beginning, she was now mired in this murder mess.

And Cecil wasn't helping, she thought, getting Jack here late to make her wait for him. Monarchs waited for no one. The silence of the rooms, even with Kat's clearing her throat from her seat by the door, seemed to scream at Elizabeth. Her stiff green damask skirts swishing, she paced to the big bay window—these rooms mirrored hers—and glared out at the river, then stalked back toward the cold hearth and perched in one of the two facing chairs.

Finally a knock on the door. Kat rose to open it. Not Cecil but one of his men stood there, Philip something or other. He bowed and stepped aside to reveal Jack St. Maur.

Jack swept off his cap and strode straight for her, his bootheels clicking on the bare floor.

She had positioned their chairs so he would be looking into the sinking sun and she at him, but she had not planned to be gazing up at his height.

His bow was steadier than last time but not polished. He swept off his hat, its proud plume attached by a big gemstone. His garments were of good cut but not what she'd seen at court lately. Yet he held himself proudly, even for a man so tall.

Despite her battery of rings to keep him from kissing her hand, she found she could not offer it to him. Yes, even in the dim light of the Tower church, she had seen well enough to note how much of Tom was in him. But, pray God, not the desire and deceit.

"I hope Cecil's man told you," she began, "that I believe it best you reside in my lord secretary's household until this confusion over Penelope Whyte's murder is seen to. Sit, Jack, and tell me what you know of the poor lady."

She noted he did not have his sword. Had Cecil presumed to take it from him? He sat straight, his big feet flat in front of him. His elbows rested on the chair arms, and only his fingers gripping them betrayed his nervousness.

"Lady Maldon was a lovely person, Your Grace, and I am deeply grieved such a tragedy occurred." His voice was not as deep or ringing as Tom's and had more north country burr.

"Do you mean lovely in face and form," she asked, "or in character too?"

"Her physical beauty was well appreciated, Your Grace—even by Penelope herself."

"Ah, kindly put. In short, the lady knew her power."

"Yes, but she had a true inner gaiety about her too, a deep interest in life and people."

"And was she interested in you, Jack?"

His eyes locked with her assessing stare. "I will tell you true, Your Majesty, because you are queen and I admire you and always have, though, ere this, from afar."

He paused a moment. Elizabeth inclined her head.

"I believe she favored me as a man," he explained, "but not as a person because I chided her. I told her it was not right that she was besmirching my foster parents' name. They have striven to live an exemplary life, and then she came to town to..."

"To..." she prompted when he hesitated.

"To amuse herself, despite their expense, and I don't mean in coin. If she didn't give a fig for her own good name, she should have shown a care for theirs. I regret to say I knew her favors. I mean not to speak ill of the dead, Your Majesty, but to come clean, even at cost to myself to ever be in your good graces."

That last subtle plea touched her, but she kept to the course. "In what specific way did she shame them and favor you?"

Despite his ruddy, windblown color, he blushed. She sighed silently in relief. Tom never would have blushed or come clean at any cost to himself. There was no way in hell

72

Tom Seymour would have been contrite, and she could read what was coming next.

"She enticed men," he admitted, slightly hanging his head but keeping his eyes on hers. "She was like a beautifully baited snare. Again, I regret to speak ill of the dead."

"Perhaps, Jack, we must do so to settle why she is dead. Say on. You were so snared?"

"I admit it. But she also cast her net at my cousin Edward, Your Majesty, and I soon saw it was not solely my attentions she coveted but those of...others too. I am ashamed of the way I responded, for I knew she was wed, even if to an old man she could not abide. I must sound the rustic clown, but she dazzled me, and until I saw you, I thought she was the fairest and most comely—"

She held up a hand and not from modesty. He was leaning forward, and she feared he would throw himself at her feet or kneel in supplication. It deeply annoyed her that she seemed to be able to read him before he moved or spoke, but at least she had never felt like that with his sire. Never had she known from one moment to the next what Tom would do. And unlike with his sire, she did not want praise or pleas from Jack, but for him to stick to the business at hand.

"Did Penelope break her marriage vows with you, Jack? Tell me plain, yes or no."

"Not exactly. I mean, she tried, and I agreed, and then I refused to meet her, even though I was sore tempted, Your Majesty."

Her heart went out to him. No defiance, no

debate from him. He was someone who knew and admitted when he was wrong, not swore great oaths and cast defiance at the heavens and his monarch.

"Your Gracious Majesty," he went on, his face and voice so intense, "I owe John and Isabella Harington a great deal for taking me in, my Lord John especially. With both my parents dead, I had no hope for any sort of father—until my Lord John. And truth is, I partly turned down Penelope to avoid all sorts of trouble with the Haringtons. I feared they might not introduce me to you, and see the mess it's made."

He looked straight at her. His jaw had that Seymour set, but it was clean-shaven with no luxuriant beard to shadow his expressions. "But to think," he whispered, shaking his head, "if I had kept the tryst with Penelope, I might have saved her from death and saved myself...from your suspicion. I know the Duchess of Suffolk accuses me, Your Most Gracious Majesty, but I am innocent! It's true that I was dallying and sparring with Penelope, but after I whispered to her that I would not meet her that last day—"

"That *last* day?" Elizabeth demanded. "Penelope wanted an amorous liaison with you at Arundel House the day of my royal procession?"

Wide-eyed, he nodded. "*During* your procession. It would add a fillip to love's cup, she said. She thought it a great lark to meet upstairs over their heads, over where you passed by in all your grandeur."

He rushed on, staring at his knees. "She said she intended to watch you, Your Grace, but that we could also enjoy—I mean," he said, looking up, "I was so furious with Penelope's plan—her using me when she fancied others too—that I said yes, just so she would go off by herself. And then I did not go to her but let her stew alone—at least, without me."

"So exactly where were you during the time she was missing, after you had words with her inside the house? At the common table, was it?"

He nodded. "First I walked around in Lord Arundel's statues. Then, briefly, I went upstairs to see your cavalcade with the others but was still too upset to stay. I could not allow the Haringtons, let alone that watchdog duchess, to see how angry I was. So I went out into the crowd when you went by and could barely see you, though I heard every kind word you spoke."

"Enough."

She stood and walked to the window to lean a shoulder there, staring at the thick panes etched with frost even inside. Her breath began to melt a circle of it. She grasped his anger at Penelope, yet she could also understand a woman of passion who wanted power over men and chafed to be stuck in the country while her youth and beauty flew by.

And Jack, Elizabeth reasoned, had admitted his weaknesses. He was not yet, thank God, seasoned in clever court ways and the whirlpool of politics and power that had sucked down so many, including his own sire and uncle.

Besides wanting to solve this murder to help Bella and John, she did not want him corrupted or ruined. She did not want him in the Fleet or the Tower—or executed—for this. In years to come somehow he could serve her well to make up for the great harm his father had once done. If she were the Lord Justice right now, she'd toss her cousin Frances's accusations of this young man in the dung heap.

"Jack," she said, turning to face him where he held his ground—he had risen and stood by her chair now, one hand gripping the back of it as if to steel himself for doomsday judgment— "I know all this is difficult, but I hope you will be ruled by me during this time of investigation... by others I trust."

He looked momentarily stunned. "But...I understood the murderer has been officially declared unknown. Of course I would ever be ruled by you, Your Majesty. And finally to be here, after living in exile, first when I was in Lincolnshire at the Suffolks' Grimsthorpe Castle—it is as grim as its name, Your Grace..."

She could not stem a tight smile. Humor and charm stirred beneath his refreshing naiveté.

"And when the Haringtons took me in," he went on, "but were in disgrace in both your brother's reign and then Queen Mary's, that was hard too. I—I blamed my dead father, Admiral Seymour, for all the evil he had done and wanted to make amends. And now, when the Tudor ruler we all honor mounts the throne, I am far from your good graces I most desire."

The boy had an impassioned poet's bent, she

thought. That must have come from John, for his own father had not an ounce of sensitivity in his entire body. She nodded her approval of that speech and started for the door. Jack tried to step properly backward in a bow that bumped him into the second chair and sent him off balance.

She jumped to steady him, one hand on his upper arm. "Do not fret or fear, Jack. I will take honesty over courtly manners any day. So I would have you now sit here with Cecil's secretary and recount to him everything you recall of the day Penelope died."

Realizing she still touched him, she stepped back. He smiled at her, the first time she had seen such from him. It was a broad smile, eager and trusting, not wolfish, thank God.

"I will send for you to go over such testimony later, just to square things in my mind before I pass it on to others—should official persons yet look into this," she said, starting for the door Kat swept open.

Cecil's man jumped aside. The queen strode straight out, anxious now to see the room downriver where Penelope had laid her pretty snare but instead had stumbled into a deadly one.

"Best hang on tight in this rough water, Meg," Ned told Elizabeth as, with Jenks, they took one of the palace's two small working barges and set out for Arundel House in the winter's early dusk.

The queen had exchanged garments with Meg, and Jenks had told the two bargemen that the queen had sent her girl to fetch special curing herbs from Lord Arundel's house. The bargemen had hardly given a second glance to the woman all muffled against the cold under her hood. Besides, since the barge was buffeted by wind and swept by rising river tide, they worked hard to keep its course steady along the north bank.

"Don't know if it will freeze enough to have a frost fair this year or not," Jenks said on Elizabeth's other side, huffing into his cupped hands to keep them warm. Where the new Spanish leather riding gloves she'd given the man were she had no idea and could hardly ask right now.

"Once when I was just a young groom," he went on, "we had a fine time at Frost Fair. Put studs on our mounts' horseshoes and rode clear over to Southwark and back across the ice, right under London Bridge, 'cause even those deadly rapids there were frozen solid."

"To and from Seymour House?" she asked in her best rendition of Meg's voice.

"Aye, the very place we're going," he said, as if she didn't know. "Haven't been inside the walls for years."

She had never been there, for when she was the ward of Queen Dowager Katherine Parr and the Lord High Admiral, they had divided their time between her house in Chelsea and Sudeley Castle, Tom's country seat in Gloucestershire. After his death Seymour House was sold to Lord Arundel.

The bargemen eventually put in their comments about the weather, warmer than last year when "that bloody she-wolf Mary was queen."

Only when her nose began to run did Elizabeth realize she had not felt chilled or remembered her head cold during or since her interview with Jack. Now too she wore only Meg's squirrel-edged wool cloak and not her own ermine-lined velvet one against this weather. It was as if Jack had some curative power, better than the herbal possets and comfrey brew Meg had dosed her with.

Few other craft plied the Thames this late, and the trip seemed short until they began to row through ribbons of river mist. They stopped their chatter when the great lords' houses along the Strand loomed into view. Arundel lay lower and less conspicuous than its neighbors of Somerset and Exeter. Elizabeth recalled that when Tom was beheaded, Arundel had picked up the place for a mere forty pounds, as if there were some curse upon it.

Their craft bumped the landing, and the queen noted Lord Arundel's barge was gone, so Cecil had evidently gotten him away. Ned and Jenks both gave her a hand out, and Jenks carried the unlit lantern. While the bargemen waited, the three of them went into the grounds through the water gate. The shifting, chilling fog seemed to follow them inside.

"The house looks much the same," Jenks declared as the pale, painted façade peered down from under its hairline of dark-shingled roof.

"Sh," Elizabeth said, "and no dawdling. The house is full of servants I do not wish to see us. We are just fortunate they do not use the rooms above the Strand side gatehouse anymore. I hardly need anyone knowing we've been skulking about to see the design of it."

Grass stiff with hoarfrost crunched under their feet as they cut off the gravel path and skirted the inner wall toward the street. Kat had reminded Elizabeth that this gatehouse had been mentioned in Tom's treason trial, for it was here he had planned the uprising against his own brother, Lord Protector of their young nephew King Edward. Besides being Lord High Admiral of the Navy, Tom had been Master of Ordnance and, though use of firepower was in its infancy, had ordered and privily stored muskets and calivers here. Tom Seymour's secret plans to seduce and eventually wed the king's sister, the Princess Elizabeth, were only a part of his grand scheme.

Around the next tree trunk, his arm raised as if to seize her, a man reached for Elizabeth. "Oh!" she cried, and jumped back into a rosebush. Its thorns seemed to grab at her too.

"Just a statue," Ned whispered, steadying her elbow, then quickly loosing her to gesture in a broad circle. "There's a whole army of them through here, see?"

"It simply startled me," she said, and willed

her heartbeat to slow. She remembered Jack had said he'd strode among the statues. As she looked around, through what seemed to be disembodied, floating patches of frost, she saw the life-sized likenesses of dead Greek and Roman rulers. They too chilled her bone deep.

But when they entered the gatehouse—Jenks had to boost Ned through a window to unlock it from within—Elizabeth of England froze. As silent as the tomb, as black and cold as one, the place seemed to surround her with a skeletal embrace.

"You all right, Bess?" Jenks inquired when she did not take another step in. His voice jarred her back to reality. "Should I light the lantern, then, so you can see?"

"Yes. We will go directly up to where the body was found. Close the door behind us, Ned."

As she climbed the stairs between her men, she felt in the pocket she'd tied around her waist. There she carried the paper on which she'd recorded, in neat columns, Frances's and Jack's explanations of where everyone was—or where they thought everyone was—leading up to and during the procession. She had added clues Bella and John had given, though she needed more complete statements from them. Unfortunately, most members of their party had come and gone once they left the house to head out here, so the clues must be pieced and patched. And she was sending Ned back here tomorrow to pretend to be one of the chief constable's men and interview that serving girl who had pointed out to the Haringtons where Penelope had gone.

When they reached the large garret room and Jenks stepped aside, she gasped. The shadowed hulks of large boxes draped with heavy cloths resembled shrouded coffins, just like her father's all those years ago.

Elizabeth's knees went weak, and she tilted back into Ned. "I'm all right," she told him, stepping into the center of the room. "Just sea legs—from the river."

A floorboard creaked under the weight of one of the men. Other than that, the place was so silent, when it had recently rung with her people's cries from the street. She bit her lower lip hard, then spun on her men.

"All right, Jenks, hold that lantern high in the center of the room and bring it over when I call for it. Ned, I want you to take this piece of charcoal I brought and on the back of this paper sketch the layout of the area, putting in what things I tell you."

"Sketch, Your Grace? Command a speech or bid me act a part, but I'm no Hans Holbein."

"Just do as I say," she said, thrusting the paper and charcoal at him. "Here, according to what I gather," she went on, kneeling, "was where the body lay. Jenks, the lantern."

"Best we be here in broad daylight," he protested, but hastened to obey.

Elizabeth saw not a drop of blood, snag of cloth, or piece of hair, yet her stomach churned to think of what must have happened here.

Surely the girl had not been killed elsewhere and then delivered. While the disgruntled Ned's charcoal whispered across the paper, the lantern did catch something.

"Jenks, closer," she ordered, ignoring Ned's annoyed grunt as he was forced to shift and bend to catch the light.

"What is it then?" Jenks asked.

"Note this glitter of fine dust the lantern catches all over the floorboards. None of it is here, where her body must have lain—or writhed—as if she had dusted the place she lay. But that fine stuff is everywhere about, see? Here, sketch the general shape of this dusted area. You know, there might be a murderer out there somewhere with dirt on his boothose."

"Just London grit that's drifted in that double casement," Ned said, but scribbled the shape anyway. Before she knew it, he had started across the floor toward the window.

Elizabeth lurched to grab his arm. "But even if it is just London grit, even if the Haringtons and others who came up here and found Penelope disturbed this dust, the killer might have too, and we'll see some pattern or even prints over here."

That hope was soon dashed under closer scrutiny with the lantern. The only place the dark dust lay undisturbed, unchurned to pointless patterns, was between and behind the big wooden chests, which they assumed held Tom Seymour's stored arms. But breaking into chests and rummaging through muskets was the last thing Elizabeth had planned tonight. Perhaps they would have to return during the day.

"I want to see the view from here," she said, and unhooked the inner latch of the double window toward the street. "Jack said Penelope mentioned they could view my parade from here while they...amused themselves."

She shuddered as a terrible image invaded her mind: Penelope leaning out the window, waving down at the passing panoply, shouting with her skirts up behind while Jack pressed close and cried Elizabeth's name....

"No!" Elizabeth cried as Tom Seymour chased her through the twisting garden paths. "No, are you demented, my lord?"

It had started as teasing between them. She had thrown a walnut to make him stop lifting her skirts with a booted toe under the table his wife, Queen Katherine, had arranged for their sunny picnic. When they were briefly left alone, Elizabeth had commanded him to stop.

"Princesses may order most men about," he'd said, grinning, "but you—and your heart—will ever be ruled by me, I swear it."

He had reached right across the small table as if to drag her to him and feast on her flesh there. She had thrown more walnuts and run. Behind the hew hedges he caught and dragged her into his arms. She did not scream because she could not bear the others should see them—to make them stop.

But before she could seize her sanity, he dared to pull his dagger on her.

"My lord, stop!" she begged. It was even treason to lift a weapon in the presence of royalty. She wanted to defy and deny him, but her voice was so soft, as in a nightmare where one's feet went all leaden. "What in God's name are you doing?"

"In love's name, my Bess," he'd whispered hot in her ear, and begun to slice her petticoats apart, shred by silken shred.

His hands and tearing dagger exposed her shoes, her stockinged ankles, her gartered, trembling thighs. She bucked and writhed to escape him and yet get so much closer before Kat and others found them and forced him to jump away.

Ned's voice made Elizabeth jump. "I said, this area below was full of folks that day of your parade, Meg and me included, Your Grace."

"Yes," she said, grateful for the darkness that hid her blushes. "I never saw so many as leaned out the Ring and Crown windows across the way. You know, since each upper story protrudes over the one below, someone at the tavern could have glanced over here to see something. Ned, I believe I will have you play a part and inquire about that around the neighborhood soon."

"Now that," he said, swearing under his breath when his piece of charcoal snapped and he jerked a jagged line across the paper, "is in my bailiwick, Your Grace, and not this artist buffoonery."

Ignoring his pique, she opened one casement several inches and leaned her hands on it to peer out and down at the dim street. The wood felt scuffed and scraped under her flesh, evidently where the casement slid in and out, though it had opened easily enough.

The street had been dark only an hour but seemed black as pitch with drifting gray mist. As citizens were so ordered, lanterns hung from hooks along the way to give some light. The entire area looked deserted and sounded silent without the tread of the night watch. Many believed the night air was unhealthsome and knew not to venture out on London's streets after dark without linkboys with cudgels, even in this good area of town.

"Leave the lantern on the top step, Jenks, and both of you wait for me on the floor below," she ordered. "I want a moment here alone."

"But I won't say a word," he insisted.

"I'm not done with my masterpiece," Ned dared.

"Now!"

They moved quickly away. If they had asked her why she wanted a moment here, she would not, mayhap could not, have explained it. Somehow she wanted to defy this place, to prove to herself there was no inherent evil here from Penelope's violent death. And she wanted to bury once and for all those dark, delicious memories of Tom Seymour's hands on her body and her life.

Leaving the window barely ajar to let crisp air curl in, she sat on the edge of one big chest, shrouded with an old velvet curtain. But as she stretched her booted feet out under the window, she heard and felt something crunch under her heels.

She bent quickly to feel the floor. More of that dark dust? A small pile of it? She could not tell with the lantern across the room.

As she bent lower to examine the floor, she heard a scrape, a faint knock at the window over her head. She hunkered down, her hand still in the grit. And looked up to see the casement creak inward as a maimed, skeletal hand reached into the room.

Chapter The Sixth

Shocked, Elizabeth sprawled facedown on the floor. It was not until the bare, bony arm extended over her that she realized it was some sort of wooden pole with a hook or pincher on the end. At least mayhap that explained the scrape marks on the window ledge.

Aghast, she squirmed onto her side to watch it pluck at the velvet drapery over the chest next to the one where she'd sat. As the hooked hand dragged the drapery out the window, it trailed heavily over her, choking her with more dust and dirt.

Her first impulse was to grab the disappearing cloth and give it a good yank. The second was to find out who was on the other end and why. Letting the drapery go, she scrambled to her feet and, keeping low across the garret floor, grabbed the lantern and rushed down the steps to her men. They waited, resigned, on the next staircase.

"Someone is pilfering goods from the garret," she told them, pushing past. "Come on."

"What?" Jenks cried, thudding after her. "Someone's hidden up there, and we're fleeing?"

"No, and keep your voice down!" she commanded, reaching into the lantern to gut out its wick herself. Hot tallow burned her fingers. She thrust the lantern at Ned, thinking Jenks's sword arm might be needed. "I mean," she told them as they ran outside, "a wooden pole came in the window and is filching draperies right off those chests."

"Anglers!" Jenks said.

"Fishermen?" Ned asked.

"Thieves who spy fine things through windows in the day and pinch them at night with ladders or poles from roofs or other windows," Jenks explained. "Heard they're so good at it folks waked up with no bedclothes on or lost their breeches right off the chair by the bed. Wait, you mean, we're going out on the Strand and not back to the barge?" he demanded when Elizabeth went to the postern gate next to the big, latched ones beneath the gatehouse and impatiently rattled the door. It was a solid wooden one but with a good-sized grate to look out at eye level.

"I want," she said, biting off each word, "whoever is at the end of that pole. Who knows what they have seen if they've been spying in windows?"

While she kept trying to look out the grate, Jenks picked the lock with his dagger point and cut his hand. They charged out into the murky street to see no one on a ladder or hanging from a roof. But the wooden arm was still busy, this time dangling a brocade drape between the gatehouse window and the narrow third story of the Ring and Crown.

"Come on," Elizabeth urged, and set off across the hard-rutted street.

They charged after her, going in the unbolted front door of the place. The common room reeked of hearth smoke, onions, garlic, and much worse, but few patrons were in sight, and no one paid them any heed. Elizabeth made straight for the narrow staircase, which had several of its own dim, horn-windowed lanterns hanging from wall pegs.

Upstairs it was colder and darker, but they plunged on. Ned sounded out of breath. At the top floor, without a word, Jenks pushed by her to go in first, and she let him, grateful as ever for his protection. Ned scraped out his sword quietly, but she still could have screamed at him for silence. The last thing the new Queen of England needed was to be caught in a tavern where all sorts of men slept upstairs. Gossip of Penelope's reputation would be pure as virgin snow next to that.

Jenks hit his shins on a crate, and they went more slowly, feeling their way along the timbered walls toward the front room that overhung the street. Walking was uneven here; floor-boards dipped and creaked and moved. Elizabeth put her hand on Jenks's shoulder both to move him on and to steady herself. She felt the urge to sneeze and jammed her finger under her nose. Somewhere nearby they heard a man's sharp snort. The sound came again, louder; he was snoring.

Jenks pushed open the door to the room. All seemed silent within, the wan square of open window barely discernible. But a black form filled it, a woman's shapely silhouette with wild hair spilling loose around her head and shoulders. If she was a witch, she had a familiar too, an imp that pulled at her skirt until she turned to see the intruders and gave a sharp shriek.

"Eh, run, Gil! Don't let 'em catch you!"

Something exploded directly at them, burrowing between Elizabeth and Jenks at knee level, then knocking Ned back. The woman hauled the wooden arm in and somehow made it shorter so she could swing it like a staff.

"Get her!" Elizabeth ordered, and ducked the first blow.

The chamber was too narrow and crowded to let the woman wield the pole with force. Jenks darted at her knees and tackled her while the pole clattered to the floor.

"Bring her and that...hook...and her booty," Elizabeth said, turning to shove Ned out of their way. "We've got to get that little Gil. No more protests, girl, or we'll call the local constable to lock you up."

But the stairs down were deserted already.

Had Gil—dwarf or child—disappeared into thin air? More likely he had darted into one of the sleeping chambers here, and they dared not roust out strangers searching. This woman would have to do to answer their inquiries.

"Eh, don't call no constable," she was pleading with Jenks and Ned. Her voice was rough and, at the first turn in the stairs that had a lantern, Elizabeth saw she looked even rougher. "And don't take me 'way, 'cause my boy needs me to eat, he does. Those folks 'cross the way won't miss those fancies," she insisted, trying to snatch at the bundle of old draperies Ned carried. "No one living in there, eh. If these is all yours, lady, I'll just give 'em back."

"You're coming with us to Whitehall, where I want you to answer some questions, and then we'll let you go."

"Whitehall, eh?" she said with a snort and toss of that wild bird nest of hair. "And then for a bite to eat at Solomon's temple too?" She hooted at her own joke.

"More like the Queen of Sheba's palace," Ned muttered, but Elizabeth elbowed him in the ribs.

Under the second lantern the two women got a good look at each other. Elizabeth was surprised how very young their prisoner looked and how sweet she smelled—like lavender. Yet her greasy, disheveled hair probably bred lice, the way she dug at her scalp with her free hand Jenks wasn't holding bent behind her back. She was not pretty, but she might have been

91

once. In skin as white as whey, a jagged chin scar puckered. Her worsted blue, tight bodice and thin petticoats emphasized a slender body but full bosoms, not fashionably flattened in the least.

The woman narrowed her pale eyes to study Elizabeth. She was going to be recognized, the queen thought, and then what would she do with this wench? Threaten or bribe her not to tell? Send her out of London?

"Law, these two lackbrains maggot pies cuffed you 'round too, girl?" the woman demanded, squinting hard. "Black and blue face and your clothes like you been rolling on the floor."

Elizabeth gasped as she glanced down to see her hands and skirts besmirched with that black powder from the garret. And her face...

"Handsome mustache and beard," Ned muttered. "You smeared that stuff all over when you touched your face, as if to play the part of a Moor."

"All over," Jenks repeated, and dared to snicker. "You know, I warrant it's gunpowder."

She was suddenly furious at these men—and that she hadn't thought of gunpowder. With the lantern up there, they could have blown themselves to kingdom come. But now she had this human powder keg on her hands.

"We can hardly question her in the barge," Elizabeth said, frowning her companions to silence, "and we have to get going to miss Arundel's return. Whitehall will have to do."

But the moment they stepped into the street, something flew at them from the sky or second-story window. A kicking, writhing, flailing mass of fists and legs that took Jenks down and staggered Ned. They gasped to see it was a young boy. With Elizabeth's help, Ned pressed him against the wall under the tavern sign, yet the lad did not cry out.

"Gil, Gil! We are not going to hurt you or this woman," Elizabeth promised, putting her face close to his. "We are just taking you to answer questions for us...and have a hot meal. Now you come along quiet too, or we'll toss you in—in the Thames."

She had been going to threaten the Fleet or the Clink crown prisons, but she couldn't bear to think of these two bold ragamuffins rotting there, however many of Lord Arundel's— or Tom Seymour's—old draperies they had snatched.

The boy calmed but didn't answer, nor did he react to her promises or threats. For the first time she got a good look at—and scent of— him. When she expected a stench, he smelled rather like the lime and water pomade Robin used. The lad's fine russet jerkin and pewter breeches were much too big for him. He could not have been more than ten years, though he could be as short for his age as he was skinny. Yet his face was like an angel's, a cherub's at least. She realized the woman must be his sister or mother, for he looked like her, yet seemed untouched by the things that must have hardened her.

The boy made a motion, touching his own face, evidently to indicate that Elizabeth's face was dirty, but she was still grand—or beautiful—or whatever that last aloof look that flitted across his face meant.

"Cat got your tongue?" Ned demanded, and gave the lad a shake.

The woman reached past Ned and touched the boy's cheek before Jenks pulled her back. "My Gil not said a word for years. My name's Bett Sharpe, and you really gonna feed us?" she asked Elizabeth. "What sort things you like to know?"

"I want to know just everything, Bett Sharpe," Elizabeth said, and gestured her little band on toward the postern gate across the way.

Amazingly Bett Sharpe talked best when her and her son's mouths were full. They wolfed down fine manchet bread sopped in gravy, Kat's leftover poached carp, and currant cake, washed down by tankards of small beer at the table in the empty chamber under the state apartments. The lad looked as if he would have liked to dive headlong into the remnants of bread pudding.

"Laws, spices just in pudding, cloves and mace," Bett marveled, sniffing it, then scratching her head with the hand that held her sticky spoon. If Elizabeth had not been so eager to continue her questions, she would have had Bett dipped in that pudding to kill all the lice.

So far she'd learned that Bett and Gil lived in a room on Chick Lane in East Smithfield. The street, Elizabeth knew, in the tanner's district, was also called Stinking Lane. That was ironic, since, as ill-fitting as their stolen clothes and as shoddy as their bathing habits must be, they smelled sweeter than any courtier. Elizabeth supposed that somewhere Bett had stolen sweet essences she had decided to use instead of sell. Gil's father, Bett said, had died in Queen Mary's war to help Spain, but she added, having a man—her Nick, she called him—was better than having a husband any day. At that shocking unchristian sentiment, Elizabeth had only nodded.

"Naw, I didn't see the queen's parade," Bett answered the next question between slurps of pudding. "My Nick took ill in the lungs. Gil here saw the parade down by the Strand, din't you, boy?" she asked, and made a series of gestures.

Gil nodded.

"I'd like you to ask Gil," Elizabeth said, "some questions with that hand language for me."

Bett shrugged. "Ask him yourself, girl. I only give him the signs back sometimes 'cause I'm the one taught him. He's just mute, not deaf."

Elizabeth tugged Ned back when he stepped forward either to smack or to scold the woman for her impudence. After all, Elizabeth had told Bett she was just the queen's herbal woman who wanted information about any possible disturbance in the crowd near the tavern on the day of the recognition parade. She didn't want to give away too much and have the likes of these make up some story just to get the food.

But you might know, Elizabeth thought, this interrogation was like pulling teeth. A boy who was dumb was bad enough, but he and this harridan Bett made all of them look dumb too.

Bett kept eating the best victuals she had ever smelled, but she kept a keen eye on the red-haired woman who ran things here. She must really be some rich lord's wife to be throwing orders about like she did, however shoddily she was garbed.

"Gil," the woman said now, sliding into the seat next to him at the table, "were you near the tavern when the queen's parade went by? Your mother said—"

"Bett. He calls me Bett. And now that we got our Good Queen Bess, maybe I'll just start going by Good Queen Bett, how's that?" she said, but she was the only one who laughed. Her captors looked a bit set back by that, so she decided she'd best soften her cant. "So can I call you Meg, then, like your friends?" she asked the woman.

"For now. Gil, did you go to the Ring and Crown in that big crowd to look out the windows to see what could be—could be angled later?"

Gil frowned, shrugged, and went back to eating. To Bett's dismay, the woman plucked

96

from Gil's sleeve a piece of paper that peeked out. It was wrapped around a broken shard of charcoal she'd seen him lift from the green-eyed rogue on the barge.

"Ned," the woman said, addressing that one, who smelled as if he'd been chewing cloves, "I take it you've misplaced your charcoal and diagram which has all my important notes on the back of it?"

"How in heaven's name did the little monkey get that?" Ned demanded, and snatched it back.

" 'Cause they're anglers," the younger man, the one who smelled of leather and horses, put in. "And look, Meg, on the back of it Ned did a real nice sketch of you sitting on the barge."

"I what?" Ned demanded.

Bett watched Meg take the paper and look long at it. She could see from here that Gil had done a real nice drawing of her with her hood up, the side of the barge, and dark waters behind. He had the sky only half done and put in a few stars, to boot.

"He's covered over the sketch of the room I did!" Ned wailed.

"As if it were worth a fig," Meg muttered to quiet him, though he still looked pretty hot. "I just wonder... Gil can't talk but he can surely see and draw. And he's agile too for getting lots of places..."

"Like back into the gatehouse to do a decent drawing?" Ned muttered.

Bett watched the woman rise and put a finger to her lips.

"Eh, see here," Bett said, standing too.

97

Her legs ached from sitting so long, and she let out a big belch. "Gil ain't for hire, and we're not gonna steal nothing no more, so you just let us go."

She stepped eye to eye with Meg, hoping the two men wouldn't try to stop her from challenging the one she had finally figured out was really in charge. Gil bounced up, ready to leave, just as a knock sounded on the door and a real fine-looking gentleman hurried in, bringing with him a whiff of river breeze.

"Kat said that Meg's in your bed upstairs, Your Majesty, and you went to—" the man blurted before he saw the angry look on the woman's face. The gentleman went down on one knee quick with his hat off and head bent and mouth shut.

Bett's eyes held the woman's—the lady's—Meg's. Had this man called her what she thought she heard? And now was kneeling to her?

"Laws, we're good as dead," Bett muttered, and crumpled to both knees, dragging Gil down beside her.

"I may have just made a bigger mess," Elizabeth said a half hour later, staring at the cluttered tabletop Bett and Gil had left, "but I think those two anglers could be useful to us, my Lord Cecil. I just hope," she confided, joining him at the window where he stood while Jenks guarded the door across the room, "that the Sharpes don't outsharp Harry and

98

Ned before they get them to Harry's house."

"Don't hope for much help from the likes of them," Cecil advised, facing her across the width of the dark bay window. "You did see the woman is branded, didn't you? Harry told me when I passed him in the hall."

"Branded?" she cried, her hand flying to her face. "That raised scar on her chin?"

"On her thumb, Your Grace. There is a *T* on her thumb for thief, so she's been caught once, imprisoned, and marked—and if she's caught again, will be summarily hanged. King's, now queen's, justice."

She shuddered and wilted onto the wooden window seat. She should never have promised Bella she would help clear Jack, never have felt sympathy for a wanton like Penelope or let herself care one fig for a Seymour again, even if he called himself St. Maur. But she could understood why he did so. He'd said he was ashamed of things his father had done and wanted to make amends. And she wanted to help him do that. And as for a woman being branded, marked for life...

"How has Jack settled in with Mildred and your children?" she asked, pulling Meg's cloak closer against the window draught. She had long ago washed her face and hands, though her garments were still smudged with gunpowder. Again, she wondered if the murderer's blackened garb could be a clue—if anyone had noticed.

"Jack's a fish out of water but trying to please. I fear he longs to be part of your court," Cecil said, and she heard papers rustle somewhere up his wide sleeves.

"Someday perhaps," she said slowly, "when Jack's cleared of this and the real culprit is discovered, that would be possible."

"Then you are working from the supposition Jack is innocent?"

"Not exactly, but I believe some things he said."

"Ah, aha," he said, perching on the other side of the window seat.

"Aha, what, my Lord Secretary? I am weary to the bone and am going to bed, so do not start to spar with me."

"Remember in the poison plot, Your Grace," he asked, leaning slightly toward her, "we agonized long and hard about *sui bono,* the motive of who would profit from the crime? Finally it helped us solve it."

"Yes, but, Cecil, that comes into play only if the murder is planned. Since we are dealing with a murder victim full of passion, who inspired passion in others, that may be all too rational this time."

"But we must cling to rationality, Your Majesty, even though we are weak humans and our emotions enter in far too much."

"And was wedding your Mildred after you were widowed a rational choice then, Cecil?" she asked, gesturing broadly. "Or did you let your emotions creep in and admit, even to yourself, in silence, in private, that you loved her—emotionally, that is?"

"Touché, Your Grace. But do you not agree

a marriage match must be a blend of desire and...well, discipline and dedication, far beyond just pure feeling?"

"I don't like the turn this is taking, my lord, as I have no desire to argue with you again—ever again—about anyone's marriage, especially a royal one."

"Then, since that is the case, you must surely begin to give serious thought to naming a living heir to your throne," he dared, slowly drawing out a piece of paper as if either of them could read it in this dim light. "As things and bloodlines go, it should fall to the Protestant Katherine Grey, not, pray God," he said—she could tell he almost choked on the words—"to your young Catholic Stuart cousin, Mary, Queen of Scots, who may well soon be queen of France."

"Never Mary, not another Catholic Mary queen in my realm!" she cried, and snatched the paper to sail it onto the floor. "This wretched head cold or not, I am young and sound and shall not name Katherine Grey either, not for years at least. Could you trust her mother," she demanded, stomping once on the paper, then grinding it under her heel, "or the groups that would cluster around her?"

Cecil had slowly stood, backed away, then gone down on one knee in her tirade. "No, Your Gra—"

"And I've seen Edward Seymour making cow eyes at Katherine Grey. Do we need another alliance of those with traitors' blood in their veins like the Greys and the Seymours here in the bosom of my court?"

She looked down at him again. "Get up, my man. You and I must not argue over crowns...or thieves." She heaved a huge sigh as he rose. "As for the Sharpes, I am not done with them yet, at least not with Gil and I need Bett— Queen Bett, as she'd like to dub herself— with help for that. 'S blood, I only hope, before they can be of help, they will not eat poor Harry out of house and home or steal his curtains either."

"Ask if you have questions while I explain," Elizabeth told Ned and Meg as they stood before her in her chamber the next morning. "Meg will ingratiate herself with the Duchess of Suffolk with these curing herbs, and Ned—"

"I shall play," he declaimed, striking a pose, "a multiplicity of parts. It's what used to be my bread and butter when I was with my family's country players, Your Grace. I shall first become the chief constable's man to speak with the servant girl who spotted Penelope heading up to the garret, then walk the Strand and visit the tavern to see if anyone heard or saw something amiss in or near the gatehouse the day of your parade."

"I wish I was going with Ned," Meg put in. "He could wait for me to see the duchess and then—"

"I told you," Elizabeth said, stopping to blow her nose, "you are to attach yourself to the duchess so she feels at ease to have you going in and out of her quarters with fresh herbs. What is all that?" she asked, indicating the basket Meg carried.

"Woodruff tonic, that smells like new-mown hay when it's a strewing herb, but soothes the stomach, Your Grace. And this is mugwort to mix with hot water to soak her joints. And I've put in a pinch of quince powder to promote cheerfulness, as I hear she's a real harpy—oh, pardon, Your Grace, for saying that about your cousin. It's only your aunt Mary Boleyn was next to a saint, and this kin of yours—"

"Yes, I know, so you must keep your head about you and take some of that quince yourself. As a matter of fact, it might do me more good than these cold remedies."

"Like love, they always say," Ned put in, using some elegant courtier's voice, "a cold must run its course. Then you're left with either the sweats or the chills."

"Be gone now, both of you, and be careful."

Chapter The Seventh

"I cannot believe you have written this letter without my permission, Adrian. We cannot be seen having aught to do with Penelope Whyte or her people. Besides, I am the writer here, the one who keeps a diary, and so should author all correspondence."

When the Duchess of Suffolk's shrill voice sounded through the heavy door, Meg's feet lagged in the corridor. She even fancied she heard the duchess tearing up the offending letter. She looked both ways and stepped closer but did not risk laying her ear against the carved oak.

"But, my dear, it is the Christian thing to do," a man's peevish voice resounded. "We should send our condolences to her bereaved husband. After all, we were, more or less, with the poor woman when she died."

"Hardly *with* her! Too soft, Adrian, always you are too soft, too...unpolitical."

"You'll not scold me for that." His voice rose, and Meg nodded, wishing she could shout in, *Good for you, my lord!* "Not after I agreed to the ultimate when you asked me."

The ultimate? Meg thought. Whatever did he mean by that?

"Adrian, 'tis only"—the duchess's voice came soothing now—"that we must keep ourselves—because of Katherine's rightful heritage—out of this in every way, including anything that smacks of mea culpas, especially signed ones."

What was a signed *make all pass*? Meg wondered. Some sort of release from a debt? Or was that foreign words? She wanted nothing to do with another language when Ned had just taught her to read good King's—Queen's—English. At least, she thought, mayhap she wouldn't even have to face the duchess in such a heat. She could tell the queen what she'd overheard, that would satisfy her for now, and she'd go back another time with these herbs.

"Hey, girl, are you eavesdropping?" a deep voice challenged her from behind.

Meg spun, planning to give some guard a dressing down for accosting the queen's herbalist. But at head height she was staring not into a face but into the middle of a man's massive chest.

She gave a little squeak. Her heart thudded.

"Well?" he said, crossing his arms and peering down at her from a height nearer seven feet than six. "Oh, the herb girl."

She saw it was the queen's sergeant-porter, Thomas Keyes, who had got his post, people said, by being distantly related to some of the queen's cousins. She'd heard he was a widower with several children. His main duty was to run errands, but he sometimes seemed to be guarding the queen's door.

"Of course I wasn't eavesdropping," she declared, regaining her pluck and tipping her head back to stare up at him. "I'm sent from the queen with soothing herbs for the duchess. But I didn't want to interrupt their...discussion."

"Oh, that," he said with a nod. "At least the duchess isn't ranting at her daughter, the Lady Mary, this time. I just escorted her outside for a walk. Usually I'm not sent for such enjoyable tasks as to fetch and carry the Lady Mary."

Though the man had turned pleasant as pie, Meg was doubly angry with herself. She'd not only been careless but got unstrung at the size of him. All in all he was not bad-looking, with brown hair and eyes of that same bland hue. As now, he always wore drab dark brown. But she'd noted how quick his temper had sparked. And with someone this big and strong, a spark seemed a bonfire.

He rapped on the door. It was opened by what looked to be the duchess's tiring girl but with a man's dirtied doublet in her hands. She didn't, however, look one whit surprised to see a giant at the door.

"The queen's herbalist," Thomas Keyes announced, nodding at Meg. "With special *soothing cures* for the duchess."

Meg had to bite her lip at the way he emphasized those words. But she need not hide her amusement, for the girl banged the door shut in their faces.

"The queen won't like this insult," Meg muttered.

"That's the way with the duchess's people," he said, as if he were an expert at knocking on this door. "But for her husband, her temper's catching like the plague. She riles me all the time. Fetch this and that. I'm not in her service. But don't fret. They'll have you in, once they pick up things the duchess might be throwing. At least this time it's not at the Lady Mary."

Meg glanced up—way up—at Thomas Keyes with new insight. Her mouth fell open even to consider it. Not only that the queen might have taken pity on Lady Mary Grey and sent her sergeant-porter to escort her outside, but that a dwarf and this mountain of a man might have anything in common.

Ned was not certain what sort of pronunciation a London citizen who worked for the chief constable of London would have, so he mimicked the speech of the elderly steward who had admitted him to Arundel House. He gave his name as Lemuel Bailey and said he had a few new questions to ask the serving girl who had already been interrogated by his master's men.

But as he waited in the front hall—with another servant evidently posted there just to watch him—he got a good idea of how officers of the peace were regarded in the city. Even this lowly lackey glared at him as if he were a thief sent to eye the place for later mischief. At least the nervous servant girl who was finally brought to speak with him was a comely wench who seemed duly impressed.

"I will just step out to the gatehouse with her then," he informed the steward. "It may serve to refresh her memory." Another thought hit him. "And we shall step into the gatehouse so she could show me exactly—"

"Your master, the constable," the fig-faced steward said, "did that himself, and don't you know he said to keep everyone out of there, being the site of a cruel crime?"

"Of course I know that," Ned blustered, using the man's very voice back to him, "but that

107

stricture hardly refers to his own men. Never mind, then, as we'll just walk near the gatehouse."

He hustled the girl out before the steward could say more. Ned saw she was shivering and realized she had not planned to be outside, so he gallantly laid his cape around her shoulders. Thin and pale, with milk white skin and periwinkle blue eyes, she smiled shyly at him. From her kerchief peeked tousled canary-colored hair to frame her sweet face.

Ned had always loved the stage roles where he played men with authority, especially generals or kings in command of entire armies and realms, but this would have to do for now. It rather added something, though, to play a scene with a flesh-and-blood woman rather than one of the boys all done up in wigs and paint. This wench's name was Sally Muncey, and she clung to his arm.

He cleared his throat, surprised that he too was nervous. "I'd like you to tell me, Sally, not only about Penelope Whyte, Lady Maldon, but anything you deemed unusual—besides our new queen's recognition progress—on the day of the murder." As he talked, he steered her through the statues and rosebushes toward the gatehouse.

"You weren't here with the constable and coroner afore," she said, and batted her eyes as she leaned slightly into him. "I'd of remembered you, Master Bailey."

"Ah, no, I was busy with another matter—helping guard the queen."

"Pity. So you want told of the time on the stairs or others?"

He nearly tripped over his feet. "Do you mean you saw the lady in question another time besides when she went up to the garret?"

"Oh, yes, two others, but the constable din't ask me 'bout them. He talked to the likes of me nary a moment and spent all his time with the important folk—and them not wanting him to keep them, I could tell. Crying the tall, handsome lady was, and others looked full of choler, and the old duchess in a fit."

"Yes, I can imagine. But now I'm here to spend time with the likes of you and pleased to do it. Say on about the two other times you saw Lady Maldon then," he encouraged gently squeezing her arm and keeping his voice soothing and solicitous.

"First, in the hallway outside the dining chamber, where they were eating," she said, glancing back toward the house.

"What was she doing in the hallway?"

"I heard her say inside that she was disposed, so—"

"Indisposed, you mean?"

"Aye, that's it—like to puke, I think she meant. But once she got away from the food, she didn't get sick. The older man—not those two handsome lads—came out and said something to her, then she reached up and kissed him full on the mouth. He didn't want to at first, I warrant, but clamped her to him hard, then pushed her away and rushed back in, wiping off his mouth like she tasted bad—or maybe 'cause she said she felt sick, but din't look it to me, kissing him like that."

"This older man—thin and red-haired or the one with big shoulders?"

"Oh, big—not the duchess's poor husband, being sent out on her orders all the time like he was one of us servants, though I hear he used to fetch her horses and then he married high. Are you wed, Master Bailey? 'Tis a dream a mine to wed high, just like a princess, and you here being on such a lofty rung of London's ladder, being a constable's man and all..."

Ned swallowed hard. Everything she'd said after it was John Harington kissing Penelope blurred by. On the mouth and grappling her to him? Hell's gates, the queen was head over heels into this because she believed in the Haringtons. There'd be a royal explosion over that tidbit. His first impulse was not even to tell her or maybe to have Cecil break the news.

"And the second time you saw the lady in question?" he prompted. She was looking at him so expectantly he wondered if he'd missed something.

"When I took the sweets and drink up in the gatehouse for the guests acoming, she was right over there." She pointed at the postern door they'd all rushed through last night.

"At the door to the street? She left the grounds?"

"Don't know, 'cause I just saw her standing there, door ajar, like waiting or maybe peering out at the crowd through the grate, so many people out there to see the queen."

110

Including him and Meg, he thought, though they'd not been down the street this far. He wished he'd been intent on more that day than Her Majesty and Meg.

"But isn't the door kept locked?" he asked.

"'Less any of us got to go on errands, a key's right there on a nail plain as day. See it hanging there?"

"Plain as day in daylight," he said, thoroughly annoyed they'd worked so hard to break the lock last night. The staff here must not have noted that yet. "But Lady Maldon was standing there before the other guests entered the gatehouse?"

"That's it, a little while after she kissed that man. I even thought maybe she was waiting for him, but he came out with his wife and the duchess and her husband, 'fore he left the gatehouse again. Up and down the stairs, all of them but the fat, old duchess, when they should have just been watching the street."

Ned swore under his breath. Not only could anyone in the gatehouse, except the duchess herself, have stepped out to kill Penelope, but if Penelope had gone out onto the packed street, any man in the whole of teeming London could have followed a pretty girl back in, darted after her upstairs, then raped and killed her.

"Hardly blamed her, as I'd like to have gone out too," Sally was saying, her lower lip thrust in a pout. "But had to work, wait in case the guests had needs, after I already spent the morning sweeping out the whole place, every floor, even if they looked clean enough to me."

"Now listen to me carefully, Sally," he said. "Once you were in the gatehouse on the first floor where you could see who went up and down, during the queen's progress, did you ever leave your post?"

To his dismay, she nodded, big-eyed, like a child caught with yuletide suckets in both fists. "I was so excited with the new queen going right by," she admitted, "that I had to run into the servants' jakes in the house twice, couldn't help it, my stomach all in knots. I thought I should just get behind a bush out here to be faster or should have brought a chamber pot, but it was pretty cold to be baring my bum out here, least on that day, but today I don't guess bare skin would be too bad."

Ned fought to separate the fact that she was trying to seduce him—wasn't she?—from the facts he'd best recall for the queen later. "I'm impressed with how helpful you are, Sally. Did you note anything else amiss?" When she sighed, he felt her shoulder heave under his armpit where she'd somehow gotten wedged.

"I didn't stay at the postern door long 'cause the view was blocked by the tallest man I ever seen. Would've needed a ladder to look over him, and he at the back of the crowd right by the door. Master Bailey, you din't really come to question me 'bout those sweets I ate myself and took some wine too, did you, and now I'll have to pay a forfeit?"

Ned cleared his throat and tried to clear his mind of the scent and closeness of this woman. What else should he ask her? Would the queen want a blow-by-blow telling of when Sally heard or saw guests going up and down the stairs? But he'd have time to get that from her if he just softened her up a bit more first.

As if she'd read, or dictated to, his mind, she darted a quick glance toward the house, blocked by trees and statues. She let her borrowed cape slide open and arched her back to thrust her tightly laced bodice against him. And tilted her hips into his.

Ned had kissed her only once, carefully, when a crow cawing on the grounds jolted him. "Caught! Caught!" it seemed to cry.

He snapped back to reality, for this was not some scene where he could write the parts. Her Majesty would have him pilloried if he messed this up. And if the grim keeper of Lord Arundel's house inquired too much into his visit, it could tip off his lordship, and he'd question the queen.

Reluctantly he stepped away and held the girl back at arm's length. "Tell me some things quickly," he said, frowning out at a crow staring from some emperor's head. "I need to know what guests went up and down the gatehouse stairs and approximately when. And did you note if anyone's clothing was smudged? I can't be shilly-shallying about if I'm to get this report to the que—constable."

The queen coughed so hard that her eyes watered. " 'S blood," she croaked, and seized an extra handkerchief from the first lady-in-waiting who offered her one to hack into, "I don't want my people to think I'm either ill or crying over something. A stout heart and smiling face from their queen—that's what they need and shall have now."

She knew her every public word and action would be reported to the court and far beyond. Though her cold was worse, she had summoned Cecil and her Privy Council for a brief meeting that afternoon. Her kingdom needed shoring up in the shifting tides in which Queen Mary had left it. In unofficial mourning for Penelope—and to get over this head cold—she'd put off Parliament once but would have to face them and England's problems all too soon. Then, too, this murder was a malady all its own.

Wishing for more of Meg's soothing honey and hoarhound, forcing a smile, Elizabeth left her women in the hall and went into the council chamber alone. Although she preferred to enter after everyone was in attendance, Cecil had sent her a terse note that he needed to talk to her first. She was surprised to find not only him but Edward Seymour standing and facing the door. Both men bowed low.

But as always, when she entered here, the huge Hans Holbein painting of her father commanded her attention. Despite the other fine murals and hangings and the fact that King

Henry was joined by his parents and Queen Jane Seymour in the piece, his figure dominated the room. His plumed and bejeweled hat perched cockily on his head. He seemed to bestride the world, his legs spread in an aggressive stance, and the protruding codpiece that emphasized his manhood on display. Someday soon, she thought, though she was not a man, her portraits would show she now held this realm and people's hearts.

"Your Majesty," Cecil began without ado, "young Seymour here seems not to understand that his friend Jack St. Maur is under confinement in my household. My lady wife says he's been to see Jack twice without invitation, the second time after being told to stay away. You had mentioned you wished to speak with Edward, so I thought this might be a good time."

Edward looked chastened as she merely glared at him, but that did not appease her. She was quickly getting in a vile mood. "You seem," she said, staring down her nose at him, "to have a penchant for sneaking and speaking to those you had best avoid." He blanched at that, though she had no idea if her subtle thrust about Katherine Grey had hit its mark.

"I—Your Grace, begging your pardon, but Jack is my best friend and cousin, and he's as good as exiled from court, unjustly accused, and lonely, however kindly the Cecils treat him. I feel great regret that but for an accident of birth, Jack would be a legitimate Seymour

115

heir, and the Duchess of Suffolk would not dare to cast aspersions on him because of his heritage or—"

"Yes, well," the queen interrupted, sitting in her big carved chair at the head of the table with her father's painted face glaring over her shoulder, "accidents of birth and heritage, as you say, can wreak havoc or be God's blessing for an entire realm."

"Oh, I didn't mean—"

"Whatever you did mean, Edward, you are to stay away from Jack St. Maur for now, friendship and loyalty notwithstanding. My chief constable and justice of the peace are no doubt still inquiring into the business of Lady Malden's murder. And you were there too, so I would not draw any sort of untoward attention to myself right now if I were you."

Wide-eyed surprise, then squinting outrage showed in his eyes, but he controlled himself. "Surely, Your Majesty, you cannot imply that *I too* am under some sort of watch...or suspicion."

"It is an unsolved murder, Edward. And if you are such a boon companion to Jack and he desires to rise above his heritage to make his way at court, why do you not help him to dress more fashionably? Are you so short of funds, or are the Haringtons? He needs to learn to bow and behave courteously with ladies. You do behave so with ladies, especially highborn ones, do you not?"

He went white again, then color stained his neck and cheeks in a slow bleed from his collar upward. "God's truth, I do," he said, shifting his weight from foot to foot. "As for Jack's style, I've never seen his clothes tawdry or unkempt, though he much prefers the traditional fashions and ways. You see, Your Majesty, Jack and I want very much to please you, but we long for the days before our families made great errors in judgment that were not our fault."

"But mayhap your own recent errors in judgment *are* your fault, Edward. I do not suggest you directly harmed Penelope, Lady Maldon, but were you swept into her pretty web too?"

If he had not already flushed to the roots of his hair, she was certain he would have now. "Too? Besides Jack, you mean? I—she—I suppose Jack told you she flirted with me, but it was only to make him fume."

"Ah. And did he fume?"

"Neither of us approved of her tactics, Your Majesty, and resented being toyed with and teased. I always resent that," he dared to say, "but we did not lay a hand on her." He clenched his fists. "I had naught to do with—"

"Of course," she again interrupted, pointing at his face, then lowering her finger toward his fists, " 'lay a hand on her' can mean more than one thing." Damn, but her voice felt scratchy. She was going to cough again and not make it through this dressing down or this coming council meeting.

"Your Majesty—" Edward began, his voice rising.

"Now see here, young man," Cecil put in, and Elizabeth startled to recall his presence, "you'll not raise your voice to the queen under any circumstance or you can cool your heels someplace much lonelier than Jack's exile in my household." With a quick sideward glance she noted that clever Cecil had been sitting in a chair in the far corner, an inkwell perched on his knee, apparently writing down every word Edward said.

"Enough of this," she muttered, and began to punctuate her words with coughs. "Edward Seymour...just see that you steer clear of your friend Jack for now...and of others you had best not be...secretly skulking about with."

"Yes, Your Majesty, I shall. I swear it."

After he had left the room, Cecil said, "I hope he takes your double entendres to heart and stays away from Katherine Grey. On the way here he didn't beg me not to tell you what he'd done—but not to tell the Duchess of Suffolk."

"So perhaps he and Katherine are hiding from her, not me?"

"Both, I warrant." Cecil took his place to her right at the council table and proffered her some wine he'd poured from the corner sideboard. It eased her throat a bit, but she still wanted that honey and hoarhound.

"Your Majesty," he went on, "if Jack's lonely in a household as big and busy as mine, it's because he's a solitary soul."

"Quite unlike his father, then, thank God," she said, and took another swig as if she drank to that. "Besides, I can sympathize with him on that, tossed about between places and foster parents, branded with a dangerous heritage, waiting for and wanting a chance to make good when others still point their fingers...."

Cecil squinted at her as he tapped his papers into a neat pile. They heard men's voices; the others were coming in.

"Your Majesty, you *are* pursuing this murder investigation for the Haringtons? Not for Jack St. Maur, as if you owe his family a debt? It's noble, but you don't see in this murder something that comes near your person like the poison plot against your own Boleyns, do you?"

"If so, you'll be the first to know, my Lord Cecil. I see not one thread to link me to that dead woman or those who might have wished her ill, save the people who were with her that day."

"Good—God be praised," Cecil muttered as her lords entered for the meeting, surprised to see her already here, announcing her presence with a wretched, hacking cough.

Chapter The Eighth

"Quick now, reports of what has been discovered by each of you in turn," Elizabeth ordered her Privy Plot Council members as they met that evening in the deserted chambers below hers.

She could only pray that this meeting went smoother than the one earlier today with her official advisers, who had argued about how to approach Parliament for funds in but one week's time. Now she and Harry had taken the only two chairs, and the others stood, but then she was hoping this meeting would be short. After all, their cause was but to solve a murder, not to save an entire kingdom.

"My throat is raw despite Meg's good tonics and cures," she went on, "so do not make me ask extra questions. Harry, please go first."

"I wish you'd given me Jack St. Maur to watch and not Bett and that boy," he said, frowning at his clasped hands. "It's not only that feeding them is like tossing wood into an open hearth, but the woman is lording it over the kitchen servants and the boy is drawing all over their whitewashed walls with anything he doesn't eat first."

"He is skilled at drawing, is he not, Harry?" Elizabeth asked, breaking her own rule to keep silent.

"Aye, I'll admit that, Bess, so—"

"Next time you come to court," she interrupted, "bring him to Kat. We are going to induce the boy to draw what he saw in the windows of Arundel's gatehouse that day. And don't feed him right before you come. Aught else?"

"Bett's distraught because her man Nick will wonder what's become of them. Do you want me to send a note to him—"

"A note?" Cecil cut in. "You think he reads?

What trade does the man follow, or is he a thief and angler too?"

"He's a saltpeter man," Harry explained, "and newly in the employ of Lord Robert Dudley, the queen's handsome Master of the Horse—Bett's wording, not mine."

Eyes and heads swiveled Elizabeth's way. She sucked in a breath and got a coughing fit.

"So what are you saying then against my new master?" Jenks finally asked.

"Not a thing, man," Harry insisted. "I warrant Lord Robert's allowed to invest in saltpeter and gunpowder and firearms if he fancies them. Evidently Lord Thomas Seymour did such once."

Elizabeth glared at Harry, then Cecil, then Kat. None saw fit to add to that.

"I am reminded that I am going to ask Lord Robert to demonstrate the use of gunpowder such as we saw all over the gatehouse floor," she said, keeping her voice calm. "It must have been there since Lord Admiral Seymour's rebellion, a powder keg of a place all these years. I have been considering another surreptitious visit to the gatehouse to see if more is stored in those trunks. Anyway, next I speak with Lord Robert, I shall inquire if he knows of this Nick whatever his name is...."

"And Her Grace said she wouldn't talk," Meg said to Kat in a stage whisper that made the older woman elbow her in the ribs.

"Cotter," Harry put in. "The man's name is Nick Cotter. But can you imagine that pair? Bett and the boy smell like pomade, and Nick Cotter must stink like the very devil."

"Why's that?" Meg piped up.

"Because," Jenks answered before anyone else could, "saltpeter men tend piles of earth and animal excrement mixed with lime and ash in cellars to make the stuff that is used in gunpowder. They wet the stuff down with urine and—"

"We get the idea, Jenks," Kat put in while Elizabeth coughed again at the mere thought of that putrid business. "You just ask Lord Robert," Kat went on, pointing at Jenks, "for a shooting demonstration for Her Grace then." With her other hand she reached out and rubbed the queen's back as if she could soothe her cough away.

"No more of this topic," Elizabeth said, taking another spoonful of Meg's honey concoction. "Mmm, Meg, you told me earlier that the Duchess of Suffolk scolded her husband for a condolence letter to Penelope's husband?"

"Yes and said it smacks of 'make all pass' or 'make all pay,' especially a signed letter."

"A make all what?" Cecil said. He and Elizabeth looked at each other and shrugged. " 'Make all pass or make all pay'? Could that be a letter with mea culpas? If so, she implies they are guilty for something, and she was afraid Adrian would admit blame in a legally admissible letter."

"I don't know why I ever forget you are a lawyer as well as my best adviser, Cecil," Elizabeth said, her voice scratchy.

"And worse," Meg said, annoyed Cecil had known what those foreign words meant when she didn't even get them straight, "I heard Lord Adrian say he had done the ultimate for the duchess when she asked him to."

"But didn't explain that either?" Cecil pursued.

Meg shook her head and said quietly, "I think, my lord, it could mean several things, including to kill Penelope for her, but don't you ever make me admissible in court on that."

"If you ask me," Harry said, shaking his head, "just agreeing to bed with the duchess was the ultimate."

"And one more thing," Meg went on, trying to ignore both Cecil and Harry. "I learned the sergeant-porter, Thomas Keyes, is real familiar around the duchess. She orders him here and there when of course he's supposed to be working for the queen, so—"

"The thing is," Kat cut in, "since Thomas Keyes is in and out of here to fetch things, the duchess could have him spying on you, Bess. Just because someone's related to the Boleyns doesn't mean you can trust them and ought to appoint them to positions that—" she got out before she evidently realized she was about to insult Harry and left off in mid-thought.

"And," Meg said in a rush, "I know it sounds lunatic, but I think Thomas Keyes is sweet on the Lady Mary, protective of her at least."

"It must be the latter," Elizabeth said, "for

who wouldn't pity the small thing—except her own heartless mother? The duchess favors Katherine for obvious reasons, and I'll wager the poor little Mary takes the brunt of her temper. I pity and will champion her for that," she vowed, hitting a beringed fist on the table.

"You know," Ned spoke—amazingly, Elizabeth realized, he'd been quiet for once—"the servant girl I interviewed at Arundel House said she saw a giant of a man standing outside the postern gate the day of your procession. You don't suppose it could have been Keyes waiting for or running an errand for little Mary Grey, do you? It's obvious from my notes Lady Mary and her sister were in and out of the gatehouse."

"So this servant girl was quite cooperative, I take it, Ned?" the queen asked, shifting in her chair to face him.

"Ah, yes, under skillful, straight questioning."

Elizabeth noted he refused to meet her eyes for once. "The thing is," he went on hurriedly, "Penelope too was standing at the gate. Sorry you cut your sword hand opening the lock, Jenks, because it has a key hanging on a nail right there. It's entirely possible Penelope stepped out or met someone during the parade—with her reputation, perhaps some lover."

" 'S blood," Elizabeth said, and punctuated the curse with a cough. "Supposedly anyone who came to London for the festivities could have killed her. That makes it even more important that you—and Meg, I'll send Meg too, Ned—speak to people in that area about what and whom they saw. Aught else? I believe there is more."

"I obtained from the servant girl," he said, producing a paper with a flourish, "a listing of who came and went from the gatehouse and approximately when. She did not recall if anyone had torn or dirtied garments. The rest, Your Majesty, is for your ears only."

"Ah," she said, leaning back in her chair, "we have no secrets here, Ned. Can you say the reason for this request for privacy?"

"Because it greatly bears on a friend of yours, someone you trust, Bess."

"Not one of us here?" Harry put in.

"Of course not," Ned avowed, his voice vehement.

"And not my Lord Robert again?" Jenks asked, and Ned shook his head.

"Stop playing a guessing game and just tell us," the queen ordered. "I've long known I cannot trust people I long to trust—in this very instance my cousin Frances, Katherine Grey, Edward Seymour, and mayhap even Thomas Keyes—"

"And Jack St. Maur," Cecil put in, barely under his breath.

The queen did not deign to look his way. "As I was going to say, though, I do trust all of you. Say on, Ned."

"It concerns your friend John Harington," he said, stiffening as if to brace himself. "The servant girl claims he and Penelope kissed hotly after he followed her out into the hall of the house." Elizabeth felt sick. They all stared at her, evidently waiting for her to explode. Why, she thought, as she fought to bridle her fury, was she surprised that a man would betray Bella or his queen too? Lies, seductions, deceptions, adulteries: She had seen them all before from men, but they still cut deep. "Cecil," she said, measuring her voice and words, "I would count it a favor if you would send several men to bring John Harington to me early on the morrow, by force if he so much as hesitates to comply."

Everyone seemed to breathe again. Elizabeth realized she was shaking. Though she'd not bring it up now, in addition to John and Bella's wanting to control Penelope and protect Jack, this meant both of them had motives for permanently dispatching the woman.

"He has gone where?" Elizabeth shouted the next morning when Cecil's man Philip Farmont reported to her that John Harington had left London for the countryside.

"Gone home, to Kelston, near Bath, hard by Bristol, Your Majesty," he said, standing far enough back from her that she surmised Cecil must have warned him she might finally blow. Farmont was one of Cecil's most trusted men, so she supposed she must trust him too and not kill the messenger. Still, all this annoyed her beyond belief.

"I know where Kelston and Bath are, man! Were you given a reason?"

"His wife said only that there was trouble at home."

" 'S blood, there's trouble here, and he's run from it! You tell your master Cecil he's to send some men to fetch John Harington straightaway for questioning by me. And his wife, until I send for her, is not to leave their home in Stepney. Is that where you went, to Stepney? And do not tell me it is just across from Greenwich Palace, because I was born there and know full well where it is!"

"Yes, Your Majesty. I shall tell my Lord Cecil directly, and he shall care for it all."

As soon as the man had bowed his way out of the privy chamber, Elizabeth strode back into her bedchamber and this time drank the honey and hoarhound straight from the goblet Meg had mixed. It had wine in it too, she'd said.

"Bad news?" Kat asked as she came in with Meg in tow.

" 'S blood, John Harington has flown, but I refuse to believe he's guilty. Oh, yes," she said, beginning to pace, "he's guilty of much, but, pray God, not that woman's rape and murder. Times past I would have trusted John with my life, and I did trust him with the life of my dear Bella when I gave him leave to wed her."

She flounced behind the painted screen, into the small chamber of her garderobe, lifted her voluminous petticoats, and plopped on her velvet-padded chamber stool. "I'm going to send for Bella, but I have something else to do first," she called out through the open door to them. "Besides this, I mean."

"Aye, get over that cold and cough," she heard Kat say in a whisper obviously meant for Meg alone.

"And, Kat, you're going with me, but we'll employ the ruse of your going off with Meg to fetch herbs from an apothecary."

"Your physicians, especially Dr. Browne, won't like that one whit," Kat called in. "He's already in a vile humor over your using herb tonics instead of their bleedings and cuppings."

"We shan't tell him. That is only for the bargeman's ears."

"Bargeman?" Kat cried.

"Bundle up, and get us both weather masks too, because we'll have to ride a ways to get from the river to Lord North's house near Holborn."

"Clear to Holborn? That's almost in the country. Whatever there for?" Kat called before Elizabeth rejoined them.

"It's where they put the dead woman's body, remember?" Meg said quietly when Elizabeth didn't answer at first. "And you can't really mean you're going to look at it—her—Your Grace."

"Now listen to me, both of you," the queen said, pointing a finger as if she were their tutor. "I am getting desperate in all this. Who knows how soon the northern roads will clear and her lord will claim Penelope's body for burial? They said because of the cold, she was not embalmed yet. I should have gone before. Now, step out and send for Jenks. I'll have him ride to Lord North's to say the queen has sent her dear friend Lady Katherine Ashley and another maid to show their respects to the dead woman, and they should have full and privy access to her body."

"I'm glad Bess didn't make me go with her and Kat to see that corpse," Meg told Ned as they walked along the Thames on their way to talk to street folk near Arundel House.

"Aye, me too," he agreed, frowning. "Bloody, bad business."

The tide was fully out, exposing twenty feet of muddy foreshore. Ned had insisted they take this route rather than the street so the queen's courtiers and household wouldn't see them go. Meg liked to be seen with Ned to keep the kitchen maids away from him, but he'd insisted there was no reason for the queen's fool—and principal player; he always put that in—to be going off with the herbal strewing girl. That cut to the quick, but she'd gladly hike through muck worse than this to be with him.

"Jenks told me," Ned said, "Her Grace actually had him dig up a body once to pull poison arrowheads out of it to match them to the murderer."

"I know. I wasn't there but heard."

Yet he rambled on about the gory details as if they were just discussing the weather, which was biting cold. She didn't like this day at all and felt a great foreboding sitting hard on her heart.

"The Thames is like a great tidal pool," Ned declaimed with a sweep of his arm as if he had a huge audience. "It not only rushes on its way but goes up and down, tossing things and people, sucking entire lives down and out into the vast sea."

He gestured toward a stranded boot and a wooden box that still held cracked and broken pots. A carved chair back and a dead dog lay farther out with heaps of other things they could not identify from here.

"Ick," Meg said only, and was glad when they headed up a narrow lane between two tall brick walls toward the Strand. They emerged not far from Arundel House on the now-busy thoroughfare, though not half so crowded as she'd seen it last.

"Let's try some of the shops," Ned said, "and save the Ring and Crown for last. I stepped in there after I questioned that girl at Arundel, but all I got out of anyone was that they recalled the boy who never talked darting in and out and thought he was someone's lackey."

That plan sounded good, but Meg's feet dragged. She kept staring at that hanging apothecary sign down the way.

"See," Ned said, noting where she looked, "you get your chance to go in there today and ask them all you want about herbs before we get on to what they might have seen during the queen's recognition parade. Come on, then, you're walking like you've still got river mud on your soles."

Got that river in your soul, echoed in her head. Where had she heard that before? Had she said it to someone? London was all new to her, yet sometimes it pulled and tugged at her. And that shop up ahead...

"Meg, whatever is it?" he said, his voice annoyed now.

"I don't feel so well."

"We're not going back before we've done what she sent us to do."

She leaned against the wall of the Ring and Crown, still staring down the street. She tried to diagnose herself—stomach cramps and head pain—but it had come on so sudden. Over Ned's shoulder as he bent toward her, his face solicitous now, she saw a blond woman waving through the half-open door across the way and shouting a name.

"Ned, that wench is yelling for Lemuel Bailey but looking straight at you."

He looked carefully over his shoulder. "Hellfire, it's Sally Muncey." He gave a quick wave back but turned again to Meg. "She thinks I work for the constable...the girl I questioned for Her Grace yesterday."

"And must have done a fine job of it," Meg muttered. Her stomach twisted even tighter because the girl wasn't acting as if she were greeting a stern interrogator.

"I'll have to go settle her down, tell her

I'm with my sister shopping or some such. Then we'll make straight for that apothecary. I'll be right back," he said, and darted across the street.

Ordinarily Meg would have been furious. Sister? He could better have put the wench off by saying he was with his wife. She could read the man clear. He'd flirted with that woman at the very least, a pox on him. But now she was glad for the respite, for a chance to decide what she was going to do.

A boy, mayhap ten years old, coming along with a bulky hemp sack in his arms, looked up at her and said, "Oh, yer back. Heard someone saw you in the crowd when the queen went by. Where you been all this time, Mistress Sarah?"

Meg turned and fled.

At the last minute Kat said she wouldn't budge if they didn't take Jenks too, so the three of them, with three horses he brought them, went by working barge upriver to the Black-friars landing stairs, then rode north toward the fields of Holborn. Lord North's huge London home, Charterhouse, was a sprawling complex that had been a religious house before Henry VIII closed them all down and took their wealth for himself.

Kat was soon muttering to be heading out-side the city proper, and a nervous Jenks kept rattling his sword. But despite the weather and her health, Elizabeth felt good to be out under open sky. To see fields and open vistas again calmed her. How fine it would be to ride out

132

hunting or hawking or on progress into the shires this summer. She inhaled deeply, trying to brace herself for what was to come as they left the city walls through Aldgate.

"Kat, you must do all the talking, and I'll just be one of the queen's maids," she said.

"Then you'd best stand afar off and keep that muffler on even inside," Kat replied. "The whole city has seen you of late, and your face will soon be on the coins. Meg may get away with playing you from time to time, but you'll hardly be playing anyone else, maid or lady, herb girl, lad, or what you will."

"Then Jenks and I will stand back as if we are a couple the queen has sent to accompany you. Say we are Blanche and Thomas Parry," she added, using the names of two of her well-born, longtime companions.

"Mmm, you're a couple of something, all right," Elizabeth heard Kat mutter as Jenks helped her down.

Kat rang the bell at the gatehouse that guarded the expanse of stone walls. Elizabeth dismounted and took Jenks's arm as they waited farther back. He was beaming like a bedlamite, and she elbowed him sharply.

"We're here to pay respects to a poor murdered woman," she told him, "so wipe that grin from your face or I will do it for you."

"Aye, but wait till I tell Meg about this— my lady wife," he dared to call the queen. He sobered, suddenly looking like a whipped puppy, though yet a rather proud and pleased whipped puppy.

Penelope Markham Whyte, Lady Maldon, lay in a lead casket on a stone bier in a small chapel within the grounds. Her temporary mausoleum was, Elizabeth thought, more like a hermit's cell once attached to a church, as the old religion used to sponsor recluses on their grounds as a reminder of penance. The chapel was low-ceilinged, not much larger than an anteroom, and bitter cold. Each stone seemed eternally frozen in time and place.

Lord North had seen that the heavy casket lid was unbolted and set aside. Both women gasped, for where a gold coin, a crown, had slipped off one of the corpse's lids, one eye was open as if to stare at them.

"I shall have someone replace that coin before we reseal the lid," Lord North's minister put in. They'd had no idea he would ask his reverend friend to be here. "If you'd like it done now while you step out—"

"No, that's all right," Elizabeth said. It wasn't all right, and she couldn't bear the death stare as if Penelope were silently pleading with her for justice, but she did not want that eye covered. The white of it was dull, its visage sunken, but it was strangely speckled with pinpoints of red she must examine further.

But for that eye, at first glance she thought the corpse looked normal, though the face looked a bit mottled. The features had gone slack. Gray light from a single window slanted in to illumine the body, arms at her sides and a prayer book on her breast. Despite what sort of woman Penelope had been, she looked almost angelic. Then the queen noted something else awry: Her nose was crooked.

"Sir Thomas," Kat told Jenks, "if you would not mind stepping out with his lordship's reverend, Lady Parry and I would like a moment alone with the departed."

Jenks nodded importantly and went out behind the churchman. Kat peeked out to be sure they had walked away, then closed the door a bit more as if against the wind.

"Let's be quick if you insist on this," she said.

Trying to hold their breath at first despite the fact the corpse had been kept cold from the first, they bent close to look for bruises on her throat to match those mottled ones on her face. At the corpse's throat the queen found the coin that had fallen from that open eye but did not put it back yet. To examine her throat, they had to pull her neck ruff awry, then put it back. Nothing noticeable there, but then smothering was hardly strangling. Penelope had been of course reclothed in finery for her lord's viewing and for burial back home. Besides, Bella had said, the garments in which she was murdered had been greatly wrinkled and smudged, especially on the back. Unfortunately they had accidentally been burned by a Harington servant who thought she was helping protect Bella from having a reminder of such horror in her possession. Kat and Elizabeth pulled the voluminous blue velvet sleeves up the white, limp arms. Yes, vile discoloration and bruising as if someone had held her down by her wrists with much weight and might. Could she have kicked her own skirts up in a struggle, Elizabeth wondered, and in haste the murderer had not pulled them back down?

She leaned close to stare into that single eye again. Yes, speckles of blood under the eye and skin, and yet Penelope had not bled one drop.

"Perhaps," Kat put in as if reading her mind, "when someone struggles against the murderer's hand or whatever smothered them, blood pops in their eyes."

Elizabeth nodded and, with the edge of the coin, closed that eye, and placed the coin on it again. Until she solved this, she'd see that blood-speckled eye whenever she so much as closed her own.

"But isn't smothering usually with a pillow?" Kat asked.

"Nothing was found by the body, but I can't imagine there being pillows up there in the chill garret—unless Tom used to have them when he worked up there years ago, to ease his back in a chair or to take a nap. We'll have to search those coffers."

"Mmm, knowing him, a pillow could be put to good use if that garret was a trysting bower for a ladylove."

Elizabeth refused to answer, but she knew full well that was possible. "I'd say, Kat, some of those heavy draperies over the chests up there could have been used to smother

her, but they were neatly placed as far as I could tell—until Bett's angling pole disturbed them. I doubt that a fleeing murderer would put them back in place when he didn't even pull her skirts back down."

At that comment they both hesitated to do what they had planned next. "Forgive us, lady," Kat muttered to the corpse as they turned up her heavy skirts to her waist to bare her nakedness to their gaze, much as she had lain when she was found.

The body wore slashed blue velvet slippers but no stockings. Though previously stiff in rigor mortis, the legs had relaxed now. Once Elizabeth and Kat saw that one area of discoloration was a rose-shaped birthmark, they discerned only the slightest hint of bruises on the inner thighs and nether privy parts. The bad bruises were across the knees, as if someone had sat hard on her there.

"Held down from kicking," Kat whispered. "And with something over her mouth to keep her from screaming—mayhap silencing turned to smothering."

"Both of her wrists must have been pinioned over her head so the murderer's other hand was free, and he pressed her face so hard, her nose was smashed."

"And it didn't discolor to black and blue like a man's who's been in a fight because she died so quickly," Kat added. "Her breath, then blood, just stopped."

"That much seems clear, but what about her thigh bruises? Are such proof of ravishment?"

Kat said something, but the queen wasn't listening now. Considering that Penelope had suggested to Jack that they couple standing at the window of the gatehouse, were these marks a remnant of rough lovemaking the day she died or soon before? Not with Jack, but with whomever she had met in the street? Or with John Harington, who had kissed her hotly?

At least, Elizabeth reasoned, her overpowering attacker must have been a man. Yet a devious and furious woman could have kneed or bruised her in a struggle, even lifted the skirts to make it seem a man had done the deed. Surely not slender Katherine or tiny Mary, and that left Bella. She would have to send for Bella.

When Kat did not move or speak more, Elizabeth wondered if the older woman was going to faint. She should have brought Meg instead. She glanced up from Kat's hands, still gripping poor Penelope's petticoats.

"Kat, are you all right? We are done here. Kat?"

"She's—she's been with the Haringtons and estranged from her husband near on a year, first in the country, then here?"

"Yes. Why?"

"I don't suppose you've seen it much, maybe never."

"Seen what? Death?"

Kat shook her head jerkily, and Elizabeth saw she stared at Penelope's belly.

"She's so slender everywhere else," Kat whispered, tears in her eyes. "She's barely showing yet, but she is—was—with child."

Chapter The Ninth

"You know, my queen, gunpowder was once thought to be evil in and of itself," Robert Dudley—her Robin—announced to the crowd of courtiers the next morning, though he looked straight at her.

"And why, pray tell us, my lord?" she responded.

"Because it is black and sulfurous, and its crack and smoke reminded everyone of hell and the devil himself."

"And so," a man called from the back of the crowd, "you stand in Satan's stead today." Elizabeth could not place the voice and did not crane her neck. She knew Robin had many enemies at court, some who still hated the Dudleys for his father's part in the aborted Jane Grey rebellion, some who feared the unwed queen favored him too much.

Robin laughed with the others and shook his head. "Not so," he retorted, "though I would ride through hell to serve my queen. But now to the weapon and gunpowder demonstration Her Majesty has requested so she might stay abreast of the art of warfare in her kingdom. After all, France and Scotland are not our friends, not to mention our dear 'ally' Spain."

Elizabeth tried to keep her mind on the business at hand to avoid being distracted by Robin or his charms. But her mind swirled with her continued efforts to solve poor pregnant Penelope's murder.

When Bella had sent a missive, claiming to be ailing as well as grieving, Elizabeth realized she herself had often taken to her bed when she was accused but not guilty. At least for a day or two she would allow Bella the sanctuary of her own bedchamber. Mayhap she was mourning the murder of her marriage as well as of her sister. And, Elizabeth had reasoned, it might be best she question John before seeing Bella again. She had sent one of her physicians to be certain Bella was diagnosed and treated—and kept in bed until sent for again.

Meanwhile, Robin had set up this shooting demonstration in the great hall overlooking the Sermon Court. It had drawn a goodly crowd of courtiers, hungry for any sort of society with the new queen, who was, as far as they knew, spending a great deal of time resting to cure a cold. At least there was no way they could know the real purpose of this presentation, she assured herself. So many clustered here that Jenks, who assisted his master, as well as Cecil, Harry, and even Ned, did not seem to be out of place, crowding close, as she was, to hang on Robin's every word.

"Good English longbows," he was saying, "may still be the dominant weapon of battle, but mark my words, all of you, firearms, gunpowder, and lead balls will grow in use to make even the best-tempered armor obsolete someday." A few laughed, but all quieted when Jenks walked into the center of the circle to hand Robin the long matchlock firearm. The carved wooden stock was unwieldy enough, but the bronze barrel, inlaid with ivory, was over four feet long. "See, who can aim that long thing in battle?" Lord Arundel goaded. "I know King Henry's soldiers began to use them, but give me a sword or lance anytime. Cannon, we've proved that, yes, but not individual firearms."

"Which is why," Robin went on, undeterred, "we must employ an aiming pole."

Jenks produced a metal pole with a V-shaped rest at the top. "This," Robin said, looking directly at Elizabeth again, though she knew he loved to play to a crowd as much as Ned did, "solves the problems of weight, aim, and recoil, which is considerable. Shall I load and shoot, Your Majesty, and then perhaps you will do us the honor on the reload?"

She nodded, and he swung into action. "First the powder must be poured down the barrel, then the ball rammed down on top."

He rested the gun on its stock and demonstrated. The lead ball was at least one inch in diameter.

"What exactly is gunpowder made of?" Elizabeth asked.

"Made of gold," Lord North put in, "as long as the English crown continues to restrict its supply, which is why Lord Robert is trying to corner the market...ah, in several commodities, eh, my lord?"

"No shots today but from that firearm," Elizabeth declared, glaring at Lord North and

141

ignoring his implication that Robin was also trying to monopolize her. "Robin, about the powder?" she pursued her questioning, coughing discreetly into her handkerchief.

"Ah, let's see, charcoal, niter, saltpeter—"

"Which is what, my lord?" she asked.

"I forgot you have such a scientific mind, Your Majesty. Saltpeter is potassium nitrate. Some places in the world, like Morocco, have natural deposits. But we poor English must import or manufacture it so that's where some expense and profit can come in. Saltpeter is valuable for everything from curing bacon to mixing dyes, and now gunpowder. It has been used to soak the match here too."

Jenks handed Robin a two-foot strand of woven hemp, lighted at one end. "This cord is soaked in wood ash and saltpeter and will burn about one foot every three hours," Robin explained as he clipped it to the gun with a piece of S-shaped metal, keeping the shorter, smoking end close to the top of the weapon. "I've heard 'tis an awesome sight," he said, waxing almost poetic, "to see an army with these weapons at dusk or dawn, for it seems a thousand moving lights are twinkling in the dark.

"Now," he went on, "I'm going to prime this firearm by placing a small pinch of powder in the pan. It's connected through a tiny hole to the main charge of powder inside the barrel. And when I touch the match end to the priming—"

"Wait," Elizabeth commanded. "I want to shoot it with you."

She moved forward to stand beside him at

an open window that overlooked the courtyard. Below, Jenks had set up a target taken from the archery butts in St. James's Park. Robin and Elizabeth stared into each other's eyes at close range while the ring of onlookers shifted back a bit.

"It makes a mighty kick, my queen," Robin said, his voice so low as to be now for her ears only.

"You think I cannot handle it?" she whispered.

"I know you can. And I know I cannot stem the flash and smoke and roar in my heart when you so much as shoot a look at me."

She felt her cheeks flame. "I love fireworks too," she dared to say in a quiet voice, not to be outdone despite the fact Robin had his wife, Amy, tucked away at his country house. "I recall times my father ordered masses of fireworks shot into the night sky," she went on, "rockets, fire wheels, squibs, and pikes...."

Her voice wavered. She tried not to cough.

"They call those pikes of pleasure," he finished for her.

"Let us proceed then, my lord," she said in a normal voice.

He stepped partly behind and loosely embraced her. Taking the butt of the wooden stock against his own shoulder, he leaned the long barrel in the pole.

"We aim," he said, his voice excited, "we touch the match—if even a bit of this powder got loose, it could blow us all sky high—and fire!"

The firearm belched smoke and noise and knocked them both a step back. Everyone rushed to other windows to peer at the target below. It had been blackened and blown clear off its sturdy wooden legs.

Later Elizabeth bade everyone good day and allowed Robin to walk her to the state apartments. When she questioned him—she hoped she sounded nonchalant and merely curious—he said he did not personally know the men at his saltpeter cellars but for his overseer, Jemmy. Elizabeth had not mentioned Nick Cotter because she'd have to explain how she had heard of him. Sometimes she thought she would love to have Robin's help in solving the murder, but some deep-seated instinct—besides Harry's and Cecil's obvious dislike of him—held her back.

The moment she entered her bedchamber and closed the door, she heard muted but dreadful wails. Kat jumped up from her chair by the bed, her embroidery spilling to the floor so fast she stepped on it.

"I did not hear that outside these chambers," Elizabeth said. "What and where is that ungodly noise?"

"The boy without a voice. Lord Harry, Meg, and his mother are downstairs with him, and he's been carrying on just terrible."

"So I can hear, and so will this entire palace if he keeps it up."

"But I made certain it didn't carry into the

halls," Kat protested as the queen hurried down the back staircase. As Kat had implied and Bett had sworn, Gil Sharpe was supposed to be mute.

With Kat hard on her heels, she tore into the lower chamber to see Bett holding the wailing, writhing boy while Meg hovered and Harry paced.

"Finally you're here," he said. "I thought it would be a lark for the lad and Bett to see the shooting demonstration, but the boy went wild. I had to gag him and cart him away before everyone saw him and—"

" 'S blood, he's acting as if he's been shot," Elizabeth said. She walked to Bett, who struggled to hold Gil on her lap. "What's wrong with him?" Elizabeth mouthed to her over the tumult.

"Once," Bett shouted, "he was in a blast that threw him near through a wall. Laws, guess he thought it was happening again."

"A blast?" Elizabeth bent over the boy, then squeezed his face between her hands to hold him still while Bett grappled his arms to his sides. Tom Seymour had once slapped Katherine Parr, who had got hysterical when she'd come upon Tom kissing Elizabeth. But the queen's touch seemed to be enough to still the boy.

Flushed, he breathed hard through his mouth. His eyes seemed to focus on her from far away.

"No one is going to hurt you, Gil," Elizabeth said. "No one is going to shoot at you or

145

make any more bangs. Bett, I thought he had no voice."

"He can wail or scream but has not talked since that explosion at the saltpeter works where I took him to see my Nick years ago. Some lackbrain made a spark, and the whole place went. I ended up with only a chin scar, but two men died. Others got burned, and the boy got thrown into a wall, then never talked no more."

"Gil, stand up like a big boy." She pulled him off his mother's lap. "I want you to draw something for me, will you?" she went on, hoping to divert him. "I thought your sketch of me in the barge was so good I'd like another one or two, and I'll pay fair for them too, in either coin or food for you and Bett and Nick."

Flushed, still breathing hard, the boy nodded. A quick glance at Meg sent her scurrying upstairs for paper, pen, and ink, though that was a mistake. The boy had never held a pen and kept breaking the nibs and splattering black splotches as he feverishly began to draw more pictures of Elizabeth on a barge adrift on the river. She ended up with a big ink puddle that blacked her out as if some curse had struck.

"Enough," Elizabeth said. "Until he can master a pen, fetch him charcoal again, but sharpen the tip somehow. Gil, listen to me. I don't want that picture over again but one of what you saw in the window of the Arundel gatehouse the day of my procession. Any face, anyth—"

Gil jumped up from his seat at the table and rushed to the window so fast Elizabeth was terrified he meant to hurl himself through it, glass and all. Harry stopped him, and Bett soon had him in her arms again, standing in the corner, the boy shaking and her crooning to him in a guttural voice.

Elizabeth hit the table with both fists, splattering more ink. "This isn't working. Nothing's working," she whispered to Harry and Kat. They followed her out to the stairs that led back up to the state apartments. Meg tagged along, and the four of them huddled there on the small landing.

"I had a thought," Meg said, "when the boy was struggling so with that pen but using it like a lunatic. I told you I heard the Duchess of Suffolk say she kept a diary and scolded her lord Adrian that she was the writer in the family."

"I don't want to even think about that woman," Elizabeth said with a shudder. She turned away, crossing her arms over her bodice as if to hug herself.

"Those fresh rumors about me, Your Majesty," Harry whispered, his voice breaking. "You—you think she's the one started them?"

Elizabeth frowned at the wall for a moment, facing none of them, though she knew these people were on her side. The old rumors had been rampant again that Harry Carey, newly created Lord Hunsdon, was indeed more than her cousin through their mothers, Anne and Mary Boleyn. Someone had been whispering that Harry had been sired by King Henry when Mary Boleyn was his mistress, before the king's eye fell on Anne.

Such infidelity was expected of kings, of course, but Elizabeth abhorred it. How many bastard half siblings might she have in her new kingdom was anyone's guess. It could include, for all she knew, Harry, and certainly John Harington's first wife, which made his daughter, Hester, Elizabeth's niece.

She turned to face them, one hand on the curved stone wall.

"It's a damned lie simply to discredit you," Harry went on, "and I shall always say so. God's truth, I resemble my father, Will Carey, and my mother would have told me if he was not my sire!"

"Your mother," Elizabeth said, reaching out to squeeze his arm, "and rightly so, feared and hated King Henry for his six wives and God knows how many mistresses, so who knows what she would or would not have told you? But you have proved yourself true to me, Harry, and I warrant we shall weather worse rumors than this over the years. The duchess may have begun them, but I think not as she does not wish to elevate you in people's eyes, but rather her Katherine. And I believe the duchess is departing court for Suffolk House not to hide from me but so that she can leave Katherine more completely in my care since I have decided to take her on as Lady of the Bedchamber."

"What?" Kat cried. "Katherine Grey, one

of those ninnyhammers I'm to keep an eye on?"

"Exactly. A sharp eye on. That's the point of Katherine kept close. But let us figure what we must do next in finding Penelope's foul murderer. Meg, what is it you began to say? Any news from your latest visit to the duchess besides that she has her servants, including her poor husband, packing?"

Elizabeth knew to wait when Meg paused or hesitated, but Harry put in, "Say on, girl. If I had to wager who would be vile enough to plan a murder to discredit the Haringtons and Seymours, mayhap drag out past evil rumors of our queen again, well, I'd still lay odds on that power-hungry duchess any day."

"I was only going to say," Meg replied, her voice almost a whisper, "since Ned taught me to read, I thought I might find that diary in her rooms here when she was packing. Then I would read what she wrote about the murder. But I had a chance to be alone when her tiring girl stepped out and didn't find a thing like a diary or loose papers either."

"Meg, you took a terrible chance," Elizabeth said. "She probably keeps it at her house across the river."

"If I take her the herbs there, I can look there."

"You're no sneak thief, my Meg. What is it? I knew you've been on the verge of tears. What else have you not said? Was the duchess cruel to you?"

"It's only that Ned's been venting his spleen for my leaving him on the Strand yesterday when I got to feeling ill. I—it means so much to me,

Your Grace, that you've cared for me and trusted me, just like you have Lord Harry."

Elizabeth ignored Harry's roll of eyes at being lumped with her herb girl, but she said, "I trust and care for you all, and Ned does too though he's sometimes a bit too full of himself. You can go on back with him to question folk on the street about what they saw or heard amiss—other than some rabid dog—that day on the Strand. And though I'd give a fortune," she said, gripping the iron railing, "to be able to peruse the duchess's diary, you'll not risk yourself again with thievery, Meg, but stick to gleaning what you can by merely listening and looking."

Listening and looking, Bett thought as she peered through the crack in the door at the queen and her friends. Aye, that was half of being a good angler, making plans for what to snatch once darkness came. And the queen had said she'd give a fortune to have the Duchess of Suffolk's diary out of Suffolk House over across London Bridge in Southwark. Eh, Bett knew the place, 'cause who could miss that pile of stones, so big and grand?

She glanced back at Gil, sitting on the floor in the corner, his skinny arms wrapped tight around his bent knees, staring at the floor. How kind the queen had been with her boy, like some folks said the mere royal touch could cure some dread disease they called scrofula, the king's evil.

150

Bett wished she herself could cure her boy from the way he sometimes slipped back into that day of the big blast at the saltpeter cellars. Wished she could make him talk again. Wished she could get him to draw what the queen wanted so they'd get more coin.

Laws, despite how fine things were at Lord Harry's fancy town house, she had to get them out of there, get home to Nick. And now maybe too filch the duchess's diary and sell it to the queen.

Buoyed up by the queen's kind words on the staircase an hour ago, Meg let herself out into the cold privy garden, where she would tend her herb beds, though she guessed she'd have to oversee ones at any of the royal palaces the queen visited.

Meg walked past the big central fountain, frozen silent now, and hurried down the gravel path beneath the bare fruit trees that lined the promenade. Pulling her cloak tighter, she went out the tiny gate that led to the tennis court, then onto the narrow, cobbled, public street that cut through the far edge of Whitehall. Out the Holbein Gate she went, then made her roundabout way through the crowds and carts toward the Strand.

With each leaden step, she forced herself on, hearing what Ned had said about the apothecary she had to visit today to find the answers. Not answers to who murdered Penelope, but maybe who murdered someone she once was.

151

"That apothecary shop was closed anyway," Ned had reported. "The old widow who owns it, Mariah Scutea, has evidently taken ill. Someone said her husband, John, was once apothecary to Queen Catherine of Aragon and later Queen Mary. And the Scutea daughter, who used to help with the place, supposedly ran off somewhere, though someone else said they even searched the Thames shore for her body."

Meg shuddered at that. Those names, that news, had rocked her. Not that she remembered any of it from her former life. But last year the Princess Elizabeth, at William Cecil's urging, had asked if she could be the daughter of John Scutea. Because the Scuteas were so ardently anti-Protestant, anti-Boleyn, and anti-Elizabeth, Cecil had wondered if they could be behind the poison plot that targeted Boleyn kin, including the princess.

Meg had denied any knowledge of the Scuteas, but that lad yesterday had called her Mistress Sarah and asked her where she'd been so long. And she had felt so—so pulled to that shop. Worse, if she turned out to be the missing Sarah, she would have to leave the queen's service. No matter how much she claimed she trusted her, Her Majesty could hardly keep her in her household. And that would as good as kill Meg Milligrew too.

She felt sicker the closer she got to that swinging shop sign. That Turk's head with a gilded pill on his extended tongue suddenly reminded her of someone who was about to puke. Had she seen that many times before the day she and Ned stood under it waiting for the queen? She had been so sure she'd never been to London, yet there were echoes of something here, especially when she looked out over the river.

Got that river in your soul, she heard some distant voice whisper deep inside her, maybe her own voice.

She rapped on the closed door of the shop, waited, then rapped again. Trying the door, she found it latched or bolted. She put her cupped hands to her face to shield the single shaft of winter sun that worked its way down between the overhang of protruding upper stories and thatched roof. Now she could see through the thick glass at the jars and crocks and hanging herbs, the narrow, deep wooden drawers and cubbyholes with their dried treasures. No, she could not see that far in, but she knew they were there. Locking her shaking knees to stand, she rapped again.

"Hey, you, the mistress is ailing, and it's closed," a woman's voice shrilled down.

Meg stepped back into the street to see above the first overhang. A few folks jostled her as they went by, but she paid them no heed. "Please, if the mistress is ill," she called up, "I need to speak to someone about Mariah Scutea." She loosened her woolen muffler to be better heard and squinted up at a form that blocked the sun. It was an old dame, her face a web of wrinkles, her kerchief clean and white.

At least that face meant nothing to her.

"That you, Sarah?"

"I—no. Someone's mistaken. My name is Meg Milligrew. Please let me see Mariah, even if she's ill. I've brought my own curing herbs for her," she said, and took a packet of the many she'd brought from her basket.

It seemed eternity before she was let in. The smells, the silence of the shop with the door shut on the street—things began to roll back over her in great waves.

She followed the old woman—a neighbor, it turned out—up the narrow steps at the back of the shop. They sagged and creaked. Somehow that sound was comforting.

"Where you been? Why'd you ever take off that way when your sire died?" the beldam interrogated her on the way up. "Was it just that you and Ben argued? Don't you think they been sick just looking for you and now this tragedy?"

As if the woman were speaking from underwater, those words hardly sank in. Meg's pulse pounded. Why could she not picture all of this place, recall the face she would see soon, the face that might be her mother's? And what would she tell the queen?

"What tragedy?" Meg asked in the narrow, dim corridor outside a door where the old woman paused. "It's not the pox or plague?"

She shook her head. "Your leaving broke her heart. She's dying from a ball and powder wound. Shot, she was, just standing in the crowd right near the queen when she rode by."

Chapter The Tenth

The queen met with Jack St. Maur in the apartments below hers, which she had taken to using as her center for working on this crime.

"I am eternally grateful you have consented to see me on such short notice, Your Majesty," he said, his voice somewhat muffled as he had not yet risen from his deep bow. But the bow itself suggested he'd been practicing. Her heart went out to him—until she hardened it by recalling how Cecil had worded Jack's request to see her.

"Rise, Jack. My Lord Cecil says you have a confession to make to me alone."

"I do indeed, and—Oh, Your Majesty, you did not think I came to say I harmed Penelope?"

"It had crossed my mind."

"Then you do not believe I am wrongly accused," he said, looking entirely crestfallen. The setting sun gilded his teary eyes.

She began to pace. "But," she said, "when one hears the very words 'confession to make'..."

He dared to keep in step with her back and forth until she stopped. "You know, Your Majesty, I have thought of confessing to her murder, I swear I have."

"Stand away from me."

He backed off two steps but threw his arms out in supplication. "But only so that you would not suspect those I love, who, unlike me, have things in this life and hopes to build on, such as the Haringtons or Edward. I swear to God it is not that I am guilty."

She sighed so hard her shoulders slumped. She leaned her elbows in the deep window ledge as if to watch the last of the day's watercraft on the gray Thames. "You are so naive, Jack, even to come close to admitting such a dire thing," she warned. "If you are innocent, and I pray you are, you must stand firm, you must declare it always to the skies." She spun to face him so fast her skirts belled out. "What confession will you make, then?"

"That I would do anything to serve you. And I implore you if there is aught I could do to clear my name that I might be your liege man until I die. And not just to compensate for my father's vile actions—"

His voice broke. Now she blinked back tears.

"All the wealth," he went on with a sweep of his arm toward the window, "the power of this vast kingdom lies in you, Your Majesty, and so I beg you to forgive that this token of my admiration and eternal esteem is so meager. But like the widow's mite in the Holy Scriptures, it is all I have to give and so my everything."

Why had she ever thought this man could not express himself? He went down on one knee again and extended his hand, palm up. A filigreed gold brooch set with a rectangular-cut topaz leaped with amber light, struck through by the last rays of sun.

156

She was grateful for the window ledge behind her or her knees would have buckled. Once his father had given her a yellow sapphire, so similar, set on a locket with a painted miniature of him in it, but Jack could not know that. Even Kat did not know that. For years the locket had been wrapped in flannel and thrust in a tiny leather box with a pair of earrings that had once been her mother's.

"I know," Jack went on when she did not speak, "that your friends and favorites must have bestowed upon you wondrous gifts for the twelve days of Christmas, but—"

"Hush, Jack. Make no excuses, I said. You must learn that: to be strong and sure whatever befalls. Rise."

He did but also came two steps closer, holding out the brooch. She reached to take it from him, warm from his skin, then extended her right hand for him to kiss.

He bent his head. His raven black hair glinted almost blue, so like his father's. She longed to stroke it or sink her fingers in the thick tresses, but she stayed stock-still. His lips felt slightly chapped against her skin; his chin stubble scraped the backs of her fingers. Her insides cartwheeled as another memory of Tom assaulted her. She tugged her hand back when his lips lingered.

"Jack, I accept your gift, and you will take my advice in turn."

"Yes, Your Majesty. I remember each thing you say to me."

"Go back to my Lord Cecil's household

and behave until I send for you again. Be content there without Edward or anyone else coming to call."

"And can I not see the Haringtons," he wheedled, "for their sakes as well as mine?"

"No!" she exploded, terrified she had now come to suspect them, John at least. "The waiting game," she went on quietly, "is best for you. I've played it, you see, and won."

"Yes," he replied, his gaze so intense. "You have played it more than once and won."

"Now I am going to ask you a question, and you will answer me rightly and truly, with God as your witness."

"Anything."

"But never promise anything. 'S blood, you have so much to learn!" she said, and stamped her foot, then made for the door, the brooch clutched in her perspiring palm. Cecil had accused her once of truly loving Tom Seymour. Aye, mayhap she had and been thoroughly burned for it. And now she was coming to care for his son when she must not.

At the door she turned back to him. He had followed her partway across the room. "Jack, do you swear you never bedded with Penelope? And I don't mean necessarily *on* or *in* a bed, so that you do not mistake my intent. No mincing words here."

His eyes widened. For one moment she feared he would guess that Penelope had been pregnant. Or had her murderer known that and smothered her to silence when she said she would use it somehow against him?

"Your Majesty, I never did. I am innocent. And taking a lesson from you this day, I know I should not even say again how I wanted to lie with her, how I, like others, was seduced by her, but I did not bed her."

He stared straight into her eyes. He did not flinch or blink. Yes, she thought, someday, when all this was past, he would learn to be her man for whatever duties she would give. Perhaps someday his truth and loyalty would compensate for the lies and betrayal from his sire.

She knocked on the door for Cecil's man to take Jack back but turned again. "Next time we meet, Jack St. Maur, I have a gem to exchange for this one, set above a portrait your father gave me once. Have you ever seen his likeness?"

"They say a fine one hangs at Sudeley Castle, which your royal father bestowed upon him once. I've never seen the painting or the place, forfeit as they were, with everything else. To tell true, I have inherited all of it, but only in my dreams."

"Dreams are good," she whispered, "if they don't become nightmares."

When the door opened behind her, she felt a cold draught cloak her. Jack said something else, but she did not look back.

The next thing Meg remembered was a wet cloth on her face. Where was she? Had a horse kicked her in the head? Ah, yes, Lady

Mary Boleyn had taken her in and would care for her.

"You fainted dead away, Mistress Sarah," a woman's voice said.

Reality rushed back. She opened her eyes and let the old dame help her up from the floor and to a chair. Beside a bed. With a woman lying there. And that woman staring at her with feverish eyes in a sunken face.

Meg blinked and looked. She did not remember the face, though she supposed she resembled this woman in the shape of the chin and nose. Her hair was white, but with the faint blush yet of auburn.

"Oh, my dearest girl, you came back," the ill woman, Mariah Scutea, whispered. One thin hand kept clutching at the covers. "Ave Maria, the Blessed Virgin has granted my last wish to see you."

Papists, Meg thought, but then anyone who had served Catherine of Aragon and Queen Mary would be. The new queen said people's consciences were their own affair, but everyone knew Elizabeth was Protestant clear through, for King Henry had ruined the Catholic Church in England to wed Anne Boleyn. All these high-flying things came to Meg, but not one memory of this poor woman.

"I had to see you," Meg said. "Because— just because I need to ask everyone around here if you saw a young, pretty blond woman on the street the day of the queen's parade. That's all I came for."

"So many people on the street," the old

neighbor woman said. "But, Mariah, remember that woman who pounded on the door when we were on our way out to see the new queen ride by? You know, the woman in a hurry who offered a handsome fee for pennyroyal or mandrake, but you told her it was a mortal sin, however much you could use her coin?"

"Oh, yes," Mariah whispered. "With the giant."

"We don't know he was with her," the old woman said, glancing from Mariah to Meg with a shrug, "though he waited outside. Then he followed her fast away, towering over everyone in that brown hat. But that doesn't matter one whit now that your Sarah's come home."

Meg tried to concentrate, but she kept thinking that if Mariah was her mother, it was a sin not to comfort and honor her, a mortal sin.

"I don't remember...before," Meg tried to explain to them. She sounded kind of foggy, felt that way too. "I was in the countryside, in Essex, and a horse kicked me, and people took me in. My name is Meg Milligrew."

"I knew, just knew you would never leave me widowed here to keep this place alone," Mariah whispered as if she had not heard one word. "Ben knows nothing of the herbs and was restless to be back on the river. Lord Banbury died and left me no money, not a groat, and we're in debt after all these years."

The name Lord Banbury seemed familiar, but Meg couldn't recall any brother Ben she'd had. The old neighbor dame was now fussing over Mariah, smoothing the coverlet and pressing the wet cloth to her hot brow.

"Here, let me do that," Meg said, rising unsteadily. "I've done nursing. I know the cures."

"Of course you do, your father's pride," Mariah whispered, grasping Meg's wrist weakly. "But there's no cure for this lead ball in my innards. They say gunpowder in a wound is poison."

"Poison?" Meg cried.

"It was as if God's judgment fell from heaven but missed that anti-Papist, Protestant bastard it should have got instead of me."

"H-Her Majesty?"

It struck her then, harder than a blast from a firearm ever could: not just that these people hated the new queen but that someone had shot at her right outside in the street and hit this woman, Mariah Scutea, her mother, instead.

It was after dark that night that Cecil's message reached the queen. His men had escorted John Harington back to London. When and where did she want to interview him? *Now and on the tennis court,* her return note said.

With Jenks for a guard, she went down to the barge landing and around the back way to avoid seeing any courtiers. It was icy cold, but she was in such a heat she hardly noticed.

"Bring a torch inside, in case they haven't thought of it, Jenks," she ordered tersely.

162

"Aye, Your Grace."

She stepped inside the large, high-ceilinged brick building her father had ordered built years ago. Only men played tennis, but there was a large gallery here for women to cheer them on. Today she would be center court, she thought, and took a white linen stuffed ball from the rack of them by the door. She bounced it hard twice, then squeezed it in her hands as she walked onto the clay court where two of Cecil's men stood waiting with John. One held a lantern. She stopped on the other side of the limp, low-hung net and stared across it at the men. One was Philip Farmont, Cecil's most trusted aide.

"All but John step aside with the lights," she ordered. "We shall speak privily."

When Jenks and Cecil's men moved away, the shadows of the net jumped and darted between her and John. She squeezed the tennis ball to keep from leaping over the net and beating him with her fists.

"How dare you leave London without my permission at such a time?"

"No one told me I needed permission. An emergency came up."

"Which was?"

"My daughter, Hester, has run away from our country home in Kelston. I thought I knew where to find her there, but evidence suggests now that she came here."

"Here? To the court?"

"To London, Your Majesty, I know not where."

"Hester must be all of twenty now, *Master Harington.*"

She could tell her formal address startled him. "Yes," he whispered, no longer looking so defiant.

"How would you feel if she were wed and accepted the hospitality of some older married man and his wife and you saw him kissing her passionately—and mayhap more?"

Even in the webbing of net shadows she could tell he blanched.

"Well, sir? And if the young woman were this older married man's wife's sister?"

"Bella knows? She told you?"

"I am praying Bella does not know, though well she should."

"It's not my fault. Penelope lured me and—"

"Not your fault?" Her voice rose to echo in the big building. "You are the head of your household, you are older, you were her host, if not guardian, first in Kelston, then in London. Perhaps it is doubtful she would have come to this big city at all had not her husband trusted she would be in your and Bella's care, just as I was once entrusted to the care of your old friend and master Tom Seymour, who seduced my heart, if not my body!"

He gaped in fear. "I...didn't look at it that way. But Penelope was not a green girl, not my ward, as you were Tom's, and she was so headstrong—"

"Oh, I've no doubt. I can read her character clear, a wanton, a seductress. Yes, that's true. But I can also see I have read your character

164

wrong from the first, and now you have become a chief suspect in her murder."

"You cannot mean that," he insisted, but his voice wavered. He grabbed the net between them with both hands to make it bob and sway.

"Let me make my worst suspicions plain, John Harington. Let us say she seduced you, then threatened to tell Bella if you did not do something or other for her—mayhap help her rid herself of her old husband, I know not. Or you got her with child, for she died pregnant, sir, and you were fearful she would claim it was yours and take you for your fortune or your reputation, which you and Bella have tried so hard to rebuild, as you have tried to have a child together."

"Pr-Pregnant? I didn't know," he said, and looked as if he'd taken a belly blow. "But I swear, Your Grace, it cannot be mine."

"Or here's another possibility for you," she pursued relentlessly, ignoring his avowal. "You did it to protect Bella. Bella does not conceive, and you wonder, since you had your Hester with your first wife twenty years ago, if this childlessness is Bella's fault or yours. And Penny, as you called her once to me, was your broodmare to see if—"

"No! Lies, all lies!" he exploded, and ripped the net from its posts. It coiled between them, catching at her skirts, Jenks and both of Cecil's men ran in until Elizabeth's raised hand halted them.

"I want to believe you, John," she said,

165

"but I have seen at close range how men can act. You are banished from court until I receive from you and Bella separate written statements of all you know of Penelope and what happened to her, accounts beginning with the first moment she set foot in your house in Stepney here—or further back if you so much as touched Penelope in the country too. Cecil's men," she said, raising her voice and gesturing them over, "will accompany you home to be certain you do not concoct something together. But Bella must eventually know of your flirtation, whether merely foolish or very fatal, with Penelope. As for Hester..."

"Hester...yes," he stammered as if he'd forgotten. "I fear she's here on her own somehow, I just know it. But..."

"But?"

"I have her maid's word in Kelston that she was coming here to Penelope, who had promised to help her find a place in London. I—we had an advantageous local match planned for Hester at home, but she didn't favor him. All she cares for is her lute and her music, but with Penelope dead when she arrived in London, if she made it here, what could have become of her?"

"Are there people in your household at Stepney who know her and can look for her in the city?"

"Yes, but look where? She knows no one here but us."

"She should have come to me, as I am, after all, her aunt. Mayhap she will turn up yet. Would she have come to me, do you think?"

166

"I...don't know. Her mother put ideas in her head before she died: that she had rights and claims on the Tudors. It's another reason I felt she should wed well in the countryside and learn to be content there."

"In other words, she was resentful at being stashed away, much like Penelope. And bitter like others who have even one drop of royal blood but no part of that wealth or power. Like Katherine Grey and her mother."

"If I'm not to search for Hester, may I see Jack?"

"Not now. Consider yourself blessed that you are not seeing the inside of a cell in the Tower until this is over. As you have been there before on my behalf, I spare you that for now. But never defy or lie to me again!"

She threw the tennis ball at him. Surprised, he did not grab for it or duck, and it bounced off his head into blackness across the court.

"Oh, that bed looks good," Elizabeth told Kat as she climbed up into it a half hour later. "That warming pan has done its work. I wish I could sleep and sleep, but my head and heart are churning with this crime. It's like trying to swim upriver."

"Mmm, and you can't swim," Kat muttered. "Someday in the country, maybe Meg should teach you, as I hear she swims like a fish."

"Why isn't she here? She knows I like that posset with the throat herbs before I sleep."

"Don't know, lovey," Kat said, using her little-girl name for her. "I sent for her earlier, and no one could find her."

"Lost in the vast reaches of Whitehall," Elizabeth mused as she flopped down and Kat covered her up and began to blow out candles.

The queen thought about John's daughter, Hester, lost in London. About Jack, lost in life, wanting to be someone, to do something grand to make up for his father's failures. She understood that. Thinking of how he adored her, she could almost drift off to slumber like this, just lost in—

She jolted at the rap on the door. It was so late that it must bode ill.

"Don't jerk like that," Kat crooned. " 'Tis only Meg's knock, and you do have *your* guards on *your* doors now," she added as she unbolted and opened it. "Meg, my girl, what's happened? Looks as if you've seen a ghost." Kat's last comment shot Elizabeth upright.

With wind-ripped hair and clothes and all color drained from her face to remind Elizabeth too much of Penelope's corpse, Meg shuffled in. Kat helped her to the bench at the foot of the great bed, and Elizabeth scooted down to the end of it with the covers ruffled up around her.

"Meg, tell me," she said simply.

"You know I am loyal to you," Meg began, her voice so shaky it was not her own. "And I never lied to you, so can't start now."

"You'd best not. I have plenty of others who

do that," she said, alarmed the girl looked so downcast. Meg sat slumped, staring at her knees, her empty herb basket dangling from one wrist.

"I think I found my mother, my other life. You asked me once, Your Grace, if I could be Sarah Scutea, and I said no, but—"

"You've been to see the Scuteas?" Elizabeth asked, trying to recall all the details of that earlier investigation. "The man who knew the poisons—he's dead, isn't he?"

She nodded wide-eyed, looking up at last. "They thought I was dead or run off. But now that man's widow, Mariah, is dying. My mother, I guess."

"You still don't recall? I'll send her a physician. Where is she lying?"

"It's too late. I looked at her wound: gangrene, and it's spread." She sucked in a deep breath. "Mariah Scutea tends an apothecary on the Strand, just down from Arundel House. Her friend said a woman who looked like Penelope Whyte came there desperate the day of your recognition parade trying to buy pennyroyal and mandrake."

"Herbs for?" Elizabeth prompted.

"You've got to get the dose right not to end up dead yourself, but they can cause a pregnant woman to miscarry the child."

"Abortion," Kat muttered.

"Mariah turned her away," Meg went on, "not so much worried about the dosage as that—that Catholics believe it's a mortal sin."

"Meg, Catholic heritage or not," Elizabeth

said, trying to leap ahead to stem her fear, "it doesn't change a thing about your being part of my household. But you're distraught because you still don't remember the Scuteas?"

Meg nodded as she stood, one hand on the carved bedpost to steady herself. "I need to beg your permission to tend her until she dies, Your Grace, whatever I recall. I owe her my life, my earlier life. The thing is, I think you owe her your life too."

"What?" Elizabeth said, drawing herself up straighter on the bed.

"The gangrene in her belly, Your Grace, she says is poison from gunpowder and a lead ball she took standing in the crowd the day you passed by in your procession. Even though she championed your sister, she wanted to see the new queen."

"Someone shot a firearm that day?" Elizabeth demanded, now trying to stem her own fear. "Into the crowd?"

"Like a judgment from heaven on her, she said, so I think she meant it came down from above, so—"

Elizabeth clamped her hands over her mouth. So many things bombarded her, then fell neatly into place. Yes, the crowds roared loud enough that day from time to time, and trumpets blared. That could have covered the sound of a firearm. And there was gunpowder on the floor of the gatehouse, especially the pile under the window. Scrape marks on the window ledge there, which she later thought must be from Bett's angling pole. That disturbance—a woman's shrieks—in the crowd when Robin rushed her away. Someone must have carried her off fast, and with the rabid dog, then in the confusion, Robin did not know the truth to tell her. And she had stood, encompassed by his arms, shooting out a palace window down at a target that was nearly blown away.

The queen clutched handfuls of the sheet to her breasts. Her eyes met Meg's, and the girl nodded, her face a mask of fear.

"Then Penelope's murder," Elizabeth whispered, fighting to control her panic, "may be tied to an attempted assassination—mine."

Chapter The Eleventh

By dawn Elizabeth had signed Cecil's pile of papers—grants, bills, and warrants she'd previously ordered or agreed to—and sat down with her little band of Privy Plot councillors. All were present but Meg who had gone back with the queen's Dr. Browne to comfort her mother.

"So it has come to that," Cecil said when Elizabeth explained the new evidence Meg had gathered. "We are investigating not some lovers' quarrel or domestic squabble that went awry but politics in the highest degree, an assassination attempt that, thank God, went awry too."

"I fear so," she said while the others leaned forward intently. "I may not only owe Mariah Scutea for taking that lead ball for me but Penelope for coming upon an assassin and perhaps delaying or jostling his aim."

"And then paying for that privilege with her life," Harry put in.

"But what about Meg?" Jenks asked. "She remembers her mother and her past now? Will we have to call her Sarah?"

"Will she even stay with us?" Kat said in more a statement than a question. "Now that she knows she's bred by Catholics and those loyal to your royal sister, who might have been behind a plot to harm you earlier, so—"

"Stop," Elizabeth ordered, gripping in her lap the ribboned pomander Meg had filled for her with sweet herbs. "I'll not have that dragged out again. Meg is not Sarah but a new self she created since her accident, loving and loyal to me. And she is useful—needful to me, to all of us, and not just to play the part of queen when I need to be elsewhere. Are we agreed on Meg's continued place with me and us?"

She looked at each until she got a nod or murmured acquiescence. In truth, she realized, she'd sat on them so hard because she did not know the answers to what they had asked. She knew only that this time in the light of day she must return to the site where someone had murdered a woman, but from which he'd meant to kill a queen.

"There may be the slightest chance I can save her if I pour seething elder oil and theriaca for an antidote to the gunpowder into the wound," Dr. Browne told the exhausted Meg in the narrow, dim hallway outside her mother's bedchamber. "'Tis a well-trusted practice on the battlefield."

"So you've seen it work before?"

"I've never been sent to the battlefield...before now, girl, if you don't take my advice straight."

Dr. Percival Browne was one of the physicians left over from the reign of Edward VI before Queen Mary. Bearded and somber, he looked formidable in his long gown and linen cap with dangling strings, which marked him as an eminent physician. And he had made it eminently clear to Meg he thought it ridiculous that the new queen preferred possets and cordials from her herb girl to his learned pronouncements and practices.

"But she's already in great pain," Meg argued. "Burning oil? Doesn't make sense to burn an already dreadful wound."

"Now see here, modern medicine is far better than your—"

"I'd be willing to try a warm healing salve of egg white and rose oil, not seething, Doctor, but—"

"But indeed! But, but, but!" he scolded as he wagged his finger in her face. "But *you* are an herb girl, that's what you are, and I shall tell but the queen of your stiff-necked—"

"No, I shall tell the queen you did not do as she commanded, and that was to help and comfort an ill woman in her hour of need." She blocked his way when he tried to get back into the sickroom. He threw up his hands, seized his packet of goods from the chair beside her, and rushed downstairs. When the door to the street banged, she hurried down to latch it behind him.

Perhaps, she thought as she trudged back upstairs, she had become Meg Milligrew indeed. She was certain Sarah Scutea would not have stood up to a learned man, let alone one in the queen's employ. Everything had changed for the best when she'd gotten to know clever, bold Bess Tudor, and she was so afraid she would lose that now. Her mother had looked up from her fever an hour ago to ask her to stay on here, to use her father's knowledge of the herbs she recalled—even when all else seemed to have slipped away—to keep this place up. But then she had told no one here that she and Dr. Browne were sent by the queen Mariah hated.

"You're back, my Sarah," her mother said again, seeming to wake from the feverish stupor that pulled her toward distant death.

"Yes, back to stay with you."

"And with the shop when I'm gone? I hope you aren't paying that physician too dear. Dusty, stuffy men, with their urine bottles and bleedings before they'd trust a God-given leaf or root. Is the sun up yet? Even in the winter it creeps in here. I'd like to see the sun."

Despite all that jumbled talk, she looked instantly unconscious again. But Meg pulled the worn curtains back and opened the window enough to shove the shutters aside, then latched the casements closed again. Wan daylight washed in, waking old Dame Nan, who dozed on a pallet in the corner, covered only by her shawl. She stirred, then stretched.

"Is she gone then, your mother?" Nan asked.

"Not yet," Meg whispered. "She—Mother—wants to see the sun."

Meg went back to sit on the bed and hold Mariah's hand. "Is the priest here again?" the feverish woman asked, her eyes fluttering open.

"You've already had him here for last rites, Mariah," Nan said, stepping to the side of the bed where Meg sat. "And the best gift of all, Sarah recalls who you are now—don't you, girl?—for you called her Mother."

"True?" Mariah asked. "It would ease me so to hear it, Ben too."

"I—yes, Mother." Meg lied, but it was a good lie. She wished she had Ned's talent for talk, his convincing gestures, but she could say no more. Mariah sighed and seemed to sink into the bed.

"Where is Ben now?" Meg later whispered to old Nan over Mariah's labored breathing.

"Betook himself to Southwark not long after you left."

Meg wondered if she'd recently learned that Southwark was the area right across the Thames from London or if she'd known it from living here before. She could not even recall that.

"Sad," Nan went on, "when Mariah had to go it alone with all the work here. Your father and you loved the herbs, not Mariah or Ben. But I've sent for him."

"Good. I hope he gets here before... What trade does he follow?"

"So it's *not* all coming back to you? Always was on the river, Ben was, said it was in his blood. I pray the Queen of Heaven you'll recall him when you see him. Started as a wherryman, but became a bridge shooter. Remember all the family fuss over him risking life and limb like that?"

Meg frowned as something stirred inside her. *You still got that river in your soul,* she must have once told Ben. But he argued, didn't he? Shouted at her?

"You remember?" Nan asked.

"A bridge shooter? Not even that."

"You know, one of those daring sorts, heroes to the boys and bargemen. When folks must go upstream, shooters take them in boats under the bridge, even at high tide, but some die trying."

The bridge. She had to mean London Bridge, Meg thought, grasping for any straw of memory. It was the only one over the Thames in all of London. She hadn't been near there and couldn't picture it, or her parents, or brother Ben, or being Sarah Scutea, and it all scared her to death.

Later Nan whispered, "I—I don't think she's breathing."

Meg's gaze jumped back from staring at the shaft of sun as it climbed onto the foot of the bed. She leaned forward to listen to her mother's heart, then felt for the pulse at her neck. "Fetch me a piece of glass, will you, Nan?"

She held the small vial under Mariah's nostrils to see if any mist or haze of breath clouded it. Nothing.

"God bless her soul," Nan whispered. "Gone."

When Meg just stared, Nan reached down to make the sign of the cross on the dead woman's forehead. She covered Mariah's face, then patted Meg's shoulder. How Meg wished it were the queen's or Kat's, Jenks's—yes, even that stubborn Ned's—touch. She felt stunned and sad but not grief-stricken.

"When I was in the country," she whispered to the old dame, "I thought my name was Meg Milligrew. Do you know where I might have found that name?"

" 'Twas Mariah's mother's. She lived here for a while. You—did you really remember your mother, then?"

Meg shook her head, but they both jumped when a pounding rattled the street door below. "That physician's back," Meg said with a sigh. "I'll get rid of him."

"If you truly don't remember, wait," Nan said, and darted to the window.

She opened it and called down, "Who's

there then?" just as she had done with Meg yesterday—or was that years ago?

"Ben Wilton, mistress," a harsh voice called up. "That you, old Nan? You sent for me, din't you? Old Mariah alive or not? Let me in!"

Meg made for the chamber door to go down to greet him. Mayhap at least she would remember her brother when she saw him.

"Wait!" Nan cried. "Ben has a temper and thinks you run off from...your duties. Since you don't recall him, best let me go down first. You two had words. He even hit you once or twice."

"But with our mother gone, it will bind us—"

Then, even as he began to bang on the door again, Meg's stunned brain snagged on something Ben had said. "Why," she asked, "would my brother have a different last name from Scutea?"

"You—you're confused again," Nan said, plucking nervously at her shawl, not meeting her eyes. "I thought if you remembered your mother now, you must recall Ben too. See, your name's Wilton, your married name. Ben's not your brother but your husband."

A quarter hour later Meg's pulse still pounded. She was out of breath from tearing down the apothecary stairs and out the back door and through filthy alleys almost all the way back to Whitehall. At least she'd avoided Ben Wilton. How she'd hated running out—not on him but on her mother's funeral and on that treasury of stored herbs. But not a one could cure this mess her life was in.

Still dazed, she managed to get control of herself before she entered the palace. When the queen heard she had a rude, rough husband, she would surely toss her out. Her Majesty got choleric enough when she sensed Meg cared for Ned, or Jenks acted sweet toward her. But a husband? And how could she ever go about the London streets now? Not only did she not remember him, but he knew and could spot and claim her.

The guards at the queen's bedchamber door opened it for her. She stepped clear in before she heard the queen's voice raised. She would have gone back out if the guards had not—wisely—already quickly closed the door behind her.

"When you bring Katherine Grey to me this evening, I'm going to let her know in no uncertain terms she'll not take up with that man," Her Grace was telling Kat. "No, rather, I think I'll subtly torment her with it. None of my maids shall become betrothed or wed without my consent, especially not one who intends to stay in favor and she does, so— Oh, Meg." She interrupted her own tirade, evidently noting her at the door only when the girl spun to let herself back out. "Come here and tell how does your mother."

"She...died, Your Grace," she said, slowly turning to face them.

She didn't mean or want to, but she burst into tears. They hurried to her. Kat held her like a child while the queen clasped her shaking shoulders as if to hold her up.

"There's something...I must tell you," Meg choked out, taking a step back to swipe at her tears. She had to tell them, to share this wretched burden. After all, she was not one of the queen's ladies. Whom she wed was no great affair of state. And the queen hated people lying to her, especially friends.

"I know what you're going to say," the queen insisted, "but do not worry for her funeral expenses. Without anyone's knowing it is because of my regard for you, and what she did for me, I will pay for mourners and a fine gravestone and say that she is being buried well because of her husband's service to two former queens."

"Thank you, Your G-Grace, but not th-that."

"It's about your keeping that shop and leaving here," Kat put in.

"No—I—yes, that's it," she said, changing her mind about admitting she was wed. After all, she'd tried to tell them, and they'd both changed the topic. Was that not a sign to keep silent about Ben Wilton?

"I don't mean," she stammered as they stared at her, "that I want to go but stay. Forgive me, Your Grace, but I'd rather not see that shop again, and it's in debt anyway. I don't recall anything but the herbs, and I want to tend yours here—wherever you go, especially outside London."

"That's settled then," Elizabeth declared. "Was that what you wanted to say then? Is that all?"

"Yes, Your Grace. I just want to be Meg Milligrew, not Sarah Scutea ever again."

By midmorning, dressed as Meg, with the girl left behind in her bed—willingly this time, as she was exhausted and had not begged to come along for once—Elizabeth, Jenks, and Ned walked the low-tide river shore, then cut up onto the Strand. She prayed Bett and Gil would meet them just outside the Arundel gatehouse as they had planned. Broad daylight or not, the anglers had to help them get inside.

Holding her muffler close across her lower face, trying to blend in with the people on the street, Elizabeth kept thinking not about Penelope but Meg. She actually envied her, an herb girl, for being able to comfort her dying mother. How she wished she'd had even as many meager memories of her own as Meg had been given at the end.

"Here they come," Jenks said.

Bett and Gil appeared as if from midair when they reached the postern door next to the Arundel gatehouse. According to plan, Ned and Bett staged an argument across the way by the Ring and Crown to draw passersby's attention, while Jenks boosted Gil over the wall on this side of the street. He dropped to the ground inside, got the key, and opened the door, for the broken lock had evidently been discovered and replaced. Elizabeth and Jenks stepped inside. Ned soon chased Bett down

181

the Strand. Then, after their audience had dispersed, they doubled back to dart inside.

They glanced around the grounds. Gil had done well. The key was back on its nail, and no one was in sight. But when they tried the door and the lower window to the gatehouse they'd gotten in through last time, they were locked out.

"Can you climb that tree, boy?" Ned asked Gil. "Maybe the second-floor window will be open."

Gil went up easily. As they watched him, Elizabeth whispered, "You're right about the trees and statues providing a screen back here, Ned. It made your interview with the servant Sally quite a privy one too."

Ned only nodded, obviously not daring to look her in the eye again. Her favorite player, her chameleon, would have borne watching had she not had this murder and her monarchy to worry for.

With his legs and one arm clasping a limb, Gil reached for the window. It was shut tight too. The boy looked down at Bett and made some sign. She searched on the ground, found a sturdy stick, and heaved it up. The boy caught it with one hand.

"If we have to break a window, we'd best muffle the noise," Elizabeth said. "Ned, take off your cape."

"Eh, he's got it now, my boy does," Bett boasted.

They watched Gil peel the stick flat with his teeth, then wedge and wiggle it between the casements. He pried it open. Before they knew it, he had shinnied along the limb and disappeared inside.

Grinning, he came down to let them in, and they latched the door behind themselves. On the third floor they surveyed the dim room in silence. This time the silhouette of the first big coffer reminded Elizabeth of Penelope's lead coffin in that mausoleum. She hurried over to the streetside window to open it and the shutters. Sharp light leaped in to reveal the coat of gray dust with its random design of footprints.

Gil and Bett began to gesture wildly to each other. "What is it?" Elizabeth asked Bett.

"He wants to know if this dust is like saltpeter, if it might blow."

"Tell him we won't let it. I still need your help, Bett, but if you want to go home, I will not hold you. I hope Gil will draw for me whom he saw at that window, though, and you can reach me anytime through Lord Harry. All right," she ordered, turning away from the surprised woman, "everyone do as we've planned."

She was pleased to see Bett and Gil confer and then stay, she hoped not just to abscond with the draperies the men dropped to the floor as they began to uncover and peer into each big box. They found two sacks of the black powder, one full and sewn shut, the other sliced into and three-fourths empty.

"Here's the source of the gunpowder," Jenks pronounced solemnly, sniffing at it, then sneezing as if he'd caught her cold.

183

"Bring the sack that's been opened," Elizabeth ordered. "We may be able to date or trace it."

When she announced they were taking it, Bett defiantly picked up and folded one of the brocade draperies, then held it in her arms. Elizabeth frowned at her but said nothing. Of the other large coffers, some were empty, but one contained curtains.

"I guess the rumors were wrong, as is often true," Elizabeth said, closing that lid herself before Bett could filch more from poor Lord North. "If Tom Seymour's weapons were ever stored here, they are long gone. It didn't make sense, if they were taken as evidence at his treason trial, that they would just be put back here."

Jenks lifted the lid to the last coffer and rummaged in it. "I fear you're wrong, Bess. Old matchlocks under these velvet curtains. Firearms something like the one Lord Robert showed at court."

"Then who's to know if they are old or not?" Ned said as they gathered around the first one Jenks pulled out.

"And," Elizabeth added, "who's to know if that gunpowder is ten years old or not? As for that firearm, the ivory inlay pattern is far different from the one Robert Dudley had yesterday. But yes, this is old...and special. See, the Seymour arms. So that at least was his. Can you tell if any has been fired lately?"

Jenks examined, then sniffed at the six he'd found. "Not sure," he said, and jumped when

Bett grabbed the inlaid one to sniff at the priming pan.

"Laws, thought so," she declared. "This one been shot recent."

"Bring it with us, Jenks," Elizabeth ordered, instinctively believing her, "but wrap it in one of these cloths. Here, Bett, you carry this brocade one for us," she said, draping another curtain across her arms. Bett's eyes lit.

Elizabeth plunged into her mental list of other things to check: There was a definite scratch mark on the center of this windowsill, and Bett said it was not from their angling pole. From its size, the bottom of the barrel could have made the marks, not only for a rest but from a recoil. Then, too, the pile of powder was still discernible under the window. Someone could have spilled a goodly amount on top of what must have been there for years.

"As dangerous as it is to be walking about in this stuff, thank God they didn't sweep this place out yet," she said, and heard Ned gasp.

Expecting him to have found something else, she turned to see him staring at her. "Ned?" she prompted.

"I forgot, Your—Bess. It seemed such a small thing at the time when I was trying to remember so much that—"

"Leave off the monologue or confession about that servant girl. What?"

"She—Sally mentioned briefly, in passing, that she had swept the gatehouse out that morning, all of it, so—"

185

"So, if you thought not to tell us that before, you had best keep to being my fool and little else," she clipped out. "Then this powder on the floor has hardly been here from Tom Seymour's aborted rebellion, but the murderer, my would-be assassin, could have spilled it all over in his haste or when he was surprised by Penelope's sudden appearance up here."

"But spilled it all over?" Jenks challenged.

"It was windy that day and with the window open to look out, to shoot out, it blew in and around," she surmised. "But now we'd best try to discover if it was stored in this coffer from years ago, who could know that, or if it was new purchased and perhaps by whom."

She felt someone tug at her skirts and looked down at Gil. A few steps behind her he had drawn something with his finger in the black powder they'd all disturbed. He had smoothed a square of it flat for his portrait.

"This side," Bett said, motioning her. "He wants you to look at it this side."

Elizabeth lifted her skirt and stepped carefully around while the others crowded behind her. The boy had drawn an open window and within it, hunched forward, two masculine shoulders and the top of someone's head of hair. But where the face and chest and hands—and weapon—would be was a cloud or big bubble.

Elizabeth jerked a step back, right on Jenks's toes. "Gil," she asked, recovering her balance and pointing across the room, "that window? A firearm blast from that window?"

Wide-eyed, he nodded.

"What color was the man's hair?" She looked expectantly at Bett as Gil signed something.

"Shadows," Bett said. "His hair was the color of shadows in the room."

"Which could be anything," she said, and sighed. "But was there a face before the blast, Gil? Can you draw the face?"

Frowning, he signed something to Bett.

"He says, he keeps seeing the explosion at the saltpeter works, but he'll try to recall this one. Eh, he'll try for you, lady queen."

"Which if it's like all our other clues," Elizabeth muttered, stepping back to lean against a big box behind her, "will lead to more and more dead ends."

She instantly regretted her own words. She was sitting next to where they'd found the corpse. If Penelope had come up here, if the shooter had already been intently leaning out the window with all the outside crowd noise, he would not necessarily have seen her unless she spoke or even walked over to touch him.

More questions than answers flew at her. Did Penelope speak because she knew him? And after all, her would-be assassin did not have to be any of the men who had been down below. Or did Penelope run to the window to try to call out a warning amid all that tumult below? Did she rush him and make his shot go astray?

"Look, Your Majesty," Bett said, ducking

187

behind the box where they had found the firearms. She leaned down to avoid the steep-gabled roof. "A man's hat back here, a fine one too, branched brocade and a smell of sweat and lime pomade still on it."

She handed it to Elizabeth, who sniffed at it too. She couldn't smell anything but dust and the faint sulfur of gunpowder. It was streaked, stained, and wrinkled—almost creased. If she remembered right, they used to call this dark hue badger brown. Her father wore one like it in the council chamber portrait that so dominated the room.

"It's a fine one all right, but a bit old-fashioned, at least at court," the queen told them. "It's probably not the assassin's, for Gil drew a bare-headed one. Just like the firearms, it could even be from Lord Seymour's day. For all we know, it belonged to one of his men or the admiral himself."

She stroked the wrinkled, smudged fabric before she realized everyone was staring at her. She flipped it over to examine the tight, even stitching. It had a maker's mark, an embroidered double star, and the velvet lining band was worn. It was old, perhaps Tom's, but it could hardly have been his ghost that had taken a shot at her.

"Even with John Harington looking so suspicious," she said so low Ned and Jenks had to lean close to hear, "the duchess's husband, Adrian Stokes, is my first choice as the shooter of the firearm. Meg heard him protest he'd done the ultimate for his wife. The duchess scolded him for trying to write a

188

condolence letter to Penelope's husband, for she wanted nothing smacking of mea culpa. Adrian was gone from the others here several times, purportedly to fetch cordials for the duchess."

"And she could have timed and arranged all that," Ned put in.

"Exactly," Elizabeth said with a decisive nod. "Also, the servant Sally thinks he came downstairs one fewer times than John Harington recalled—if he's telling the truth. That one time Adrian could have gone up, not down."

"And killed her instead of you," Jenks whispered.

"And," Elizabeth went on, "the Suffolks are the only ones in attendance that day who would directly profit from having me dead and Katherine Grey, though unnamed by me as heir, next in line for my throne. The duchess controls her daughters' doings, so that would as good as put Frances Brandon Grey Stokes in control of my country."

"But it would help," Ned said, "to establish that Lord Adrian or someone in their employ was here before your procession to reconnoiter this place and make sure the firearm and powder were here or bring them in himself."

"So we've got to step up watching Adrian and the duchess," Jenks added. "And here they're leaving court for their house across the river."

"Unless..." Elizabeth said.

"Unless?" Ned prompted. "You're not thinking of sending Meg along with her?"

"No. I mean unless Edward Seymour means to marry Katherine Grey. If he killed me, he could rule as king with her."

Chapter The Twelfth

Lady Katherine Grey is here to join your ladies, Your Majesty," Kat informed Elizabeth. Her women were helping her dress for the first time she was to dine in public since her coronation banquet five days ago. Her cough was relenting a bit, yet her runny nose was still worse than the Thames.

She stood in her embroidered linen smock while they laced her canvas corset on, then tied on four petticoats and the wire-and-whalebone bell-shaped farthingale around her waist. Next came her brocade underskirt and the velvet one, cut to reveal the brocade. Her boned bodice was pearl-studded and richly worked with gold filigree thread. It was laced tight across her small breasts, though its pointed waistline and tabbed pickadils fell over her skirts. They began to tie a pair of ivory silk sleeves to the bodice while Elizabeth stood like a statue. She inclined her head and smiled at Katherine when she came up from her curtsy, but she intended to make her wait. "Those hues are wonderful on you, Your Grace," Katherine gushed before she was spoken to. Elizabeth tried to bridle her pique at the girl. After all, she gave her ladies leeway to speak their minds.

But in this case the monarch should speak first, and Katherine knew that full well. Mayhap she knew a lot more she wasn't saying.

"Do you think I must stick with pale golds, insipid canaries, and tired tawnies, then, Katherine?" the queen asked as deft hands fastened a stiff, small, lace-edged ruff to the velvet band around her slender neck.

"Oh, no, I didn't mean that," the girl amended quickly.

Katherine Grey, Elizabeth thought, was a still-waters-run-deep sort with a deceptively placid demeanor. Though she could seem both delicate and frivolous, Elizabeth believed she was neither. She had a long, oval face, red-gold wavy hair, and deep-set hazel eyes that made her look more Tudor than her sisters Jane or Mary. The queen felt pity for her cousin only because she'd had to live with the Duchess of Suffolk.

Yet partly for that reason she felt she could not trust this simpering young woman any farther than she could throw a horse, especially now with her parents and her paramour under suspicion for murder and attempted assassination. But for all that, she would keep Katherine under sharp scrutiny here. "The amethyst necklace and earrings, please, Mary," Elizabeth said with a smile at Robin's sister, who proffered one of her jewel boxes for her selection. She had also decided to wear Jack's gift to her. Though she had not even told Kat about it, no one would notice the simple brooch among the rest of the glittering array.

"No, not that box; yes, there. Katherine, I am pleased you will be staying in my household," the queen went on as another lady clasped the necklace around her throat. "I believe your mother and her Lord Adrian have removed to Suffolk House across the river."

"Oh, yes, business, I believe, as she dislikes to leave you."

"How kind. I rely on you to keep her posted about things at court. And I must tell you, cousin, I insist that my unwed maids remain in that single estate and marry only with my express permission. That ring there, and fetch me that small box in that other jewel case, Lady Mary," she said, glancing away, "the white leather one."

Though she feigned being distracted, the queen watched Katherine's face closely. At the mention of steering clear of entanglements with men, annoyance, then anger had flitted across the fine features before the set smile returned. Elizabeth had first considered forbidding her to so much as speak with Edward Seymour, but it might simply be best to give her some rope to hang herself...and him too.

"And I believe," Elizabeth went on as she herself pinned Jack's plain brooch on her sleeve, "a certain young man has been showing you marked attention of late."

"Edward or Jack, Your Grace?" she inquired with raised eyebrows as if she were surprised indeed. "They are both simply friends, though I believe two ladies meant to besmirch that fact."

The other maids' hands stilled as they scented a whiff of rumor—or mayhap a display of royal temper. "And those ladies would be?" Elizabeth asked.

"One's dead and the other ill, I hear, so I warrant it doesn't matter now," Katherine countered. The queen felt they might as well be fencing.

Mary Sidney lifted the small jeweled and lace cap that was to be pinned upon the queen's upswept, piled hair. Ordinarily Elizabeth would simply bend her knees so the shorter women, often Kat, could place and fasten it for her. But damned if she would bend even one knee in Katherine Grey's presence.

"Fetch the mounting stool, Mary," Elizabeth commanded, "and then let Katherine begin her tasks in my service by putting it on my head."

"Oh, thank you, Your Grace," Katherine said with another sweet smile as she flounced forward. "I shall pretend I am crowning you. Just think, I've seen you crowned, and before that your sister, Queen Mary...and before her, my sister, Queen Jane."

No one so much as breathed. The queen's gaze locked at close range with the woman's hazel eyes. Elizabeth had liked Jane Grey the times she'd been with her while they were growing up. Jane's brilliance had flashed forth however plain she was. Yet when Tom Seymour was widowed and Elizabeth had been taken from his grasp, he had set his sights on Jane as a possible wife to solidify his power.

But it was not the stab of jealousy that upset her now. It was that sweet, simple Katherine—her mother's description of her— had shrewdly thrown down the gauntlet of her heritage in public. Since some rebellious English had risked their lives to make Jane queen, surely someone with a firearm aiming from a window had risked his to make Katherine queen hereafter.

Late the next morning, the Sabbath, Bett Sharpe and Nick Cotter leaned together against a tree trunk and watched Gil and other boys throwing snowballs at a crude target Gil had drawn with packed snow on a brick wall. The snow, Bett thought, was nearly as scarce as pickings had been in these tough times. Still shouting—all but Gil—the boys bombarded their bull's-eye.

"I told you I was scared you'd got caught again," Nick said. " 'Cause with your thumb branded, they'll hang you sure. But you got snatched by the queen herself. And she liked you?"

Laws, he was handsome, her Nick, but clever only between the sheets. Yet what other man would let her wash him with rose-water and rub on lime pomade when he came back from that stinking work he did?

She inhaled the crisp, clean country air on the low hill, for the wind was right today. East Smithfield was on the edge of the city, with a distant view of the Tower, the Thames, and Southwark. If she squinted, she could make out the tall walls and four turrets of Suffolk House from here, standing big as you please on Borough High Street right across London Bridge. Nick could not know what she intended, Gil neither, or they'd try to stop her.

"Eh," she said, putting her arm through his, "she liked me too, or wouldn't of let me take that one drapery and give me the other. If I can just get Gil over his fits from that first blast, he'll draw that face. Then she'll give us a fine reward, I know it."

"So you're going back to tell her that?"

"Right," she said, not looking at him. It was sin enough, 'specially on a Sabbath, to be angling folks' goods, but worse to lie to Nick. "So you'll watch Gil?" she asked. "I'll be back quick as I can. And one more thing. You ever met that Lord Robert Dudley friend of Her Majesty's, the one owns the saltpeter cellars?"

"She ask you that? Wanting to know what I thought of him?"

Though her stomach was tied in knots, Bett had to grin. "Not 'xactly, but she wants to know who came to Jemmy's shop there, got powder."

"A few folks, I guess. I seen Lord Robert twice, but once recent. With another gent'man 'bout a fortnight ago, come to buy two bags from Jemmy, and with the very saltpeter stuff I been tending," he said proudly.

"Two bags, eh? If one man was Lord Robert, who's the other then?"

"Don't know but can ask. Cloaked and hooded, came in a sleet storm and fussed about keeping the powder dry, Jemmy said. But I know what was bought for."

"Laws, Nick, tell me then."

" 'Cording to Jemmy, one gent'man wanted fireworks to cel'brate the queen's cor'nation."

Trailed by courtiers, Elizabeth had no more left the chapel at Whitehall after morning service than she caught William Cecil's eye and read the look he gave her to mean *urgent business now.* Hoping the French had not egged on the vile Scots to start a rebellion—surely not in the depths of winter—she gestured him to follow her into the privy chamber and shut everyone else out except someone's yipping lapdog which scurried in. She picked up the spaniel to quiet him.

"Tell me then, my lord. More bad news, I warrant."

"It depends on how badly you want to solve Penelope's murder, Your Majesty," he said, producing yet another piece of parchment from up his sleeve. She put the dog down and snatched it.

"I must warn you," he went on, "this is a real confession for the murder, nothing like that other little lapdog of yours—Jack St. Maur's—ploy to see you."

"From Adrian Stokes or Edward Seymour?" she asked excitedly, choosing to ignore his snide comment about Jack. "But...this is signed by

John Harington. You don't mean he admits..."

"It's the sworn statement you ordered him to write. He's confessed to Penelope Whyte's murder, an accident in an argument where she fell back and hit her head on a large coffer, he claims. Your friend Isabella, on the other hand, insists she has such a migraine she cannot see to write and refuses to dictate to my man lest he change her words. Needless to say, I've ordered the Haringtons still not be permitted to confer, so they're being detained on separate floors at their house in Stepney."

Elizabeth sat in a chair he pulled out for her. She skimmed the letter while the spaniel darted through Cecil's feet and bounced her skirts.

"Damn him," she whispered. "He forms an amorous liaison with his flighty, flirty sister-in-law behind Bella's back, argues with her...about *her* besmirched reputation...murders her, and now suddenly admits it? *Guilt and loyalty to you, Your Gracious Majesty, has kept me on the rack of conscience,* he writes, devil take the man!"

"He's rather sketchy on the details of the crime, as you see, but claims he did not ravish her, just pulled her skirts up to shift the blame—to some outsider, he claims."

"Is he mad? Outsider? Did he not think someone on the site would be blamed?"

"Read on, Your Grace."

"I see no mention of him getting her with child. He even denies he bedded her, just as

197

Jack did. Do you think he didn't know she was with child?" she demanded, looking up at him. "The fact she was pregnant and not by her lord means she did not just lead men on but coupled with someone, for heaven's sake!"

"I've been trying to read between the lines, but you know Harington far better than I. Oh, by the way, my man Philip Farmont says Harington drank at least a keg of claret while he wrote this."

"Hence the sloppy writing and disjointed thoughts. So these blurred speckles are claret and not the tears he mentions here. He begs me at the end to release Jack from your care and free Bella from any cloud of suspicion. And please to put out a hue and cry for his lost lamb, his daughter, Hester, here in London. The fool had best beg for his own life!" she cried, and let the paper roll itself noisily closed. Cecil put it back up his sleeve.

"One way or the other, Your Grace, this letter is a hue and cry for protection," Cecil said with a sniff. "But for whom?"

"Bella or...Jack," she whispered, pressing her knuckles into her lips.

"So, you do recognize all the possibilities?"

"Of course I do," she said, jumping up so fast he stepped back. "Do you take me for some rustic milkmaid or tavern dolt? I see it could be Jack or Bella who killed Penelope, but hardly who took a shot at me. Things just aren't fitting together, for I think her murder and the attempted assassination *must* be by the same person—and a man."

198

He held up both hands as if they would hold back her anger. "I simply wanted you to see your old friend's letter before I ordered him sent to the Tower, where you can find a way to question him—"

"*Not* in the Tower."

"But he's confessed in writing to murder, and you know he must have information at the least concerning who shot at you. And it is proper procedure that any person suspected of a crime be removed from the presence of the sovereign. Or do you mean," he added, frowning, "send him not to the Tower but the Clink or Newgate or another pris—"

"I mean," she said, accidentally stepping on the dog's foot so it darted away with a yelp, "*I* will not go to the Tower to talk to him but will see *him* in Stepney before he goes to the Tower."

"But it's been snowing off and on. With the river ripping along, a barge, even your big royal one, cannot risk shooting those rapids under London Bridge to get to Stepney. Not to mention that with the assassin still possibly loose you should not be in a royal barge or going about openly where you could become a target again."

"Don't you think I know all that? I'll take a coach and six surefooted mules and go well guarded by men who can arrest John and convey him to the Tower after I interrogate him, if need be. I shall tell people here that I am going to console Bella. Everyone has heard she's ailing. Katherine Grey even alluded to it, the brazen baggage."

199

Though she usually stood erect, her shoulders slumped. "John Harington—I cannot believe it," she repeated. "Oh, perhaps in a rage or thwarted passion he struck Penelope, but not that he meant to kill her or would ever try to kill me. After all, longtime loyalty and friendship aside, I am the Haringtons' best hope for their social resurrection. Can it be the two things, Penelope's death and my would-be one, are somehow *not* related?"

The spaniel kept whining and scratching at the door. She hoped that meant only that its mistress waited outside and not that anyone would dare to listen at cracks or keyholes.

She stood, dabbing at her runny nose and quickly at her eyes so even Cecil wouldn't see. She wanted to deny John's guilt completely, but she'd seen too many men's betrayals. This needed to be probed, perhaps lanced, to get the infection out, whatever sort it was.

The royal coach jolted her so hard her teeth rattled, but it at least enclosed her so someone could not shoot at her again. She wanted desperately to be loved by her people, to earn their loyalty. But what chance did she have of that if friends like John Harington could turn against her?

Mingled with the rattle of harnesses and clatter of hooves on cobbles, Meg's shaken words before Elizabeth had left the palace today came back to her: "I just pray, Your

Grace, you'll not turn against me for my ties to Catholic traitors."

"Meg," she'd said, and clasped her shoulder, "your words are too strong. Many preferred my sister, Mary, and the old religion, and I do not brand them traitors unless they act against me."

"But you don't have them working close for you either," she had choked out between a river of tears and sobs.

Elizabeth had been surprised by the girl's continued display of nerves when she thought things were settled in Meg's heart. "Nonsense," she'd tried to comfort her. "Even Lord Arundel's a Papist, though he attends my services to please me. You are just distraught and exhausted, so I want you to get some sleep. Kat will be here, should you need a good shoulder to cr—"

"There is something else, Your Grace," the girl had blurted.

"Yes?" she'd said, and waited, impatient to be going now.

"It's just something else the old woman caring for my mother said, that's all. That when Penelope—or the pretty blond woman—came to her for those abortion herbs, she was followed by a giant of a man."

"Indeed?" Elizabeth had asked as her sergeant-porter popped instantly to mind. Thomas Keyes would be on duty first thing in the morning, available for questioning. If his being with, perhaps guarding, Penelope pointed to the Suffolks again, yet if John Harington said he had committed the crime, was there some sort of vast conspiracy? Surely not. This was getting to her, that was all. She had to be certain it was solved and she was safe again within five days, when she rode publicly through the streets to open her first Parliament.

Feeling trapped inside this rumbling, jolting coach, she slid over on the padded bench on her side, shifting her feet and skirts past those of Mary Sidney and Anne Carey, who sat facing her. She peeked out through the leather flap, wondering how far they were by now, as the trip in this newfangled thing already seemed endless.

"Just past the bridge," she muttered.

"Ooo," Anne said, leaning sideways to peer out too, "I hate to look up there and see those parboiled, rotting traitors' heads on pikes at the Southwark side, but I do love shopping there."

Snowflakes drifted in and clung coldly to Elizabeth's lashes before they melted to make her blink false tears. "Like life," she said, smacking down the flap, "the dreadful seems to guard what's most desired."

Bett decided to be bold to see how far she'd get. She walked right in the garden gate at the back of the Suffolk estate. Then, with a big basket balanced between hip and arm—

202

mayhap some would think her just a new-hired washwoman—she sauntered in the back entry and through the huge, busy, open-hearth kitchen.

It was just after midday meal, and scullery maids and cooks alike were busy. She'd planned that, thinking it was better to stroll through chaos than chance meeting a single nosy servant who had a moment to talk. At least it was the Sabbath, so other than kitchen staff, people might have the day off or be at rest.

She found the back servants' stairs easily enough. She knew better than to be hauling cheap laundry, so in her basket lay the two fine fabric curtains she'd gleaned from the Arundel gatehouse. Still, she'd rather be doing this from a distance, in the dark, with a long picking pole through a window.

"Eh, you," she called out, bold as brass, to a young boy who looked like a page or linkboy, a sleepy one too. He was just a little bigger than Gil, with the same color hair, and that made her want to trust him. "I been hired," she told him, "for an extra wench to help with the duchess's laundry, her fine draperies, see." She tipped her basket so he could look inside. "She said get them back in her privy chamber when they was done, so which one is it, then?"

Stifling a yawn, he pointed down the darkened, wainscoted hallway. "Second door that side, her lordship in the adjoining chamber."

"Thankee."

She'd seen that in other rich folks' homes, though only from looking *in* windows. Separate bedchambers as if they couldn't abide each other, even at night. Bet that meant the duchess's lord wasn't good as Nick in bed, or she'd want him right on top of her.

She smiled grimly at her own jest. She'd feel a lot better if she could have come traipsing into this pile of rooms with a couple of strapping men like the queen took with her into the gatehouse yesterday or like she'd snared her and Gil with at the Ring and Crown.

Holding her breath, she rapped lightly on the duchess's door, then his lordship's next to that. If they were adjoining ones, she didn't want one or the other popping in on her.

Nothing. She lifted the latch and darted into the duchess's fancy chamber.

Laws, Bett thought again as she got busy searching for the diary, this wasn't her style at all. It must be hid, 'cause that herb girl, Meg, had looked in other chambers and not found it.

She tried not to leave a mess or trail. Some books were here but all in print, 'cept a ledger type that listed rows of numbers. The man she sold stolen goods to had taught her how to read, more or less, especially if she took a long time over it, which she didn't have today.

She was getting desperate now, looking in odd places. Under pillows, behind pots of face paint. She was tempted to take the jars of pomade, but if she got caught leaving, she'd never explain that. She just sniffed at them, the wonderful, expensive scents of roses and gillyflower cream, for one. "Vi-o-lets of Ven-ice," she sounded out, but quickly put it back. "Naw," she muttered, "that's good English gillyflower and wild roses."

And then, maybe, there it was, not hidden at all. A book on the padded seat before the small looking glass. A leather-bound and tooled book of rich-smelling leather with lines of slanted writing inside and numbers for the days of the month and year.

And sticking out of the book was a letter that said clear as you please, in the same hand, though it took a moment to sound out even these short words, *BURN THIS IF NEED BE.*

Bett hid both book and letter, then froze to listen. First off, the duchess must not be too far away since this was left out. And there was some distant whack, whack, like someone beating a carpet over a bush outside.

The sound stopped then, so Bett covered her booty under the draperies in her basket, then grabbed the letter back out, folded it small and wedged it in her bodice between her breasts so she could feel the edges and points of it. If she had to make a run for it and hide the book till later, she'd have something on her to show for all her pains. *BURN THIS* made it sound real important.

Footfalls sounded in the hall. That boy's voice: "She come this way, but Her Grace already got draperies!"

She darted for the adjoining chamber, lifted

the latch, and plunged in. A woman—the duchess?—stood beside the bed, naked, fat, taking a leather belt to a skinny younger man's bare bum while he bent, willing as you please, over the big bed.

Bett gasped, the duchess screeched, and the doors of chaos swung wide.

Bett shoved the basket at the first man who darted through the adjoining door. Another man ran in with the boy pointing at her. "That's her!" he screamed over the duchess's wails. Bett tried to make it to the window. It was just instinct because the drop to the cobbled courtyard would have killed her. Hard hands held her, dragged her to the floor, and shoved her down before the two men hauled her to her feet to face the livid duchess and her lord, now wrapped in robes. "Who sent you, thief?" the duchess cried, her face in a blooming blush.

"No thief, madam, just bringing back the laundry like I was told."

"Look," one of her captors said, wrenching her wrist hard. "A thumb marked with the *T*! A thief indeed."

"Then she couldn't have been sent—not by the ones I feared," the duchess murmured to her lord, who nodded. "Bind her and haul her off to the constable."

"No, good madam, I was sent, but only by a laundry woman give me a groat to deliver these to you. I just couldn't of got the wrong house, could I? Please—" Bett begged. "Lookee,

Your Grace," the other of her captors cried. "She got draperies here all right, and this book in them too."

"Ha!" the duchess declared, snatching back the diary, while her husband stood behind her nodding. "This bitch says those are my draperies, so be it. Tell the constable she's stolen them then. With that mark on her, she'll hang instead of draperies she's lied about. Good riddance to some of the vagabond rabble in our streets. Now get her out of my lord's chamber." Bett tried not to cry, but she couldn't help it. Fear of death, of losing everything, made her bones turn to butter. No one would know her fate till it was too late, for Nick and Gil thought she'd gone to see the queen. Is that who the duchess feared had sent her? Bett dare not say so. Besides, Good Queen Bess would probably hang her with her own hands if she made a peep to anyone that she so much as knew her.

Chapter The Thirteenth

Elizabeth fancied she saw Bella's pale face at the window as she alighted from the coach, but it might have been a servant or even a reflection of shifting sky. As she went in, Cecil's man, Philip Farmont, told her they had given John Harington the freedom of his library and dining parlor while Bella was kept upstairs. An armed guard stood sentinel at the bottom of the carved staircase.

Elizabeth was surprised to see Cecil hurry to greet her as she had not ordered him to attend her here. Then he must believe John was indeed guilty and mayhap dangerous.

"I will ask the questions now, my Lord Cecil," she said after she let Anne Carey take her cloak. While both ladies went into the solar to await her, Cecil nodded, handed her John's written confession, and followed her in.

Since Elizabeth had seen John two days ago, he seemed to have aged two years—and twenty since the happy day of her recognition progress but one week ago. She bade him rise from his bow and sit across the dining table from her while Cecil seated himself at the far end of it.

"I recall as I went by the Arundel gatehouse last week," Elizabeth began, fixing the nervous Harington with a piercing stare, "I glanced up to see you and Bella leaning out the second-story window, radiant and happy for me. Surely that was not the face of a man who had just committed murder one floor above."

She almost added, *nor who had just tried to kill his queen,* but that was the trump card she was still holding close to her chest.

"I looked down flushed with panic and desperation, for what I'd done upstairs," he admitted, "yet with guilty relief Penelope would no longer sully our good name nor shame her poor lord back home. And yes, I still felt joy for you, Your Grace."

"According to what you wrote, you had run upstairs during my stay in the street and had met up with Penelope as the two of you had planned when you kissed in the hall at Arundel House. You quickly argued, struggled with, but did not force her carnally, then smothered her? Is that yet your sworn testimony, John?"

"I—yes, as I wrote it. I did not run upstairs but walked. I had met with her briefly ere this in other...ah, precarious situations with but a few moments snatched between us." He tensed as if waiting for her explosion. She saw that and kept calm. "And what excuse did you give the others in the gatehouse so that you might leave?" she asked.

"Why, no excuse. They were rapt, gazing at you. Others came and went upon occasion. Bella leaned out one window, peering down the street at you, and the Suffolk clan was intent—Adrian and Frances then at least."

"And their girls?"

"Katherine and Mary came late upstairs, very late," he said with a stiff shrug. "Earlier Lord Adrian came and went at the duchess's bidding to fetch more of her medicine from the house, but as to times for all this, it was a blur, and I cannot recall."

"Cannot recall," she echoed, producing from up her sleeve his written confession in a ploy she'd taken from Cecil. Slowly she unrolled it on the table, staring at and smoothing it out to let him anticipate what was coming next, as if she were a wily lawyer.

209

"Just as you cannot recall many details of the murder itself?"

"I was so furious with Penny—Penelope. She had led me on and then dared to flaunt that she was doing the same with Edward and Jack." Perhaps without realizing it, he repeatedly hit his knee against the table leg so hard it shuddered to a beat. "And with boys, when the sap is up, of course they were taken in. I had to protect them from her."

"Oh, an effective way to protect them—and not a bit extreme," she said mockingly. "Tell me then," she plunged on, leaning toward him across the table, "exactly what words and actions passed between you and her in the—I would estimate—no less than the quarter hour in which I listened to my people's play scene in the street, spoke to them, and then went on?"

"You were rushed away by Lord Robert when he saw us there, as if he feared you would give Bella and me special notice," he blurted. "Aye, he looked up and saw us just before he took you off and glared at us. Your Grace, do not rely overly on that man so that he becomes—"

She shouted an oath and stood so fast her chair tipped back and smacked on the floor. His confession letter noisily coiled itself back into a roll. "Cecil," she cried, "have you been prompting this man? Lord Robert Dudley has naught to do with any of this, and I will not be baited or sermonized by anyone on him. Do you want to go to the Tower for the third time, man?" she demanded of John, leaning stiff-armed on the table toward him.

He scrambled to his feet. "If I'm to die for a woman's murder—even an accident—I warrant I shall speak out. As for the Tower, I know not why I am not cooling my heels in its familiar confines already. I have gone there once to protect Tom Seymour and once for you, and now I will go for..."

"Yes?" Elizabeth goaded. "Whom will you go for now? To protect whom?"

He stood gaping at her. His flush faded to ashen. She realized he had thrown Robin at her to get her off course. Yes, she must admit, John could have killed Penelope in the heat of the moment, but her own attempted murder must have been carefully calculated. As they glared at each other, the room went so silent they could hear the cold beams creak over the crackle of the fire and the quick footsteps of someone pacing back and forth overhead.

"Take him to the Tower, and question him there, my Lord Cecil. I am grieved to lose you, John Harington, but grieved more so for Bella."

"May I see her before I'm taken?"

"I am going to see her first. Then perhaps, if she wishes. It will be better for her to see you here than a supposedly sick woman coming to the Tower in this foul weather."

"Not supposedly, Your Grace, for she is sick at heart over what I've done. Even as I am." He threw himself down on both knees, nearly at her feet but with his face lifted to her. "I beg you to care for her when I am gone, Your Grace, for Jack too. And, if you would be so gracious to send someone to look for Hester here in London, I will bless you from my grave."

"Yes, I shall care for those things for old times'—for friendship's—sake."

"It was a crime of passion, Your Grace," he insisted as she turned to go out. "You know—passion. You remember how it can lead one astray—"

She swung back, leaned toward the kneeling man, and cuffed him soundly on the side of his head. It jolted her arm to her shoulder; she felt as if he had struck her too. He was going to throw not Robin at her this time but his dead friend and master, Tom Seymour. She knew it, feared it, because she still cared for the beloved bastard too.

He lifted one hand to his face and stared into her shocked one. "Yes," he dared, "it happened just that fast when I lost control with Penny."

Bett, bound hands and feet, was taken in an open garden cart on a long, bouncing ride across the bridge and past St. Paul's to Newgate Prison. There she was manacled and tossed in a thimble-sized cell with seven other women, whose filthy bodies stank to high heaven, as did the fouled straw on the floor. But from above, a chink or shaft shot down a single stab of sunlight and fresh air.

Though still stunned, she snarled back at

the other prisoners and told them to steer clear of her. She remembered the dog-eat-dog world behind bars too well from her few days in the Clink seven years before. She hunkered down against the wall and sucked in that single shaft of air. Then she dug out the duchess's letter still wedged between her sweaty breasts and unfolded it.

Something in it had to save her. Today might be the Sabbath, but on the morrow the justices would be back about their work. Hanging recaptured thieves was as sure as sin. That was the only good thing about this hellhole. One way or the other she wouldn't be here long.

She sounded out the words in the letter, writ in fancy script that was hard to untangle with its loops and swirls. You might know a high-up like the duchess would write like this. She might be Bett's better, but she was demented to treat her man like that. He'd obviously do anything for her, and her being the rich and titled one and him once a servant, she held the reins—or belt.

The letter bore no date, but there was a big space for one, like the duchess could put one in whenever it suited her. Bett gasped to see it was for the queen. Laws, then it couldn't be anything kept secret from her, like the murder of that woman in the gatehouse. Bett's hopes fell, but she tried to read on, taking such a long time that the sunlight moved, then left, and she had to squint.

Finally she figured the most important part

was: *I am of course sorely set against it, at least without your most gracious permission, but my dearly loved, eldest living child...*

Bett stopped and swiped at her tears. Her Gil—she might never see him again now this side of heaven and was scared she was going the other place anyway.

...to wit, my daughter Katherine, Bett read on, moving her finger across the lines and her mouth to form the words to be able to hear them, *has be-beseeched me to pet-i-tion you that she might wed with Edward Seymour, for they would pledge their love and loyal-loyalty...to each other as to you, Your Majesty.*

There was much more on the page. "Can't they just write short?" she muttered.

"Eh, you. You demented?" a poxy-looking prisoner shouted in the darkening cell. "Wha's 'at yer reciting there, witchcraft spells?"

"Keep clear, you pig's bladder, or I'll put a curse on you for certain!"

"I'll tell 'em yer cursin' me, and they'll burn you at the stake!"

Bett ignored her and went back to the lines of words. No one listened to prisoners, and it would soon be black as pitch in here.

Laws, she realized as she sagged in the corner, these words didn't even touch on murder, but marriage. Her goose was cooked for sure now 'cause everyone liked weddings.

Even more furious at John, Elizabeth lifted her huge hems and stomped up the staircase of the

Haringtons' town house. The first guard jumped aside. The one at Bella's door stood his ground only until he recognized his queen or Lord Cecil, running behind her.

Inside she found Bella not in bed but pacing and wringing her hands. No, she was twisting a piece of needlework before her as she walked. The two women with her jumped up and went out with the royal physician when Elizabeth flicked her wrist toward the door.

"Cecil, you may wait outside this time too," she said.

"Your Majesty, I shall just sit in the corner and take notes, for she has refused to give a statement up to this p—"

When she turned to glare at him, he bowed and backed hastily out. She saw he kept the door open a crack, and did not protest. She knew desperate people could do desperate deeds.

Bella, like John, looked pale and anguished. Her curtsy nearly tipped her over into the mussed bed. Elizabeth reached for her arm and helped to right her.

"If you are still ill, you must get back in bed," she said, her choler ebbing now that she saw her old friend so in need.

"Just ill with grief, Your Grace. If I might sit but a moment."

Elizabeth helped her to the padded bench at the foot of the bed and perched on the end of it, turning to her. Bella stared across the room into the low hearth fire. At this close range Elizabeth noted she had wrenched huge wrinkles into the stiff piece of crewel in her hands. It was, she saw, a picture of a man and a maid in a bower of red roses.

"You stitched this of you and John?" Elizabeth asked, trying to smooth it over Bella's knees to see it better.

"Oh, that," Bella said as if surprised she held it. "Penelope did it for her lord husband. Can you believe it?" she asked as a tear plopped on it, but her voice was bitter. "Hardly loyal, this Penelope, not as in the tale of *The Odyssey,* where as faithful wife, another of that name wove a tapestry and waited for her wandering lord."

"Turnabout of the sexes, yes," Elizabeth said. "Times are different now."

"Perhaps not," Bella said with a sniff. "My brother-in-law, Lord Maldon, is of the old school. That's why I ordered that my dead sister's face be washed of all remnants of her fancy kohl eye tints, face and lip rouging in death, so he doesn't die in a fit of apoplexy when he sees her body. A pretty, young woman always painting up—that tells you she was a seductress. But the old school of her husband, they avenge their wrongs."

"Exactly what do you imply? I heard her lord is even too old to ride here to escort her body back."

"Oh, I don't imply he would get revenge in person for the way she carried on. You, of all people, know you can hire men to do your will."

Elizabeth almost flared at such insolence, but Bella had stirred something that in all her agonizing over this, she had not considered. Could Lord Maldon have hired someone to make his wife pay the final forfeit for tarnishing his honor? He had been in her father's court but was never one who took to the new ways of exchanging women and wives when it suited his whim or shifting fortunes. But had Lord Maldon finally followed her own father's example to execute an unfaithful wife?

"Bella, do you have some proof of this, that Lord Maldon could have reached down from the Blackwater through someone else to make his wanton wife pay for her sins?"

She shook her head weakly. "I only know I detested her but didn't stop her when I should have so she would not hurt my marriage and my son. Oh, yes, Jack is only my foster son, but he's all I have, and he loves me. And now he's sitting like some felon in Lord Cecil's household with Cecil's wife to care for him when she has her own sons to love."

"If John goes to the Tower," Elizabeth mused aloud, "I could release Jack on his promise to stay close."

"He'd stay close to me. But John—to the Tower?"

"He's confessed and asked me to take care of you, Jack, and Hester. I could have Jack search for your stepdaughter. Did John tell you she's lost?"

"We're all lost, all lost...." Bella began to keen, then gripped Elizabeth's right wrist so hard it went quickly numb. She wrenched it back, picturing Penelope's slender wrists, bruised and blue from someone holding her down. She wished now she and Kat had felt on the back of her head for some sign of the blow John claimed must have killed her, but she could not face returning to that dim mausoleum.

"Cecil told me Hester's lost," Bella said. The queen rubbed her wrist as Bella talked. "She and John were always close. I...the stepmother...it was different. But...John confessed he loved my sister?"

"Not loved but carried on for a while as if he did."

Bella jumped to her feet. "It cannot be he who fathered her child!" she burst out so loud Cecil opened the door and stood there. "I guessed her condition the day before she died," Bella explained. "She told me she had 'caught the babe'—that's how the whore said it—from another lover, that the child would be handsome and tall to look down upon us all."

Bella brought both hands to her face and swayed on her feet. Then she suddenly hurled herself not at Elizabeth but upon her bed. She landed facedown, half on it. Clutching at the coverlet, she slid slowly off to her knees, sobbing wretchedly.

Elizabeth motioned Cecil over, and they lifted and laid her on her back upon the bed. The queen leaned down to study her face. Bella's eyes were wide open, staring up at the underside of the embroidered canopy. "Bella, I am telling you that John has confessed to killing

Penelope in a rage over the way she was behaving. Now listen to me," Elizabeth plunged on. "John is the one who rode directly to Penelope's Lord Maldon to tell him she was dead. You do not believe—cannot know, do you?—that John killed her at the behest of her lord...or perhaps for all of you?" The irises of Bella's eyes widened, then shrank to black points, but she did not move otherwise. The strong, lively woman looked struck dumb, an effigy of wax or stone.

"Cecil," Elizabeth said, "fetch my physician back in here." He nodded and hastened to obey.

"I heard you—about John—and knew it in my heart before," Bella whispered when they were alone again. "I just can't—don't want to believe it. But he came into a small fortune from somewhere lately, from the gaming table at some tavern, so he said. I accepted that. I love him."

As Elizabeth stared at her, the woman struggled to sit up, and her voice went from cold to heat.

"But if he got Penelope with child after how hard we've—we've worked and prayed for one," she cried, staring into space with her hands gripped so hard together her fingers went waxen white, "the next time I see him, I will kill him with my bare hands."

Monday morning, just after dawn, Betty Sharpe, as the bailiff insisted on calling her, was led in manacles and leg irons before the crown's red-robed justice of the peace for the City of London and sentenced to die the next day by hanging for the theft of "two fine draperies" from Suffolk House in Southwark. No jury was needful since the accused had already been adjudged doubly guilty by the brand of "thievery" upon her thumb.

The so-called neck verse, from Psalm 51, was read aloud in Latin, then English. She was so shaken that both readings sounded like gibberish to her: *Have mercy on me, O God, according to thy loving kindness and blot out my transgressions.* Amen.

"Lucky we're not common murderers," the woman behind her in line said, but Bett, feeling dazed, ignored her. "They burn or boil them, you know, and behead the noble ones. I only lift linens off bushes."

By nine of the clock Bett was thrown into the lower dungeon of Newgate, called the Limboes, a holding cell with a single central candle to illumine the last hours of those heading for the gallows. As she had no "garnish" to bribe the gaoler with but the useless letter she had hidden on her person again, she ate the gray gruel that was the day's fare and tried to pray.

But with her belly so hollow—her heart too, longing for Gil and Nick—she couldn't. She sat in a corner and tried to recall those succulent odors of bread and spices and meat from that meal the queen had bribed her and Gil with in the royal palace of the realm. The Lord of all heaven Himself couldn't have a sweeter, fancier place ready for those who were deserving, and Bett figured that was hardly her.

Chapter The Fourteenth

"You said you wanted to see Thomas Keyes when he came on duty, Your Grace?" Kat inquired as Elizabeth sat at her desk in her privy chamber, trying desperately to list what steps must be taken next in this discovery of murder and attempted assassination. She'd only gotten as far as *Send Ned and Meg to haberdashery row on London Bridge to trace who bought that old hat. Don't send them with it, but make all male suspects try it on to see if it fits, in case someone kept it all these years.*

Though Kat stood waiting, the queen angrily crossed out the last about everyone trying on the hat. Since it was to be worn atilt, almost any man could make it look as if it fitted—or didn't—depending on the angle at which he wore it. But for her, absolutely nothing seemed to fit right now. If John hadn't confessed, she could almost suspect Bella, but was that why he had confessed? With only four days left before she must open Parliament and parade herself in public again, she was clutching at mere straws, and those were swirling out of reach.

"Ah, yes, Thomas Keyes," she said, looking up at Kat. "Send him in before my ladies hear that despite my cold, I'm up this early. And, Kat, bid him carry in that big, carved bench from just inside the presence chamber."

221

Kat looked puzzled but hastened to obey. Elizabeth rolled her list and put it, Cecil-like, up her sleeve, and stood. Though so tall, Thomas Keyes was not a deep man but, thank the Lord, not devious either.

He came, upended bench first, through the door, and had to almost stoop to get in. The size and strength of her sergeant-porter always surprised her.

"Morning, madam. Where'd you like this then?" he asked, peering around it.

"Is it heavy, Thomas?"

"I'm used to it. But a bit, aye."

"And unwieldy too, to cart such about with you. Just like some burden you have on your chest, which you should get off."

He stared blankly at her, then stooped to put the bench down. It was heavy oak with scrolled, bulbous feet and long enough for three courtiers to await an audience with their queen.

"No, not there," she said. "I haven't decided about it yet."

She stood, staring up at him as he shifted his weight to keep its weight off the floor. "I repeat, Thomas, do you have anything to tell me I should know?"

Awareness dawned on his face. "That I been running errands for your lady cousin the duchess when she was here at court?" he asked, concern creasing his forehead.

"Indeed, let us start with that."

"I was off duty then, Your Majesty. I figured I'd best not turn her down, her being a Tudor and a duchess and all."

"Then how much more important you not turn me down. Perhaps the bench would be good over here," she said, moving clear across the room. "No, I'm not sure that's what I want at all," she said when he shuffled over with it.

"I told your herb girl I was escorting the Lady Mary Grey outside, madam. Maybe someone saw me," he said, out of breath now and sounding strained. "No harm there."

"Thomas, I am still not satisfied with the bench. Over here perhaps," she said, striding across the room again.

"I need to put it down, Your Majesty, else my hands will snap clean off. Then I'll move it anywhere you want," he grunted.

"I want you to tell me what those hands did the day you followed Penelope Whyte down the Strand to the apothecary shop and then away from it where you spoke to her."

Clutching the bench to him, he gaped down at her. Kat came in and wheeled one hand as if to tell her that her ladies were coming.

"Then close the door, Kat, and tell them they cannot attend their queen until she is quite finished moving furniture," she said. Kat closed the door. "You do realize, my man," she went on, "that being related to my Knollys cousins, though they are tied to the Boleyns, will do you no good if you are keeping information from me about a murdered woman?"

He set the bench down hard and collapsed on it with his face in his hands. His arms were trembling, but it could have been from his burden.

"Tell me straight, and tell me now, Thomas."

He jumped up, for he knew not to sit in her presence unless bidden. "It was before your procession hove in sight, Your Majesty. You got spies?"

"Stop stalling."

"I wanted to go to the constable with what I knew. But since I was your man, didn't think it would look good."

"Get up and pick up that bench again. I'm going to put you on it and set you adrift in the wild Thames myself if you don't tell m—"

"I—I'm friends with the Lady Mary. And her mother doesn't know it."

"Friends? Is that right? Say on."

"She—the Lady Mary—told me she would be at the Arundel gatehouse that day. So I went to the postern door next to it."

"I approve of the truth so far, Thomas, as a servant girl saw you there."

"You mean your herb girl, Meg? I saw her on the street near there with your fool."

"Not Meg. Just tell me what you did next."

"I talked to Mary—Lady Mary—at the door once, me peering in through the grate. She said she might sneak back to talk to me later. But she'd have to get her sister to reach the key. I told her to slip out when you go by. Then I would hold her up in my arms to see."

"In your arms..." she repeated. The image was ludicrous, but she liked the idea of the duchess being appalled, however much the queen must protect any maid with Tudor blood in her veins like Katherine and Mary Grey.

"So I waited awhile," he went on, "but another woman came out. She was wearing a hood pulled up. But I could see she was comely with blond hair, and no servant. A friend of Lady Mary's, I thought, one of the guests. And she was alone and darting out into the crowd like that. So I just tagged along to protect her, like I would have done with the Lady Mary."

"And she went..."

"The Lady Mary or the other one?"

"The hooded blonde!"

"Just a short way to an apothecary. Went inside, then headed back with nothing in her hands I could see. I asked her if she knew the Lady Mary and to tell her I was waiting. She s-ss-aid," he stammered in a sort of hiss, "that s-she..."

"What?" Elizabeth encouraged, her voice calm. "You might have been nearly the last person to see her alive. What?"

"That the only way the Lady Mary and I would ever fit together is if we were lying down. Then we'd be the same height," he said. She thought at first he would hang his head, but his face flamed, and he clenched his big fists at his sides. "She laughed at me real cruel, but I saw she'd been crying. Then she ran back inside. That's it. I swear I forgot about her right after."

The man was so simple that she believed him, though the expression that had flitted across his face—and those big fists—made her tremble too. "You forgot about her because the parade was coming and you saw me?" she prompted.

225

"Wasn't you got my attention, but a mad dog. I kept waiting for the Lady Mary, even when your parade came and stopped. But then this dog, foaming at the mouth and growling, ran past me, squeezed in the door onto Arundel grounds. See, the blond lady left the door open a bit, and 'course I left it open, hoping to see the Lady Mary, and then she could step out to see you. Well, when that dog ran in, I was going to find a tree limb to kill it afore it could attack anyone."

"Especially the Lady Mary..."

"Right, but then I saw through the grate—didn't open the door wide enough to get me in—one of the other guests, John Harington. He was running all about in the rose briars and even threw a couple of handfuls of soil."

She gasped. Thomas's admission of being enamored of little Mary had surprised her, but this shocked her. "Because the dog was chasing him?" she asked. "He threw it in the dog's eyes?"

He frowned. "May have been, or else he was trying to get dirtied up for some reason. But then he did chase the dog back out, right past me. It darted somewheres into the crowd. Your Majesty, please don't tell the duchess about the Lady Mary and me!"

"You do realize she too and not only her mother and sister have Tudor blood, Thomas?"

"That's why she needs a protector. If her own mother cuffs her, who knows what else could befall her? I shudder to think some murderer was lurking nearby."

"She is fortunate to have you for a friend. But I believe, Thomas, you knew you had seen and spoken with the lady who shortly thereafter was murdered, yet you did not come forward. No," she said, lifting her hands, "I realize you've been trying to protect the living at the cost of helping the dead. But don't you realize that the witnesses who saw you hurry after the blond woman could draw the conclusion that you had something to do with her death?"

"I thought of it," he admitted. "Guess I was gambling to save my position here with you, Your Majesty, and protect—

"The Lady Mary," they said in unison.

"Then take this bench back where it belongs, and see to it that you keep me better informed—especially about the duchess. If she is cruel to Mary or anyone else, you come and tell me promptly. Do I have your word on that, Thomas Keyes, sergeant-porter to the queen?"

"You have my word and my strong back—long as they last."

"Then I shall hold the door for you," she said, and shocked Kat and her ladies by opening it herself.

"Although your foster father's confession allows me to release you from Cecil's household, I have a request, Jack."

"Anything, Your Majesty," he declared. "But first I would beg you to pardon him—for his lies. He simply cannot be guilty."

227

"I asked you not to argue that with me. It is to be decided by others now."

"Yes, Your Grace, but you also told me to be strong and sure when I believe in something."

Their gazes snagged and held. She had chosen to stay seated at the table in her presence chamber while he stood. She was afraid, if she did not keep something massive between them, she would have hugged him in her sadness for this looming loss of his second father. Let Bella comfort him, and he her, for the queen admitted to herself that her feelings for Jack were not maternal.

"The favor, Your Majesty?" he asked when she just stared at him.

"Yes, twofold, really. First, that you help your foster father by inquiring in town for his missing daughter. I realize you knew Hester when you both lived at Kelston. Did you know her well?"

"Well enough. We were kindred spirits in both being discontent there when we wanted to be in the heat of things elsewhere. She is a fine lutenist, Your Grace, and light-fingered on the virginals too and she can sing like a bi—"

"Then I shall have her play both instruments for me when you locate her, and I shall play and sing too. Now, Jack, my second favor is that in searching for her, you take Cecil's man Philip with you for protection. I do not delude myself that you might need to go into a shady place or two."

"Philip is not to keep an eye on me—for more than safety?"

"Not in the way that you imply. And you must go see your foster mother to help her bear up, to cheer her. No doubt, it would be best to look for Hester in all the normal places she might turn up first anyway, starting with the Harington household in Stepney. I have just been there, but not for that purpose. And I take it that your foster mother did not get on as well with Hester as she does with you."

"True. Indeed, it is my fondest hope that I might serve you in any way I can. Your merest wishes shall be commands to me."

"Then I still want one indulgence, and do not vow anything until you hear me out. I do not want you to visit Edward Seymour until I give you leave—later."

"But if you are convinced that my foster father was the one, is Edward still under suspicion?"

"Must you question everything?" she demanded, standing and leaning on her hands toward him. It was only when she felt the fragile chain wrapped around her wrist that she recalled what else she meant to say.

"Forgive me," he said, though he did not look abashed at her outburst. "It is my nature to consider and question. I think, truly, my queen, that gives us yet one more thing we share."

My queen, he had said. Only Robin called her that, and it was so strangely possessive an address. Jack was looking at her avidly. She felt such a bond with him that she almost tilted toward him like a magnet to true north.

"I swear, I shall ever do as you ask," he

229

vowed, and swept her a bow that could have outdone Robin at his best.

"Then two things I give you in return," she told him, speaking quickly now, knowing she must send him away before she showed how much she had come to care about him. "A sturdy mount for your use which you may receive from my Master of the Horse, Robert Dudley, in the royal stables. And this, in return for your kind gift last time."

She unwrapped the chain from her hand and snapped open the locket. She did not glance again at the painted miniature of Tom Seymour, and had not for years. Anyway, it did not do justice to the dead man, who lived still inside her head...and heart.

Jack's fingers brushed hers as he took and looked down at it. "So much he could have done for good," he said, and his robust voice broke. "I will keep this put aside to show my own son someday and give to him the command to be loyal to his sovereign too."

"What is all that clamor?" Elizabeth asked her companions as they sat over a game of primero early that evening. She was having trouble keeping her mind on the card count, and then some disturbance in the courtyard had carried clear in here.

"Some lout got inside the privy garden where he should not be, Your Majesty," her scarlet-liveried door guard came in to report

230

to her. "Drunk, I expect, and yelling that the queen has kept his wife again."

"No wonder his woman's left him," Robin put in, and trumped her queen with a king. "I'd wager it's not Your Majesty but some knave who's delayed his wife."

"You've won this hand, Robin," she said, and shifted her skirts under the table when he pressed his knee to them again. She liked his attentions and his touch, but didn't he know others would notice such tomfoolery?

She blew her nose, for somehow her cold had taken a turn for the worse again. She grieved for Bella and for John, their whole family, though she had not allowed a formal announcement of his guilt yet. She'd much rather the culprit had been the Suffolks or at least Edward Seymour, but she must face facts.

It seemed indeed John had done the deed, for according to Cecil, he was sticking to his story in the Tower, including admitting he'd made a windfall at a tavern in Maldon when he'd gone to tell Lord Maldon his wife was dead. He had not, he claimed, been rewarded for ridding the world of Penelope. Cecil, however, had sent one of his men to question the widower and speak to people in the tavern.

Even Thomas Keyes's surprising detail about John's intentionally sullying and snagging his clothes made sense: He had just murdered Penelope and was trying to cover up gunpowder on his garments from struggling with her on the floor.

Yet Elizabeth still hesitated to allow his captors to use the rack to question John further about trying to assassinate the queen. He had not been told about nor charged with that. Yet she knew she must let them put him to the question soon; if he had not shot at her, he must have seen or had some idea who had.

She frowned at the cards coming her way while Robin dealt the next hand. Then she saw Kat nodding toward her privy chamber, maybe even her bedchamber. "Play on," she told the others as she rose. "Lady Katherine, will you not sit in for me?" she added.

"What is it, Kat?" the queen whispered as she caught up with the older woman at a near sprint down the corridor.

"That man the guards grabbed outside claims his name's Nick Cotter. And Gil just climbed in your window."

"On this floor?" she cried. "Over that rushing river?"

"Dropped down from the roof, best I can tell. I heard a knocking on the window glass and opened it to see his foot while he hung from the eaves."

Gil sat wrapped in a blanket before the hearth, drinking steaming ale. "Kat," Elizabeth said, "get word to Jenks to find Nick Cotter. Tell them to bring him down to the barge landing. Gil, what is it? Are you ready to draw that face for me?"

He shook his head. Then he popped up and began to look under her bed. He shrugged, then pretended to look out the window, then shrugged again.

"Where's Bett?" Elizabeth asked, realizing he was pantomiming a message.

Nodding, the boy pointed at her and raised both eyebrows.

"She's not with you or Nick?"

A violent frown and shake of his shaggy head.

"Could she have gone to Lord Harry's or even Cecil's?"

He shook his head again and made a running, darting motion with two fingers as if he'd been both places.

Kat came back in. "Jenks was just downstairs waiting for Lord Robert," she reported, "and he's gone to find Nick. So where's Bett and why did the little monkey come in through the window, devil take him? Do we have to put guards on the palace roof?"

"No," Elizabeth said, "because Gil is on my side. He doesn't know where Bett is, and we must find her. And the roof and window were the only way he could get in after he and Nick got stopped below, yes, Gil?" she asked.

He gave her a brave smile, and his eyes lit with hope. "Get my cloak, Kat, then go out and make excuses for my turning into my bed early."

Everything Nick knew about Bett's disappearance tumbled from him in a rush. He'd been looking for her at friends' houses, in some local shops, everywhere. She had said she was going to see the queen yesterday afternoon, but somehow she had vanished.

"She never got to me," the queen told him, holding her hood tight beneath her chin as river wind whipped across the barge landing. "If you find out where she went, send Gil to me at once. Or bring Bett here, but find Jenks in the stables to get to me and do not try to walk right in."

"I lost my head, Majesty." He darted an occasional glance at her but kept his gaze lowered otherwise, as if a long look at her would blind him.

"Oh," he said, "one more thing, Majesty. At the saltpeter cellars I asked today. You know, 'bout the man who came and bought the gunpowder a fortnight ago, the one with Lord Dudley."

"Dudley? Robert Dudley?"

"That's the one. Bett asked me who else 'sides him come to the cellars where you can buy powder."

"Yes, I see. Lord Robert no doubt came to look around at his investment there."

"What about the two sacks of gunpowder?"

Elizabeth felt dizzy. She stuffed her handkerchief against her nose to keep it from running like a sieve and leaned her other hand on Gil's shoulder to steady herself.

"Lord Dudley," Nick went on, "he takes gunpowder when he wants it. But the other man bought two bags, that's what I mean. Wanted to keep it dry in the sleet storm. Wanted it for fireworks for your cor'nation."

"Thank God you don't mean Lord Dudley bought two bags. But this man was with him? And this other man's name?"

"Jemmy didn't recall. Something like Harry Carrot."

"Lord Harry Carey?" Jenks blurted.

Elizabeth felt Gil's shoulders tense. It could not be Harry, of course, even if it sounded somewhat like his name. He was loyal to her and cared naught for firearms—did he? As for motive... Those whispers about a plot around him, which she'd ignored. That he was really her half brother with Tudor blood, a male, unlike the Grey girls.

"Jenks," Elizabeth said, but her voice came out so shaky he didn't hear. She grabbed his arm and shouted in his face, "Go bring Lord Robert back to see me, and then go for Lord Harry and tell him naught of this."

"Where you want to meet with them, Your Grace?"

"Separately—and in my presence chamber— alone."

Chapter The Fifteenth

"My queen, I will come day or night when you send for me, but why here, like this?" Robin asked as he came in to see her seated on her throne under the crimson canopy of state in

235

the large, empty chamber. A sconce flamed on either side of her. His bootheels clicked on the floor as he approached. Obviously uncertain how to proceed, he knelt.

"I thought it best I remind us both who we are, Lord Robert."

"I am your adoring subject and you my queen."

"So you always say. Rise. And tell me who the man was you took to the saltpeter cellars your man Jemmy oversees in Smithfield, the man who bought two bags of black powder a fortnight ago."

"What?"

Of all she might have asked him, he obviously had not fathomed this. His eyes widened, and his lower lip dropped before he recovered.

"I asked a simple question, and I must know now. Parliament sits soon, and I must go out in public," she tried to explain, and her voice broke. "Everywhere I turn I lose someone I trust—want to trust, thought I could trust. I believed once I was queen I would feel secure and safe."

"What are you talking about? You are safe with me. I would defend you with my life," he said, and started toward her.

She held up one palm to stay him. "Then answer my question."

"You are just distressed over having to send Harington to the Tower. My dearest queen, everyone is talking about it, and I know you are distraught about his betrayal, and I long to comfort you. It is human nature that friends may turn, even against sovereigns. Consider Brutus and Caesar...or Judas and the Lord Jesus."

"You do hate John Harington then—hate him—to imply such comparisons. But I will not take your bait to go wandering down some path away from my intent," she insisted.

"All right. Of course I have been many times to my new investment at the saltpeter cellars in Smithfield, sometimes with others, but a fortnight ago..." He frowned, as if deep in thought, then shook his head. "No, there was no one with me." He held out his hands beseechingly.

"In a sleet storm, Lord Robert," she said to jog his memory. "The other man wanted to keep the powder he purchased dry so he could have fireworks for my coronation."

"That may be, but I know naught of it. I was there and left in a sleet storm when someone else was riding in, but no one was *with* me. Jemmy's a wit only over too much ale, so mayhap he is mistaken. The only one I know who even talked about trying fireworks in January when it could be raining or snowing— I hear the things are damned touchy—was Lord Arundel, and he obviously decided against it. What is all this about? I would just as soon die as have you speak of not trusting me."

"Robin, you say so much but tell me naught. Try this, then," she continued, feeling herself soften toward him despite herself. "Did you hear a blast that day there was such chaos outside Arundel's gatehouse when you rushed me away, the place you later returned to and found out about the rabid dog?"

"You're thinking Arundel had fireworks shot off from his grounds when you passed by? But he was in the procession. I heard those women screaming along the route but didn't see a thing otherwise. But then," he said, approaching and going down on one knee nearly on her hems, "as I have said, I get blind and deaf to all but you in a crowd or alone like this. You know that you can trust me more than any other man on earth, do you not?"

She let him kiss her hand, then the inside of her wrist to make her pulses pound before she snatched her hand back. "Yes, I know I can trust you that much."

"Meg, would you stop whining?" Ned scolded as they walked the broad avenue of Cheapside early Tuesday morning. They had already stopped for oysters, but Meg had given him hers to eat, claiming an edgy stomach. "After all, you've been wheedling to come with me on one of my jaunts to gather information for Bess, and here we are."

"I know, but not to London Bridge."

"Whyever not? I hear some of the best city shopping is there, especially on haberdasher's row. Not afraid of being out over the water, are you? If I recall from our days in the country, you can row like a sailor."

She nodded but felt even more sick. It was

true that she could row and swim. She was quite sure she could sail too, and now she knew why. Ben Wilton must have taught her.

As they cut down Bridge Street, that old child's rhyme ran through her head, and she wondered if her mother had taught it to her: *London Bridge is falling down, my fair ladies.* She was scared her whole life would fall down around her ears if Ben Wilton recognized and claimed her, not that Ned Topside would give a fig.

"A pox on it," she muttered under her breath.

"What? You're still grieving your mother's loss, that's why you're acting out of sorts. Just do as I," he went on with his usual grandiose gestures, "pretend you are someone else for a bit, become a persona, and escape your other self."

She didn't even answer. Being out with him—and the queen had said to playact they were married—ordinarily would have thrilled her. She should have begged off, but she dared not give Her Majesty a reason to start looking askance at her, because she'd become mistrustful of about half the populace of London, including lately Lord Robert Dudley and her cousin Lord Harry.

Meg had heard the queen tell Kat that both Robin and Harry had pledged their loyalty to her last night and their ignorance of the gunpowder. Harry had vowed he hadn't even been near the saltpeter cellars. But the queen was still on pins and needles. She'd even said the only ones she could trust were Cecil, Kat, Jenks—and Meg.

"Now our story is..." Ned chattered on, explaining the elaborate ruse he had concocted for them as if he were writing an entire drama. He recited the street they lived on, his trade as a bookseller at St. Paul's, their children, their two servants....

"You think some hatmaker will ask us one bit of that?" she protested. "Gracious, Ned—"

"Alexander Carlton."

"Alexander. If that hat Bett found is as old as it looks, its maker could be dead anyway."

"Stop fussing, Gwendolyn," he scolded. "We're here."

Meg tugged her neck scarf farther up on her face. No one would know she was thinking of this as a double disguise.

The wind was even more bitter on the bridge, though the timber and daub shops and houses would soon shield them somewhat. Three to seven stories high, they stretched on both sides across the river. With its own drawbridges, chapel, constable, and guilds, London Bridge was like a miniature city in its own right.

"Gwendolyn, will you look at that water?" Ned—Alexander—said, leaning over the railing before the buildings began.

"I'd rather not," she protested. "It makes me feel like the bridge, the whole world, is moving. The river's up so bad this winter and in high tide..."

He wasn't listening. With others lining the wooden rail, he peered below at the frothing rapids. Meg shuffled a bit closer, staring in fascination into the mesmerizing, dancing foam.

No wonder there were suicides from here, and she'd heard a terrible tale of untended children dropping from the back windows of the houses above the shops. They got sucked down, battered, and drowned against the wooden platforms called starlings that protected the piers and arches. She'd heard folks found their bloated bodies seventy miles upriver, where the tidal surge spent itself, or if it was going back out to the sea, they'd be lost forever in the Channel. She shuddered and stepped back to safety.

"Even too wild for those reckless shooters' boats to be goin' through today," someone said.

At first she felt relieved Ben Wilton would not be about, but what if, since it was a day off, he was walking the bridge? Best get this over and get away, she thought.

She tugged at Ned. "Come on, Alexander. You promised me this day out of the house to get a new hat." The queen had given them each money for a hat, but not one with long plumes, she'd said. Meg's gaze kept darting to men's faces as they passed.

"The shops and stalls look prosperous here," Ned observed. "I'll bet, with their backs out over the water, Bett could never do her sort of shopping here, long pole or not. I can't believe she's just run off," he confided, lowering his voice even more. "Not with just those two draperies the queen let her have, and she dotes on that boy and Nick, I can tell."

Their eyes met. She nodded. Their feet slowed until someone from behind bumped into them. Meg whirled about and gasped.

"Would you calm down?" Ned muttered, and this time took her arm to pull her on. But she had noted he kept looking back too.

On the large center section, traders and stall holders had to bellow to overcome the noise of the shoppers and the roaring river. The lane was only two carts wide now, and they were continually jostled. They huddled against a shopfront while Ned produced the tiny sketch the queen had made of the maker's emblematic stars embroidered inside the hat. They squinted in the wind to see if one of the swinging signs sported that same symbol.

"There, up two doors. Our lucky day," Ned shouted, and they went on against the wind.

The chaplain who visited the condemned—men and women together awaiting the death cart—had asked each yesterday if there were kin to be summoned to view the hanging or to be informed after. Bett had given Nick's name for after. No way she could bear to have him or Gil looking on. Even if half of London turned out to see her die, she prayed they wouldn't be there. Laws, like most Londoners, she'd seen hangings, when she didn't stay in town to haul things out of deserted houses while everyone else attended them. Besides, the condemned were blindfolded at the end, so she'd never get a last glimpse of Nick or Gil anyway.

But to be one of those wearing their white shrouds, laughed at and watched, and pelted with garbage—this all still seemed so unreal.

She wondered if she should ask the churchman to take her letter to the queen. She could say she was to have delivered it from the Duchess of Suffolk to Her Majesty. But they would laugh and call her a liar or forger or send to the duchess to see if it was true. She might get in even more trouble, maybe tortured before they hanged her. Except for leaving poor Gil, it was best to make this quick.

And what would become of Gil? He'd not be able to do the angling without her, and he'd never let Nick take him to the cellars to work. Other than Nick, who would her boy use signs to talk with now? God's truth, it was the queen came closest to getting him out of himself. Maybe over the years, Bett dared hope, Gil could work for Her Majesty, drawing pictures of her sitting in barges.

"You there, girl," the gaoler was saying, and pointing straight at her. "You want bread and gravy 'fore the cart comes or not?"

She shook her head and turned away from the common trencher of the cold, congealed stuff. She couldn't bear the others sobbing or standing there struck dumb, just like her boy. Besides, she thought, she'd found something to sniff in this stinking place that lightened her heart some. The duchess's letter smelled of her own sweat now, but of gillyflower and wild woodruff too, like new-mown hay.

Bett huddled in a dark corner, closed her eyes, and hid her face and fears behind that folded piece of paper.

Meg kept a good eye on the door to the shop while Ned described the hat to the shopkeeper. He was an elderly man, and his eyes lit to hear of it. "Aye, old King Henry himself made those stylish, always with a jewel or pin right in front and the hat aslant just so," he said. His smile made his leathery face break into a wreath of wrinkles around his mouth and eyes. He touched his big brimmed hat with a shaky, mottled hand, then tipped it to the side. "I've not made or sold one like that for nigh on—oh, since the boy king died, I'd say. The Lord Protector fancied them too, used to buy from us." He grinned proudly. His teeth were blackened from eating suckets and sugar. "You mean Lord Edward Seymour," Meg asked, "the one his son is named for?"

"Aye. I have the dubious distinction of both Seymour brothers going to the block wearing my hats, I hear, but don't know if they were buried with them or not, losing their heads and all."

"Right," Ned said, obviously uncertain if that was a jest.

"Edward Seymour," the old man went on, scratching his chin, "now he went reconciled to his fate with the headsman's ax, they say. But Thomas Seymour, he struggled and fought. Guards had to hold him down. But, you know, it was those royal ladies I couldn't believe an angry husband, even a king, could bear to have beheaded, e'en for being unfaithful, and I don't think..."

He rambled on about Anne Boleyn and Catherine Howard and their ghosts he'd heard haunted the Tower and Hampton Court Palace until Meg was ready to scream. Even Ned's eyes glazed over with his tales of terror. They made their excuses and ducked out without buying anything.

"I'd rather have a new cape with a squirrel-lined hood than a hat bought here anyway," Meg muttered.

"There are only about ten other shops, and if the queen gave us money for hats, we're buying hats," Ned said, then yanked her back hard into the entry to the next haberdasher's.

"What is it?" she cried.

"I didn't want you puking up on me, so I didn't tell you. I think we're being followed."

She clapped both hands over her mouth. Had Ben Wilton spotted them but wanted to be sure before he snatched her? "Let's be off," she said, tugging Ned back out into the crowd and ducking in and out to pass people.

"Aye, all right," he said, glancing back and nearly stumbling over his own feet to keep up. "I don't like this. Being in so many plays, I have a feel for when someone's standing in the wings who shouldn't be, you know."

She breathed a partial sigh of relief when they were off the bridge. All she needed was to have

245

Ned with her when some lout came up to yell that she was his wife. Once, for a while, she'd hoped Ned would not be so grand and would in time become just half enamored of her as she was of him.

"Can you describe the man you saw?" she asked. Not, she thought, that she had the slightest clue what Ben Wilton looked like.

"Tall, very tall. If I didn't know better, I'd almost swear it was the queen's porter, just stooping down a bit to blend in with the crowd. Mayhap she's going to have to question him again."

Darting looks back, they retraced their steps to the city. On this side of Eastcheap it suddenly seemed everyone was walking with them instead of against them.

"What's that tolling bell?" she asked as, out of breath, they paused to look carefully around before their last leg to Whitehall. "It's Tuesday, not the Sabbath."

"They always ring bells on execution days, Jenks says. Newgate Prison's just ahead. They take the condemned in open carts to Tyburn Hill in the country so the crowds can see the hangings better. High drama, I'd say. I'd love to have the masses coming to see me in a pl—"

"All you think about is yourself, Ned Topside, no matter what name you take or person you play. Let's walk way around."

But the bell got louder, and the crowd thicker. "Look," he cried, "here comes the cart."

Despite herself, Meg looked at the condemned.

She couldn't even see the faces at first—both men and women—because fists bounced from the crowd ahead of them and arms heaved clods or dirt and dung. Meg tried not to stare, but they fascinated her, especially that pale woman with that bush of stringy, tawny hair—

They gasped in unison. "Bett?" Meg whispered to Ned, grabbing his arm and pointing.

"Bett!" Ned shouted over the chaos, bouncing on the balls of his feet to see better. "Bett, that you?"

The woman squinted into the crowd and did not see them, but it was her. She still searched, then her eyes lit. They ran along in her direction, shoving people out of the way to get closer. Bett lifted her tied hands from the side of the cart toward them, until she jerked off balance and had to grab for the wood railing again. Though those bars held twenty or so people crammed in, Meg could see their coffins stacked in the middle of the cart.

"Tell the lady," Bett screamed over the taunts. "Tell her I was grabbed trying to find the duchess's diary. I found it, but she took it back. I have a letter. Beg the lady to take care of my Gil...."

They stared after the cart as it turned toward the city gate and Tyburn.

When Meg and Ned reached the queen's apartments, they were both so out of breath they could hardly talk. One of the door guards told them, "Her Majesty is with Lord Cecil

247

and is not to be disturbed." At their determined look, he and his matchpiece crossed their ceremonial pikes before their faces.

"She said," Ned gasped out, "I was to come to her at once...to discuss a dramatic entertainment...for her tonight." The pikes did not budge.

Meg decided to playact this time. "I'm going to faint," she said, then shrilled, "Help me! Help me, Ned!" before she put a hand on the crossed pikes and slid to her knees.

It was the queen herself, with Kat and Cecil behind her, who opened the doors.

"Your Grace," Ned blurted, "we need to tell you something of utmost, urgent importance."

"What ails Meg?" the queen asked as Ned hauled Meg to her feet and she squinted at the three of them standing astounded in the door with the annoyed guards looking on.

"I'll be better," Meg said, trying to look as if she were swooning, "if I can just have Kat tend me a moment inside."

"Ned, bring her in and be quick about it," the queen commanded.

Cecil too moved fast to close the door on the guards behind them. "You found who bought the hat?" he asked while Kat brought Meg ale in a goblet.

Meg and Ned both talked at once until the queen hissed, "Silence. I cannot listen to you both. You said you found Bett hanging about on London Bridge?"

"No, Your Grace," Ned said. "On her way to her hanging."

Chapter The Sixteenth

Elizabeth listened intently as Ned and Meg told everything. " 'S blood, trying to steal the duchess's diary for me but found some letter?" the queen repeated. "But you said, Meg, you heard the duchess ripping up that so-called mea culpa one." Pressing her hands to her head, she began to pace.

" 'Tis a pity," Cecil said, "but this Bett's evidently the sort who wanted to sell things to you for a fancy fee, Your Majesty. And it's obvious she's been eavesdropping."

"It's obvious," Elizabeth countered, walking faster, "that she and Gil would be of utmost benefit to me—and to you, my lord—in this and other delicate situations. Besides, what will that poor child do without her? Children who lose their mothers young—" She stopped walking and cleared her throat. "The point is, Bett was taken acting to help us."

"But there are city marshals and constables guarding her," Cecil argued, though Elizabeth noted his voice and demeanor were more conciliatory. "I'm afraid she's doomed, so—"

"Never say that. I've been doomed, and here I stand. Now, the cart was just setting off, you say, Ned and Meg? How long ago?"

"Can't be—oh, a quarter hour, Your Grace," Ned said. "Of course, Tyburn is a ways out in the country."

"By the time," Cecil added, "they parade

the condemned through the streets as a warning to others and stop for a respite near Holborn, it's about three hours. But, Your Majesty," he went on, his voice its most diplomatic, "even if it is not too late, you cannot publicly pardon a second-time thief. Everyone will wonder why, and you will compromise the secrecy of your Privy Plot Council and your part in this murder invest—"

"We are wasting time," Elizabeth interrupted. "Anyone who gainsays me step aside, because I mean to rescue her."

"Rescue?" Cecil remonstrated, choking on the word. "But—"

"Kat"—Elizabeth cut him off again—"you said Nick Cotter came back this morning and Jenks took him into the stables to calm him down. And you are having Gil fed in the kitchens. Fetch all of them to the chamber below, and tell Jenks to bring the match from Sir Robert's firearm demonstration. I have that partial sack of gunpowder hidden here, so I shall bring it. Well, fly, woman!" she shouted when Kat hesitated.

"Ned," the queen went on, ignoring Cecil's sputtering protests, "do we still have that angler's pole we got from Bett?"

"I was keeping it to hang a back curtain from when I did scenes for—"

"Ah, that gives me another idea. Well, don't stand there. Fetch the pole, and join us below." She was already rummaging through a coffer in the corner, throwing out night rails and shifts until she produced the sack of gunpowder. She

250

ran to her mirrored table and rummaged through the rouge pots and kohl brushes there, then grabbed a glass jar with lip color.

"Meg, I hope you don't mind playing a part in front of half of London at a hanging. And not playing me this time."

The queen stood, holding the neck of the sack, which she'd put in another bag so it would not smudge her undergarments in the coffer. Ordinarily Meg was determined to be part of things, but now she looked afraid.

"In front of half of London..." Meg murmured.

" 'S blood, girl, you look as if you'll faint again, and that was a ruse to get to me, wasn't it?"

"Yes, Your Grace. Poor Bett—I'll help. Just tell me what we're all going to do. They'll surely stop the cart when they see you."

"See me? We're not stopping any cart, and I'm not leaving this palace, though I've a good nerve to."

Cecil sighed so hard with relief, they both looked at him. "Come on then, anyone who will help," the queen said, and darted toward the privy door that led downstairs. "And if you don't, it bodes no good for your being consulted in future scrapes."

"Scrapes?" she heard Cecil say, but both of them hurried after her, grabbing candles to light the way down.

"The hat, Your Grace," Meg said in the dim stairway, "is an old style they don't make anymore, and lots of people had them: both Seymour brothers—"

"That hat is one reason we're going to rescue Bett before it's too late," Elizabeth replied as her voice echoed in the narrow, enclosed staircase. "She could have hidden that hat, then tried to sell it to me or others for a pretty penny, but she handed it right over. That's why I think she went to Suffolk House not for her gain but mine. Crown justice be damned—and if you repeat that, I will have your heads—I'll not hand her over to a hangman."

Meg was amazed how soon they were back into the thickening crowd, first thundering down the Strand, then cantering through the lanes of Covent Garden, then walking the big beasts through Lincoln's Inn Fields toward Holborn, where Lord Cecil had said the procession would stop for a late-morning respite.

Jenks, Ned, and Nick sat ahorse, though Nick had no real idea how to control his big beast, so Jenks handled his reins too. Meg held tight to Ned, and Gil to Jenks. The boy had the long match, not yet lighted, the sack of gunpowder, and the other small sack stuffed with Meg's small herbal bags, taken from the queen's coffers at the last minute. Ned held the angling pole at his side as if it were a lance and he a knight charging in the lists. None but Jenks knew exactly how they were going to use these weapons or handle the situation. She only knew they had the queen's orders to bring Bett back alive and to kill or maim no one, including themselves, in the process.

"Can't believe it," Meg murmured in Ned's ear as they surveyed the busy scene where Holborn crossed Gray's Inn Road. "It's raucous as a country fair."

They rode past street vendors selling hot pig's ears and trotters. Hawker's cries for beef pies and hot cider and ale swelled. "Pepper and saffron!" a woman's voice kept shrilling. "Pepper and saffron! Hot, hot, hot."

"Get 'em here 'n' treasure 'em the rest of your life!" another man hawked his wares in a singsong voice. His breath made puffs in the cold air. "Snatches of cloth and locks of hair from Highwayman Hank, 'bout to be hanged for ungodly, bloodthirsty deeds on the queen's highways and byways!"

He had quite a crowd, Meg noted. So it was Highwayman Hank folks were pressing close to try to touch in the distant cart of the condemned. Evil as they were, highwaymen with a reputation were the crowd's darlings.

They passed a cockfight, then a fistfight with two men stripped to their waists and already bloodied while gamblers urged them on. People of some means hung out of upper windows, as they had for the queen's progress, but no sills were draped with Turkey carpets or fine tapestries for this.

Ned and Meg's horse just missed getting hit with a shower of waste and the chamber pot, which must have slipped from someone's hands and clattered away on the cobbles. When the horse shied, she held Ned's waist hard until he calmed the chestnut mare.

Despite the crowd milling between them and the prisoners, Meg saw Jenks pull back on Nick's reins, so he wouldn't bolt for the cart.

"Listen to me, or we don't try this at all," Jenks reminded them. "She said I'm in command, and if anyone disobeys, they need never darken her door again, that's what she said."

"But we got to get nearer Bett!" Nick protested, and Gil nodded wildly. "If they get out in the country, we'll never angle her. This is our last chance!"

Jenks's eyes skimmed the scene, then he motioned them to bring their horses closer. "Here's how we try what our mistress said to do," he shouted over the noise.

Elizabeth paced back and forth in her bedchamber. Her people had set off only a quarter hour ago, and she was already going mad with worry. As she wrung her hands, she saw they were still stained from opening her paint pots to show Ned and Meg what to do.

" 'S blood," she muttered, and stomped over to her mirrored table to wipe the stuff off. And then a suspicion struck her.

She ran to her coffer and pulled out the hat Bett had found. What really were those stains on the top of it that she had assumed were gunpowder or soil against the dark creased and wrinkled surface? She was learning to assume nothing.

She yanked the counterpane down to bare

her bed pillows and stripped off the closest linen pillowcase. She put her hand inside it, then, in good window light, carefully wiped it against the stains on the top of the hat nearest the front side.

Some stains were gray, but a darker gray than dust or gunpowder. They were almost black. Squinting in good window light, she could discern two areas of this stain. One for each eye? Though the corpse's face had been cleaned, Bella had said her sister always went painted up, as she put it. This could indeed be lantern black kohl from those eyes that had popped with blood when they beheld her attacker and she had known that she would die.

To see if it was a color match, Elizabeth went to her mirrored table and lightly smeared a bit of her kohl she seldom used next to the black stain. Yes, so close.

She went back to the window and rubbed lower on the hat, where the stains should be a redder hue. If the other was kohl for eyes, the rouge—on both sides of that nose shoved askew—would be about here. Penelope's cheeks had looked mottled, perhaps from severe bruising.

She gasped. Yes, it seemed so.

She ran back to her cosmetic jars and scrabbled about for the one she wanted. It was called French Rose, but she knew it was the common English concoction of crimson cochineal, the white of a hard-boiled egg, fig milk, and gum arabic.

Carefully, bent over with her knee on the stool

by the table where she herself sat to be painted, she smeared a bit of the rouge next to the reddish stain on the pillowcase. A match. A double match. Two cheeks.

And what about down where Penelope's mouth would have been, gasping, gaping, perhaps pleading, as life was smothered out of her?

This time, as if she could predict what she would find, she touched her finger lightly to the lip rouge, a mix of herb madder and red ocher, and spread it thinly on the linen. Then she gently rubbed the space just above it, like the upper lip, against the dark brown cloth's lowest stain.

Elizabeth stared at what she'd done. On the pillowcase, draped over her left fist, was the ghostly, blurred image of Penelope's painted face as she was forced from life to death. In her other hand, she held the hat, the smeared and stained murder weapon.

Bett was glad the crowd noise had drowned the ringing of that infernal, tolling bell, but she supposed it would have faded as they got away from Newgate anyway. This constant roar was easier to close out, despite the insults, ridicule, and occasional slimy splat of garbage that found its mark. Sometimes she got a whiff of food. Mostly she kept her eyes closed, with an occasional glance of the wintry sky. She wished she could soar into it.

The noose around her neck—all wore their

nooses and shrouds already—hung heavily against her breast as a reminder of what was to come. She fought to picture the quiet, calm days she'd had with Nick or Gil, even that last Sabbath on Smithfield Green but two endless days ago, when the boys had thrown snowballs and she and Nick had talked. If she could just get back to that precious hour, if she could just not go to Southwark and Suffolk House to face that she-devil duchess...

It annoyed her too that they were being hanged with someone called Highwayman Hank, and the man was lording it over everyone. What a jackass to be smiling and nodding as if he were the King of England on progress when he was a thief on the way to the gibbet.

She shuddered as something smacked the middle of her forehead. She tried to turn away—until she realized it smelled sweet. At first she thought she had imagined it until the second one hit her right in the nose.

It *was* sweet. Soft too. A bag stuffed with rose petals and lavender?

She seized the second one from her lap where it had landed and looked out to see who could have pitied her enough to throw it. Laws, she'd hold it tight to her nose all the way up the hanging ladder the condemned had to climb and jump off. She'd jump, that was sure, and not because if you didn't, they turned you off it. She wanted this over fast.

Her eyes locked with Gil's. She sucked in a breath of shock. Sitting on Nick's shoulders, he was aiming another herbal packet. He dropped it and began to sign something to her. Nick looked like he was crying, but Gil was totally intent. His two fingers, pretending to jab his own eyes, shouted a silent *Pay attention!*

At first her eyes watered so hard she could not see to read the signs. They'd found her, come to say good-bye. The queen was saying good-bye too, Gil was signaling. No, that was not it.

The queen sends five to save you. Go to other side of cart. Stand. Look up. Window.

This was still unreal, she thought, all of it. First a nightmare and now a wondrous dream. She did not want to stop looking at Nick and Gil, but Gil was already off Nick's shoulders, and the crowd had devoured them. She clutched the small bag of sweet smells—eh, like the Queen of England herself. She slowly shuffled along, shoving past others to the side of the cart under the two-storied windows instead of the more open street side. She looked up, but not so someone else would notice.

"Here you, this place's mine!" It was the poxy-looking woman who had accused her of witchcraft the other day. "Don't want to be over there and get pelted!" she muttered, jabbing an elbow into Bett so hard she bounced back into the stack of coffins.

"Trade you my last good thing for this place," Bett pleaded, bouncing up. "Just for a minute or two. When the cart starts again, I'll give it up."

Though she loathed to do it, she pressed the tiny sack of potpourri to the woman's nose and then into her hands.

Looking surprised, even moved, the woman nodded. She shoved someone else away until everyone sitting shifted farther down. But Bett stood, now and then pretending to glance up at the sky.

Whatever was coming, she knew there would be just one chance for it. Would Nick vault down from a window or would someone drop a rope for her? But then they'd all be caught. The constables were enjoying cheese and meat pies off a ways, but two guards kept a haphazard eye on them.

The earth shook, and windows rattled. Bett ducked. Her ears popped and hurt. People screamed. A battle begun? The blast of doomsday?

Across the way, she saw a huge puff of smoke that sent tree limbs flying. An explosion had gone off way up in a tree? She ducked as twigs, then shattered window glass rained down. People shrieked and fled or threw themselves flat. Bett hunkered down, not sprawling like the others, though even Highwayman Hank was cowering.

When no second sound followed, people got up and trampled one another to flee. A booth collapsed with a bang to make people duck again. Bett had forgotten to look above her until a tree limb hit her on the top of her head.

No, her own angling pole! With Nick's face and that queen's man who smelled of horses at the top of it, half hanging out a window. Though her feet and hands were tied, she reached for the pole. Thank God she wasn't tied to the cart or the others. The men lifted. She started up, then slid back.

"Hey, there!" someone shouted at her over the noise.

Caught! It was the poxy woman she had bribed for this place. Bett held tight to the pole but slipped farther down. Despite the chaos, if the woman made a row or held her back, she was done.

But when she looked down again, she saw the woman grin and clasp her tied hands. Thinking she'd drag her back, Bett wanted to kick her in the face. Then Bett realized she had made a foothold for her—if she read her right. If she didn't, that might as well have been a doomsday blast.

The woman cupped Bett's foot and shoved. Nick and the queen's man pulled. Her hands were filthy and sweaty, and she didn't recall all these splinters on her pole. But they had her hanging on it straight out the window before they hauled her in. They dragged her hard over the sill, scraping her belly and thighs, and yanked her to her feet.

"Oh, Ni—" she got out before they stripped the noose and shroud from her and pulled a plain gray woolen gown over her head. It smelled so clean. She gaped to see two people on the floor—this must have been their window—trussed like pigs. She barely had time to dive for the duchess's letter, which had dropped to the floor, before they grabbed her and ran.

They thudded down a dark hall, then the back stairs, so narrow they had to go one by one. From outside came dreadful shrieks.

"They know I'm gone," Bett panted. "They're coming for me."

The queen's man put a hard hand over her mouth and peeked out into the back alley. Gil stood there, holding two horses. She tried to hug him, but Nick threw her up on one, then got on behind her while Gil swung up behind the queen's man.

"That's just Meg's screams," the man said. "She's got gunpowder spread on her like burns and cinnabar face paint like blood on her arms and legs. Ned's making a show of rescuing her to keep them from looking our way. Let's ride."

Elizabeth's eyes grew moist as she observed the family reunion on the barge landing and listened to Jenks's account of how well her plan had gone. She led everyone up into the apartment under hers, which was now more completely furnished and stocked to abet her privy plans. Kat kept blowing her nose, and Cecil still looked pale as bleached linen when the rescuers and the rescued fell on the food and ale laid out for them there. Afterward Elizabeth had Meg drag the exhausted Bett off behind a screen by the low fire where a hip tub of rosewater warmed on the hearth.

"I've gone to heaven, and you're the queen of it!" Bett called back. Though Elizabeth liked proper veneration, it had become a bit wearisome that Nick, Gil, and Bett had knelt and kissed her hems and her shoes. She'd already tripped twice over Gil. She'd told them to stop, but Nick had just turned his attentions to the embarrassed Jenks and smug Ned.

"Don't thank me overmuch, Bett," Elizabeth called to her, walking over to the screen. "I told Meg she must cut your hair to one hand width and get it hidden under a kerchief. I may have Ned darken it with some of his blackamoor face paint for a while too. Should there be a hue and cry put out, I don't want you recognized. Nor can any of you return to your lodgings since you gave them Nick's name. You'll have to work for me here at the palace."

At that Nick carried Elizabeth's chair to the screen while—she could tell from the sounds of delight—Bett sank gratefully into the tub. "Laws, this is better than a swim in the summer Thames," she called out.

Elizabeth didn't tell her she was considering having her thumb burned again to see if they could permanently scar over that *T* brand on it. If the woman was to be safe in her employ, she could not risk her being taken and sentenced to hang again.

Over the swish of water Elizabeth heard Meg murmur, "You know, I remember swimming in some river when the tide was low."

"And wash her hair even though you're

262

going to cut it," Elizabeth added, speaking through the painted velvet screen.

"I owe you my life, Your Majesty," Bett said.

"You do indeed. Now tell me everything you recall about the diary and whatever letter you found."

"I'll do better than that, though I didn't have time to read the diary, Your Majesty," Bett called, and splashed water so hard, some puddled at Elizabeth's feet under the screen. "And wait till I tell you what else I saw in the duchess's bedchamber."

"Tell me now."

"Both naked as jaybirds, the duchess whipping her lord's bare bum and him willing as you please."

The queen jerked rigid in her chair. If a man would submit to that, would he not murder at his captor's command? She flushed, swept with revulsion at the image of it all, but with excitement also, not for the sexual aspect of it but the heady sense of power over men. In a different way she wielded that now too.

"Didn't mean to shock you, Your Majesty. Oh, there on the hearth by that gown...what I want her to have," Bett said, speaking low to Meg now. The girl came around the screen with a tiny, folded piece of damp paper.

Quickly, over by the candles on the table, Elizabeth unfolded the paper and tilted it to read the lines amid the blur of sweat marks and web of folds.

"Anything of use to us, Your Grace?" Ned asked, shooing Nick away.

"It proves my cousin has been lying about not wanting Katherine to wed. On the contrary, she is pulling strings to align old allegiances. And if she lied to me about that, what else is she lying about? Murder? And she hoped…my murder? Also," she said, jabbing her finger at the page, "it is proof Edward Seymour has designs on my throne through a forbidden marriage."

"So," Jenks said, "you are going to summon the duchess and her husband for questioning, even if John Harington did the deed?"

Elizabeth looked up from the letter. She knew Jenks did not believe John guilty, but he was so blindly loyal that he had never believed treason of Thomas Seymour either.

"No," she replied, "because the duchess would just lie again, and it would tip them off."

Kat came closer. From the look on her face Elizabeth knew she'd been listening. "Will you give Edward Seymour or Lady Katherine another dressing down?" she asked.

"Not yet. I'm going to send for the only witness I have perhaps wrongly ignored, one easily overlooked who could not possibly smother anyone nor hold a firearm. But nothing is as it seems in this maze, and I cannot risk more dead ends."

Chapter The Seventeenth

Waiting for Lady Mary Grey to be brought to her from Suffolk House, the queen and her ladies—she pointedly ignored Katherine Grey—walked in the walled privy garden that afternoon. Elizabeth could tell they were appalled to be dragged out of their hearthside seats, but lingering cold and cough be damned, she was so pent up she could not abide sitting still.

The Thames rushed by on the other side of the rose-brick walls topped by carved and gilded figures of heraldic animals. Surmounting a painted column, each held a pennant that snapped in the stiff wind but did not batter those walking below. Hedges trimmed in the form of seats encircled grassy grounds and now-dormant herb and flower beds. None of this but the wild river and wind suited the queen's mood today.

"Is she not here yet?" she asked one of her guards Cecil had insisted attend her whenever she so much as stepped outside lately.

"Who has been sent for?" Lady Katherine piped up, looking alarmed as if she knew what was going on.

Elizabeth glared at her, then said to the guard, "Signal me for a privy audience when my guest arrives, and the ladies will continue their constitutional without me. Well, man, go to be certain, then report back."

She paced past the sundial, which read three of the clock in the wan winter sun seeping through thin clouds. Only half listening to the chatter around her, she had just passed the fountain when she saw the guard starting down the gravel path toward her again.

"I shall rejoin you later, ladies," she announced, and left them huddled like a group of chicks without their mother hen. "What news?" she called to the guard as he approached.

"No Lady Mary Grey as of yet, Your Majesty, but there is a Jack St. Maur—not to be said Seymour, he insisted—waiting for you just at the entrance to the Sermon Court."

He hurried to keep up with her as she swept past. "He is with Philip Farmont," he called after her, "one of Lord Cecil's men."

She went inside under the archway, cut through a corridor, and stepped outside again. The Sermon Court was another grassy area with broad walks for promenades and a central pulpit for outdoor preaching or speeches. The palace's wings that overlooked and sheltered the court held the privy chamber, council chamber, guardroom, and great hall.

When she saw Jack and Philip waiting with their horses on the far side of the court, she recalled this had been the last place she had seen Tom Seymour. She hadn't been living in his household then—she had been sent away in shame—but he had come to try to see her. She had risked much to sneak down here after dusk....

266

"News of Hester Harington?" she called to Jack as he strode toward her, leaving Philip with the horses. Her guard stayed at the entry she had come through.

Jack went down on one knee with head bowed but not before she saw his complexion looked burnished by the ride, his high cheeks a hectic color.

"The news is, Your Majesty, that I have searched high and low here in the city but have not seen or heard of Hester." He sounded breathless but might only be nervous. "I have described her to many—ask Cecil's man there—but no leads. I am stricken I failed you, at least thus far, in the first quest you have given me. But I have come to tell you more than this."

They began to walk the circumference of the court, slowly, as if they had all the time in the world to stroll for pleasure. And she admitted, as she laid her hand upon the arm he offered her, despite the dire note in his voice, it was her pleasure to see him. Though he went bareheaded when his father seldom had—he must have uncovered his head in respect for her—she could almost recall that last bittersweet time here with Tom....

She stumbled, and he steadied her. "What else did you come to say then?" she asked, and turned to face him in the shelter of the corner farthest from Cecil's man.

"So much...but dare not."

His eyes shone, and his face was fervent. He took her hand, and though they both were gloved, his heat seemed to burn through. For one moment she almost fancied he would declare his undying devotion. Tom had done that here, but he had brought only destruction.

"I came to tell you, Your Grace, that I believe my father—John Harington, I mean—did more than just murder Penelope. I have wanted to believe it is not so, but I fear I must accept it. For I—I heard him talking in his sleep one time when we were out hunting at Kelston together. We were exhausted, so lay down under a tree after we ate. I swear I just did not piece it together before, but, Your Gracious Majesty—"

"More than murder?" She was suddenly sure he would tell her that John had tried to kill her too. "Explain," she whispered, but her voice still broke.

"You know how desperately my foster parents longed to lift themselves from the shame of being sent to the Tower in your brother's reign and then in Queen Mary's. I understand that too, as I—"

"Say on about what more besides murder you believe John Harington intended."

He nodded, but she could see him grit his teeth to set his jaw. He flexed his hands to fists as if he could not bear to tell her but was forcing himself to.

"He muttered in his sleep something about covertly shooting a firearm at you, but intentionally missing, then claiming he had saved your life by forcing the shooter to miss his mark and run. He hoped to get quicker preferment and wealth and your trust."

He hung his head. "I know I am dooming him, my dear foster mother, and my own future too, but I had to tell you. Please temper your justice with mercy, for he surely killed Penelope by accident and never intended to harm you."

He looked so distraught she lifted her hand to clasp his cloaked shoulder. "Jack, if I believed in guilt by blood ties, I would have to send half the nobility of England to the Tower or worse. God bless you for telling me."

He nodded jerkily, too upset or shamed to meet her eyes.

"Tell me how you think it happened," she urged.

"I believe he slipped away while you spoke below the windows and took a firearm and perhaps gunpowder that had once been stored by my father there for a treason of his own.... He was my father's man and could have known where arms and ordnance were hidden. Or he could have hidden it there, visited there, more recently."

He sucked in a breath and blinked back tears. "I sought out Lord Arundel but yesterday," he went on. "He told me that arms and even a bit of powder were still stored up there. He had never wanted to touch the stuff as it was tainted and had once been evidence in my father's treason trial."

"Lord Arundel knew there was gunpowder

there from years ago?" she muttered. Her mind raced, for she had been certain it was newly purchased at Robin's saltpeter cellar. "Then I must talk to Lord Arundel too. I was starting to think somehow Edward Seymour had bought some."

"He could have, I suppose," he said with a shrug.

"But, Jack, you are saying you believe John Harington—I know it pains you to give evidence against him—decided to shoot at me, then—"

"I surmise," he said with a heavy sigh, "that Penelope saw him go upstairs or just stumbled upon him. She probably caught him at it and said she'd give him away. I don't know. If it wasn't a—a lovers' quarrel between them, that could have been why. So he killed her, maybe even accidentally, as he said, and then mayhap it was too late to take the shot at you, but I saw the powder all over the floor, so I guess he spilled it. That hardly could have been there since my father's time."

He was sounding more distraught, but he had chosen her over his beloved foster parents. At first she thought he knew too much, but she herself had reasoned out almost all that, and he had not known John had actually taken that shot. How clever Jack was. She wished she had him in her Privy Plot Council, but perhaps she could in time. Then she thought to ask, "When? When were you up there to see powder spilled on the floor?"

She watched him closely, but he did not so much as hesitate. "I wanted to see her when the constable and coroner were there," he admitted. "They'll tell you I insisted on looking. I could not believe what they said, that she was dead, and had to see for myself. And now I've failed to find Hester, and the glimpse I got of Penelope in death is haunting me. Your Majesty," he cried, meeting her eyes at last, "what if Hester is out there somewhere unprotected, where she could be harmed? Worse, what if he had shot and had accidentally *not* missed as you rode by?"

She gripped his quivering chin with her other hand. She almost blurted out to him that John *had* shot and killed a woman. Though she had as yet told no one outside her Privy Plot Council that there had been an attempt on her life, she nearly confided in this man. She was so desirous of comforting him and felt so grateful to him that she did not step back when he slowly lifted both hands to her elbows to hold her against him.

"I cannot tell you...what you mean...to me," he whispered, and tugged her even tighter.

She saw her silhouette in the wide pools of his eyes. She tried to speak, but words snagged in her throat.

"I want it all destroyed," he said through gritted teeth. "My father's place of treason— and my foster father's too. I want it gone to keep you safe."

271

She nodded, transfixed, and mayhap he took that for acquiescence. One leg shifted into her skirts as he came closer to touch—

To touch the queen. She was not some heartsick green girl longing for a forbidden kiss from a man who could really love and adore her the way her father never had. No longer declared bastard, not even princess. She was queen.

Shocked they had almost kissed in the open air where the walls had a hundred glass eyes, she pulled away.

He looked flushed again with agony, no, this time it was anger.

"I—forgive me, Your Majesty. I would ask that I be allowed to exile myself from you for a while. I would help my father—foster father, I mean, of course—whatever he has done, by finding Hester. I assume he will die for his deeds, but he could go to his grave at least knowing she was safe. I would ask your permission to ride to Kelston to inquire if she might have passed along that way or be there yet in some house or inn."

"A good idea, but not yet, Jack," she said, recovering her poise to begin to walk again. "But when your foster father confesses, then yes. And I must use your information against him to make him tell everything. You will have to dictate all this to your companion Philip for Lord Cecil, you did understand that?"

She was appalled he looked so stricken. "Jack, will you still obey me?"

"In anything!"

"Go with Philip back to Cecil's town house, give him your sworn statement, and stay there until I send for you."

"Will it be soon?" he blurted, his thick brows hunching over his eyes in a frown. "I want things settled soon."

"I pray so. Go now. And if Cecil is at home this hour, send him to me straightaway, or tell his staff to do so."

She sensed he would argue or refuse, but she was wrong. Even forgetting proper leave-taking, he spun away and hurried to where Philip was waiting.

Though the queen felt she had all her answers now, she still sat down with Lady Mary Grey, this time by the hearth in her privy chamber. She might as well take this opportunity, through her, to warn Katherine and the duchess to behave. Yet when Cecil arrived, she would end this interview forthwith.

As ever, each time she saw the tiny person— for she must stand but four feet—she was amazed she got about as she did. Some called her Crouchback Mary, for her entire body was misshapen—but not her sharp mind.

Elizabeth observed two other things about the lady. Her eyes seemed to dart as if to take in everything. Even at the young age of fourteen, she was surprisingly exacting in her dress and care of her tiny person. Just as the queen herself, she was elegantly gowned and sported the most fashionable new ruff. The embroidery on her shoes matched the underskirt that peeked from her slitted velvet gown. Most would have thought a person of such shape would not call attention to herself with such fine array. Yes, Mary Grey was both bright and bold.

Elizabeth inquired about the duchess's health and was told she was still ailing. It was more likely, the queen thought, Lord Adrian's backside was ailing, for she'd never believe a thing she heard about the double-dealing duchess again.

"How does my sister in your care?" Mary asked.

"You know Katherine even better than I. She will get on wherever she is but, I dare hope, not without my guidance."

Mary sighed. "I do envy her living here with you instead of with Her Grace."

"Yes, I know your mother can be trying, though I have heard some say that of me."

Mary smiled shyly, as if not to agree or disagree. Suddenly Elizabeth sensed a kindred soul. That was exactly the way she used to handle her father and later her sister so she would not make a mistake.

"Your Majesty, Thomas Keyes told me you did not forbid him to be my guard and escort upon occasion," she said to surprise the queen with her sudden shift of subject. "I am entirely grateful and beholden to you."

"Then, Mary, as long as we are here together, will you do me a favor in return?"

Another shy nod and gracious smile.

"I see that you are observant not only of your own pretty garments but of what you see around you."

"Your compliments mean a great deal, Your Majesty, for all your beauty and finery quite outdazzles us all. I am touched that you so much as noticed me."

Elizabeth liked Mary more and more, unlike her silly but insidious sister, but she knew she must remember the girl was the duchess's daughter and of Grey blood. And whatever was taking Cecil so long?

"I will ever notice you, Mary, and you may tell others in your family the same. But here is my request. On the day of my recognition progress do you recall what the others with you on the grounds at Arundel House were wearing and if their garments were smudged or dirtied? I am thinking particularly about men's garb and hats."

"And hats?" she repeated. "Do you want to hear of each of them?"

"Yes, Mary, beginning with John Harington's."

Elizabeth fled to her bedchamber the moment Mary Grey finished her recital of the finite facts of fashion. Let her think her queen rude or ill, she could not help it. She banged the door open, then closed it behind her.

Kat had been napping on the trundle bed

across the room, sitting up, fully dressed, her head against the wall, her mouth agape, snoring.

"Oh, lovey," she said, startled as she awoke, "I thought you were outside walking. I hope I didn't catch your cold, but I'm so tired and— What is it?" she said, struggling to her feet when Elizabeth sagged back against the door.

"I've been—I may have been played for a fool," Elizabeth whispered. She strode for the coffer in the corner where she'd kept the proofs of this murder discovery. Most of the gunpowder had gone in the blast to save Bett. Jenks had the firearm. But she still had the duchess's letter. And the hat.

"What is it?" Kat repeated, getting slowly to her feet. She came over to the window where Elizabeth dragged out the pillowcase with Penelope's blurred face and plucked from it the badger brown flat hat. She lifted the hat to window light and squinted sideways at the material. Yes, she might have seen and used the smears of cosmetics on it to learn some things, but she had missed this: two snags where a pin had been with something of weight on it.

"Did Ned and Meg recall something else about the making of the hat?" Kat asked. "Or are you going to look for more smears on it?"

"Fetch my jewel box, the ivory inlaid one."

Kat bent over another coffer. The many pieces of the queen's growing wardrobe were stored in separate rooms, but she kept all except the crown jewels close at hand.

"What do you want from it, Your Grace?"

"The whole box."

Kat brought it over and opened it, propping its weight against her bodice and one arm. Elizabeth knew exactly where the brooch she wanted was, but her hand was trembling so hard she dropped it back into the box at first.

"Are you ill, Your Grace?"

"I just talked to Mary Grey, and she recalled exactly what everyone wore in the gatehouse at Arundel. I should have asked her...all of them long ago."

She saw her brooch fitted the tiny snag holes perfectly. Her voice began to quaver. "Mary said Jack St. Maur's hose were smudged on the knees—not early in the day but later. Though he tried to keep them covered with his cloak, at her height she noticed when others might not have."

"Jack—not John?"

Elizabeth nodded jerkily. "Worse, he wore an old-fashioned brown cap but after the murder was bareheaded. He told her he'd flung it out the window in his excitement over seeing me pass by. And—and before they ate, she also recalled, he had a certain brooch on it that was missing later before the hat was lost. She mused he must have given it to Penelope."

Kat gasped. "But he had not?"

"No, damn him." She threw the hat down. "He gave it to me."

The queen had begun to shiver while she waited for Cecil to arrive. Thank God she had not allowed John to be questioned under duress yet, for she felt she was now stretched upon the Tower's rack.

John had confessed, so there must be some harmless explanation for the fact that Jack's hose were soiled. After all, he had told her he went up to view the body when the constable and coroner were there. Perhaps he had thrown himself to his knees beside it. She could check that truth with them, of course, but she'd tried to keep her part in this a secret from outsiders.

But the hat. The hat in the garret was Jack's. How had he left it behind a chest there? And Jack had given proof against John, and she'd believed him, heart and mind.

"I will have Cecil's head for this delay," she told Kat, pacing. "Whatever is keeping the man? If he doesn't come soon, I'll have to send my own guards to arrest Jack St. Maur. Then everything will get out about my playing constable in my own court."

She had fastened the brooch back on the hat now. Aye, she recalled Edward Seymour had said that Jack favored old styles. Did he favor the old style of lying to her, as his real father had?

Someone knocked on the door, and she darted for it, then stopped and motioned Kat to open it. The queen stood back, trying not to look overly distraught in front of Cecil, though he'd been her adviser and bulwark of strength through this. He'd help her know what to do.

But it was William Cecil's wife who stood there.

"What?" Elizabeth cried. "Mildred, where is your lord?"

"He left home in a great hurry, and I found a missive on his desk. And then I arrived here only to discover his man Philip had been killed."

"Killed? No, I saw him but a half hour ago. You are mistaken, or they would have told me."

"I take it his body was just found. Everyone's buzzing about it outside. They said they were going to inform you, but your guards were running hither and yon, looking for the perpetrator. Philip was killed after a brief scuffle, they say, for both sets of footprints were in the river mud."

The queen's heart thudded hard clear through her. "This day died in your lord's and in my service a loyal and good man," she pronounced, then had to clear her throat from threatening sobs. "But where is your lord, Mildred?" she asked. Still stunned, she took the letter from the woman when she dug it from her sleeve.

It was supposedly from herself, the queen, ordering Cecil to come quickly to the Arundel gatehouse through the Strand street door. The signature was similar to her own, but forged.

"Kat," she cried as she sat Mildred on the bench at the end of her bed, "fetch Ned, Meg, and Jenks. They are to meet me downstairs. Guard!" she shouted, but it was Thomas Keyes who was hovering just outside her door.

"The guards are in the hall and downstairs, madam," he explained. "They've thrown up a protective hedge around the grounds. It's odd, you know, how Lord Cecil's man was found."

"By the river, you mean? How was he killed?"

"His throat was cut. But the thing is, he wore a skirt right over his breeches, a woman's skirt. Pulled up it was too, like—"

"Like Penelope Whyte's," she said with him.

"I'll stay out here till Lord Dudley comes," he went on. "He's searching the stables, but said he'll stay with you till the killer is caught. Oh, and the dead man had a crude crown of plaited cords on his head too."

"A crown?" the queen heard Mildred Cecil mutter behind her. She had risen and come closer. "But that makes no sense."

Elizabeth thought her head would explode because it suddenly made sense to her. "Yes, guard the door, Thomas, but keep even Lord Dudley out," she commanded. "I feel ill from all this and am going to bed. Mildred, I must send you home, but I swear I shall find your lord and get him safely to you."

"But—from your bed?" Mildred questioned. "You said you were meeting people downstairs, Your Grace. My lord's been taken by some enemy, has he not? By who killed Philip Farmont? Are you saying it was the same man who murdered Lady Penelope Whyte?"

A woman after her own heart, the queen thought, but she had no time for this now. Jack must have known she'd been investigating the gatehouse and could command Cecil to meet her there. Now she must set her own trap before Jack could spring his.

"I will see my Lord Cecil is safe," she promised Mildred. "Go now, and let me care for things."

Though Mildred obeyed, Elizabeth rued her own vow. "It's Jack," Elizabeth whispered when the door closed to leave her with Kat. "All along, Jack, as if Tom, vengeful and furious, were back from the grave."

Kat clasped her hands and began to cry.

"Stop it, Kat. We are out of time. Jack killed Penelope and Philip, but they are only substitutes for what he wants to do to me."

Chapter The Eighteenth

"Lord Harry's missing just like Cecil," Jenks reported as he ran into their hastily called Privy Plot Council meeting.

" 'S blood, don't say that," Elizabeth insisted. "He can't have trapped them both."

No one was seated, but all stood about nervously. They had Nick, Gil, and Bett with them, for Elizabeth needed an extra pair of strong hands from Nick and someone to climb a tree to get them in the gatehouse window. All but Bett, Meg, and Kat were cloaked to go out, and Elizabeth had donned men's garb.

"Harry's probably just off on business," she went on, trying to assure herself Jack could not be heading a conspiracy and one of his cohorts had taken Harry. Surely Jack was not in league with Edward Seymour or the Suffolk clan. She might have made a mess, a royal mess, of investigating this so far, but she refused to have the others arrested until she had captured and questioned Jack.

She bent her knees while Kat pinned her netted hair up under her hat. At the last moment she had almost grabbed Jack's to wear as a challenge to him, but it might be needed as evidence in his trial. She waited but a moment until everyone stopped talking and turned to her, then explained what she knew.

"Jack St. Maur murdered both Penelope and Cecil's man?" Ned cried as the hubbub began again. "But you trusted him, Your Grace, and you said—"

"Silence! I know what I said, but there is no time left for—for—"

"Mea culpa?" Meg put in.

Elizabeth rounded on the girl. "Go upstairs, and take to my bed. I see I've got to get Cecil back to help me with the thinking around here since no one else is capable of it!"

"We shall be watching out the window for your return," Kat said, tugging at Meg's arm and motioning to Bett. "But you aren't going by barge since the river's up and—"

"I'm not going into the streets, as it will be dark soon."

"Lord Cecil and I were so grateful," Kat whispered to her alone, "that you didn't go yourself last time...for Bett. Must you go now?"

"Yes, I must," Elizabeth told her. "Cecil is indispensable to me, and Jack will not get away with murder—nor playing *me* for the fool." Her voice rose again. "I will stand far back and not go in with the men. I will take precautions, Kat."

"Are we to be ourselves or play a part?" Ned asked.

Elizabeth gritted her teeth and didn't answer him at first as she led the men downstairs. Besides, she didn't *have* answers anymore. She had been so certain, she had wanted it so badly, that Jack would somehow redeem Tom's lies and betrayals.

On the windy landing she spoke again. "We must all play the part of hero to stop these murders and save Cecil."

Ignoring the big royal barge, which was battened down at the landing, they rousted out two oarsmen and took the larger of the two working barges. Supposedly queen's men out to visit Lord Arundel, they had to shout to speak in the wind on the swift-running tide.

"But I think Lord Arundel's been sent for

to the palace, Master Jenks," one bargeman protested having to put out. "You know, with the man being kilt on the bank, the queen's advisers been sent for, that's what I heard."

"Did you see anything of the murder on the tidal bank?" Ned asked the man before Elizabeth could.

"Takin' our bread and beer, saw nothing. Say, you're not gonna make us set out farther from the bank or pull past Arundel, are you? This outgoin' tide's way high, and till it goes down, we'll never even row or sail us back."

Through the chatter Elizabeth stared out over the swirling rapids. Random chunks of ice and unrecognizable clumps of things lunged along at the mercy of the outgoing torrent. Sitting safe between Ned and Jenks, she clenched her gloved hands in her lap. Nick and Gil in the next seat blocked some of the wind from her. She was facing away from the bargemen so they couldn't get a glimpse under her hat and the hood of her cape. Her thoughts raced faster than the current.

I want it all destroyed, my father's place of treason—and my foster father's too, Jack had said so passionately today. Had he been referring to the gatehouse or all of Arundel? She recalled he had admitted he coveted his father's Sudeley Castle. *To tell true,* he had said, *I have inherited all of it, but only in my dreams.* She had told him dreams were good if they could keep from turning to nightmare. Did he covet her like that? And want to destroy what he could not have?

But now, as dusk descended, nightmare

loomed just across the narrowing stretch of savage river. She was risking herself but she knew she had to be present this time to save Cecil and outsmart Jack. And she had to know from his own mouth if he was working alone.

The barge bumped the landing hard, and the oarsmen scrambled to secure it. She poked Jenks in the ribs so he'd remember what she had told him to say here.

"One of you should remain with the barge and keep your eyes open," he ordered. "You, sirrah," he said to the older man, "wait at the end of the landing. If you see us coming, be prepared to cast off forthwith."

"I said," the man retorted defiantly, "only if the tide goes down and the current calms. This was a short trip with the tide and safe enough near the shore, but you'll need to be goin' back another way."

Elizabeth bit her lip to keep from boxing his ears for his insolence, however sound his advice. "Let's go," she whispered in her deepest voice. Ned, Jenks, Nick, and Gil followed her across the landing. "If we must return to Whitehall through the dark streets after we get Cecil back, we will. You are all armed to the teeth so nothing will go amiss."

From tree to tree they crept closer to the gatehouse, then each hid behind a statue in the event that Jack was watching or had others aiding him. Elizabeth believed this rebellion had been all his. No allies, probably not even his cousin Edward Seymour, who had no doubt been just as cozened and used as Penelope, as the queen herself. And she had thought Ned Topside a master actor. He could not hold a candle to the scenes Jack had played.

"Gil," she whispered, as they surveyed the too-familiar gatehouse in the wintry dusk, "do you think you can get on the roof and peer in the single top window on the street side? If he's on the top floor, he'll have to have it open to see out and allow light in."

The boy nodded.

"Then you will have to walk back across the roof and signal down to Nick what you have seen. If they are not on the third floor, you'll have to get back into the tree and look in the second story. We need to know how many men are inside. You know what Lord Cecil looks like. We must know if he is free or tied, how he is—is faring."

Another nod.

"Then the three of you," she went on in a stage whisper to her men, "will rush in while Gil stamps loudly on the roof. If that brings Lord Arundel's household out, Jenks will do the talking to them so they don't recognize me. Remember, there is probably still powder loose on the floor in the gatehouse. However, I am betting that Jack St. Maur has no desire to commit suicide, at least until he settles with me."

She knew she was talking too much, stalling.

Her voice quavered. She was terrified. This could not be happening.

Jenks and Ned drew their swords, and Nick a knife. Gil had already darted toward the gatehouse to go up a tree when Jenks said, "Remember, men, surprise is the best thing here, not a frontal assault."

"I don't want St. Maur hurt if he runs out unarmed," she said. "I want to question him—and make him pay for his crimes. And if he tries a shot—he does have several firearms and probably powder in there..."

Her voice again faltered as she realized she knew now the identity of the hooded man who had bought gunpowder at Smithfield cellar in a sleet storm. "If we are quick," she added, "he will not get off more than one shot." She didn't say it, but it must not be Cecil who took the bullet.

Jenks looked her way and whispered, "You just keep quiet and stay back here, Bess, unless we need to negotiate with the whoreson bastard." He shook his head. "My Lord Seymour's own son, I can't believe it."

She stayed behind the toga-clad marble statue while her men crept forward from tree to tree. Perhaps, she thought, they should have come in through the postern gate by boosting Gil over the fence again, but Jack might not think they would come by barge with the river up so high.

Freezing, shaking, she clung to the back of the icy statue. Gil disappeared over the top of the roof to look in the front window. Her men were plastered to tree trunks at a distance now, waiting for the boy's signals or some sign of Jack.

Someone pressed to her back, smashed her against the stone with a dagger point to the side of her neck. A leather-gloved hand clamped over her mouth. She tried to buck free but was held fast.

"I am so pleased you have come, my love."

A man whispering in a thick voice. His breath clouded the air beside her cheek. Jack. Surely Jack, but he sounded so like his father that her stomach cartwheeled.

"I was thinking," he went on, "how fetching you look in men's garb to show your legs. Did you ever dress that way for him when you led him on?"

She dared to look sideways at his face. Flushed. Almost demented. Her eyes darted toward her men, but they were intent on the gatehouse, and Gil was not in sight.

"They'll find Cecil there," he whispered. "At the very moment they rush in the match will burn down, and they'll blow sky high."

She gasped, but his hand clamped closer over her mouth and nose. Was this how Penelope felt? Pressed tight with her breath cut off?

She decided to use the rest of her strength to wrench free and scream a warning to her men. One knife cut—she would risk that.

But the glint of blade flashed at her, and the world went black.

Where was she? She was dizzy, drifting. Reality seeped back slowly with her throbbing head pain.

When she opened her eyes, the first thing she saw was her own long hair loose, sopped, under her face on the floor.

The floor of where?

Stunned, shoving her heavy hair back, she sat up in her own barge only to see the windows and walls of Arundel House slip away and disappear into the gray evening sky.

Then she remembered. Jack had taken her. She looked for blood on the floor, on her hands. He must have hit her but not cut her. She looked up, hoping to see her bargemen, but it was only her and Jack. When she moved her right leg, she felt, then saw, a leather thong holding her fast to an empty oarlock.

"The oarsmen?" he asked, rowing himself with a steady, ear-grating creak of the oars in their icy locks. "One man's in the river with a cut throat, the other fled for help."

At least, she thought, someone would surely chase them then.

"Ah," he went on, "you looked so restful like that. I craved to sample you fully, but we really had to be going."

She remembered his threat to blow up her men. "Did—did you hear a blast?" she asked, glancing back. "All that powder..."

"You didn't hear it?" Jack asked as his teeth flashed white against his ruddy face. "No doubt, it blew Cecil and the others to kingdom come. You'll be next if you don't do exactly as I tell you."

She felt sick. Cecil. Ned and Jenks and Nick. Young Gil.

She saw Jack had a firearm, a short matchlock, stuck in his belt, but its match looked yet unlighted. Then he had not left it behind to blow up the gatehouse. And out here on the river, she could hope it or his powder got wet. Damned touchy if it got wet, Robin had said.

She tried to accept the fact that because of her mistakes and stupidity, Cecil and the others had died in a gunpowder blast or fire. She craned around yet again but saw no light in the sky. Jack had lied before. That gave her hope, until her fuzzy brain grasped the fact that he had rowed them out into the river.

"What are you doing?" she cried. "Where are we going? Not out in the main current!"

He laughed. She realized she had never heard him laugh before, and her blood ran cold. He sounded just like his father.

"Didn't I tell you I wasn't one for backwaters, my queen? And what better way to put a great distance between us and those who will soon be our pursuers?"

"Then my men are safe at Arundel?"

"I refer to your guards at Whitehall when they realize you're gone, not that they'll know where to look. I really was expecting you to come after me with an armed force with your Lord Robin prancing on his steed, but you didn't even deem me worthy of that. I expected you to be in battle dress with an armor breast-plate. And I would have fired at you and not missed this time—breastplate and all." When he laughed again, the sound grated worse than the screech of the oarlocks.

She knew it could be hours before she was found missing. Do not panic, she told herself. Talk to this man, talk him back in.

"If," she began, lifting her quaking voice over the sound of the rushing current, "you are thinking to abduct or—"

"Elope. My father didn't manage it, but I shall."

"Or elope," she said, forcing herself to play along with him, "you are going to get us both killed when we get to the bridge, if not before. Where do you plan to put in?"

He laughed yet again. Was he drunk or demented?

"I am going to put in between your queenly virgin thighs and treat you the way my father should have for your desertion of him."

"You mean the way you treated Penelope? Was she with child by you?"

"I do regret that, for I would like an heir. So you knew Penny was pregnant? No wonder you are queen...so clever," he mocked. "But not clever enough to outsmart me."

For more than one reason she did not argue that. "As for your father, he is the one who led me on," she shouted. "He deserted—"

"I knew the Tudor temper would come calling," he yelled back. He let his oars drift and leaned back in his seat, as if taunting her with his nonchalance. Without some control the barge slowly began to spin and even tilt.

"You could have tried to save him when he had his trial," he accused, pointing a finger at her in his latest swift shift of mood. "Or you could simply have wed him when his wife died. That would have saved him, Tudor bitch."

Those last two words lashed across the face. When he called her that, she knew he did not intend to let her live. She'd thought perhaps she could offer making the loss of his father up to him by promising him much at court. But his hatred ran too deep. She'd have to find another way.

She sat up straighter, and taking her bearings when she saw Whitefriars go by, she glanced behind her, praying that someone would be pursuing. Except for the few craft clinging close to the banks, none was out as the high tide rushed back toward the Channel. Day was dying, and even the city streets looked deserted.

"I did love Tom Seymour, you know," she said. "It's only since you've come into my life that I've been able to admit that. What woman would not love him? I imagine he was like—"

"Like men felt toward Penelope?"

"I was going to say like you, Jack. Your foster mother adores you. I'm sure others— yes, Penelope—did too."

"Penny did, but she got in the way, rushing after me upstairs at the gatehouse and threatening to tell if I didn't run off with her. Hester I like. But you I adore."

"Have you harmed Hester? Did she come here to be with you?"

He only grinned and shrugged. Her blood ran icy again. If she plunged in the river, she would not feel a thing.

"Jack," she went on, forcing her words, "couldn't you tell that I too was falling for you?"

"I thought so, until you stepped back from my kiss today. As soon as we put in, you won't draw back."

She needed to get closer to seize that firearm. At least she could use it as a club.

"Jack," she said, steeling herself to flatter and cajole, "I'm amazed you planned all this alone."

He dared to lace his hands behind his head as if he basked in her praises. "Ah, my chance to have my cousin Edward arrested, assuming I would free you to give the order," he said, and snorted a laugh. "No, my queen, I could not be encumbered with him, his beloved Katherine, or that damned duchess. They'd hardly favor my possessing and impregnating you when they want you gone. They want their Katherine as queen and her and Edward's child—not a St. Maur bastard's—to reign after."

So he had worked alone. "I'm cold," she dared. "Why can't you hold me now?"

"I've lain in a lady's lap a lot of places, but not in a moving barge, though we could try that," he said flippantly before his voice darkened again. "I want, my queen, to hear you say that you are sorry you ruined my father's life—and mine."

"I never wanted—"

"Never wanted to, that's good." He hooted over the sound of the current. She saw they were turning again, passing old Bridewell Palace wharf. If only she could get him to put in there.

"When your father went to trial," she tried to explain, "I was afraid for my own life."

"Be afraid for it now!" he shouted. "You don't deserve to live! You should have stepped forward to say you loved him, that you wanted to wed him, save him."

"But I was not in command of things then. He tried to rebel against—to abduct my royal brother. It was Tom's own brother, the Lord Protector, not I who had him arrested and tried. Now, please, let's put in. I can use a strong, clever man like you to raise high in my court, and—"

"Liar. Liar!"

He lunged and pinned her flat to knock her breath away. Imagining poor Penelope, she gagged and dry-heaved, but nothing came up. If she could but get his firearm away now, just hit him with it, but it was still in his belt, pressing against her belly, making her sick....

"My father wanted to live," he muttered, "but it was you who went blithely on." His breath scalded her ear when she was so cold her teeth chattered. "He even fought for his life on the scaffold as they held him down and chopped his head off."

She gasped to see he had the knife again, held horizontally against her throat. His hand shook; the barge seemed to bounce.

"You deserve the same," he said as he forced her thighs apart and leaned even harder into her. With one hand he pinioned her wrists over her head and half knelt, half sat upon her legs to stem her kicking. His free hand came near her face, the knife edge pressed to her throat....

Penelope. But for the knife this was how he had killed Penelope.

Elizabeth fought to free one wrist. She grasped a bobbing oar bouncing in its oarlock just above his head. She'd never lift it, but if she could just slide it...

It hit him on the side of the head, a glancing blow. Enough, though, to make him drop the knife. She bucked against his leaden weight and kicked at him, then clawed his face. As her nails ripped flesh, she grunted and shuddered.

He reared up, covering one eye. Still on her back, then twisting to her side while he straddled her, she fought him for the knife. He held it again, but she kneed him hard in the groin, and he exploded off her.

His shift in weight made the turning barge sway even more. Both pairs of oars ripped away, sliding heavily out of their oarlocks. Jack was howling, doubled up, his palm pressed over his eye, but where was that knife now? When Elizabeth tried to scramble away from him, the thong around her ankle yanked her back.

295

As she pulled his firearm from his belt, she was horrified to see the spires of St. Paul's rotate by. The tide was rushing faster toward the stone piers of London Bridge. She tried to recall what they looked like. Wooden buffers, but could she leap upon them in this tilting ride? And with her foot fastened... Where was that knife?

When Jack reached for her again, hunkered on her knees, she wielded the firearm like a club. It hit his wrist. She heard bone crack. He screamed and swore.

"All right," he shouted, "you don't want to live with me, you can die with me! You should have died with him, had your body rotting under the stone floor of that Tower church with your mother's. I first saw you kneeling at her grave and thought I would sell my soul to have you kneel to me. Get on your knees to me now!"

She swung the makeshift club at him again, but her ankle thong tripped her and made her sprawl. Jack fastened a fist in her loose hair. He yanked her head back so she looked up into his bloodied face and eye. She dragged herself to her knees for leverage, then jammed both forearms into his throat.

She fell free again, on all fours. Darting glances back and aside, she could not get her bearings. Then the heights of the bridge loomed ahead. The sound was like a roaring waterfall.

"Jack, the rapids under the bridge. We're going to die!"

"Your fault," he shouted, gasping. "I said, get on your knees to me, or I'll throw you in now!" Again she struggled to her knees, but he screamed, "No, I'll kill you first!"

He lunged, but in that instant Elizabeth shoved at him, thigh high. She ducked, and he toppled over her. The barge tilted, and he rolled off her shoulder and, with a shout, over the side.

She screamed, but her voice, like Jack's bobbing head, was eaten by the roar and crest of rapids. She only stared after him in relief and shock but one moment, then, thanking God for that deliverance at least, turned her attention to the river.

She saw she'd have to ride it out. If the barge broke up, try to grab something. No oars left, no control.

She noticed Jack's knife where it had slid to the end of the barge. She had to lie flat to reach it with her ankle bound. Icy water washed in, smacking her. For all the good it might do her to be loose, she sawed through the thong. In the darkening dusk she could see the sprinkle of lights nearly overhead on the bridge. No one there would hear her over the cresting rapids.

The queen looked behind and to both sides one last time. She was going to die alone in the heart of her city and realm. She braced herself for the impact. Then, just ahead of her, in swift-moving silhouette, she saw another craft sucked toward the torrent.

She raised her hands to her mouth and screamed, "Help me!"

One man crouched in the craft while another rowed. A barge, smaller than this one. But then she saw the folly of her hope. If the two crafts collided before they were swept under the bridge, under the water, no one had a chance.

Elizabeth thought she heard a scream above the roar. Was it her own?

She gasped when the next turn of the foaming tidal pool bumped the barges together, then pulled them apart. Were those women in the other barge?

A huge wooden oar reached toward her, and she grabbed it. No, it was an angler's pole.

The queen squinted through flying spray. Bett. No, it couldn't be. She must have hit her head again. She was so shocked she almost let go, then remembered the small hook at the end of the pole. Bett had snagged draperies with it, but now...

Elizabeth fought to force it through the empty oarlock, then opened the hook to hold it there. Bett pulled the barges closer.

Elizabeth held hard. Beyond Bett, the one rowing—Meg!

"Edge us toward the bank!" Elizabeth commanded, but the wind and roar ripped her words away.

Silently she and Bett struggled to grapple the barges together. As long as she held on, could Meg keep both from the piers? Like a madwoman, she pulled her oars, her back bent to make her look headless.

"Yours is gonna go," Bett screamed. "Come over!"

The crash of Elizabeth's barge against the bridge threw her to the floor as water rolled in. Sopped, frozen, she held tight to an oarlock. Under her the floor crunched, then crumpled. A wall of water came at her, cold and black and white. She dragged herself toward Bett's pole, then her outstretched hand. But the pole was cracking. If she missed their barge, she'd follow Jack down, down into the maw of it.

"Jump!" Bett screamed.

Elizabeth fought to stand. The floor of the barge was split in two. She took a step back, then threw herself headlong. She smacked into Bett and took her down into the water on the floor of their barge. The grinding wood sounded like thunder.

"Help me row!" Meg shouted. "Row!"

Bett and the queen scrambled for the other set of oars, the paddle ends of them bouncing in the swirl of foam, but their handles lashed firm to the barge. Side by side, they bent and pulled, bent and pulled.

Too late. The barge hit the pier closest to the shore. The corner of it caved in with a deafening crunch.

Helping one another, shouting encouragements and commands, they scrambled out on the wooden starlings. They pulled Meg up last from the maelstrom and, shaking, huddled together while rapids boiled and seethed at their feet.

Pressing back against the stone support, Elizabeth sobbed with relief, but no one knew in all the blow and roar. What mistakes she'd made, trusting a man, getting caught in the past, looking back. Like finding rescuers on the river, she must look forward now, for surely God, and these brave, loyal women, had saved her to do better.

Huddled together, they heard shouts and looked up. As darkness fell, ropes and lanterns dangled from the bridge. Soon rescuers slid down to pull them to safety.

"Ben! Hey, don't drop her, Ben Wilton."

Meg gasped. Were they referring to her rescuer?

His arms hard around her, she dangled and spun in his embrace, lifted by the rope looped under his armpits. She began to tremble even more than from the cold. She shoved her sopping hair over her face. She might not recall him, but he would her. At least his lantern, like most of the others they had lowered, was doused by spray. She held her breath and prayed he would not know the river rat he pulled to safety was his long-lost wife.

Other hands reached for them and pulled them over the bridge railing and put them on solid ground. Her face in her hands, Meg collapsed between the other two rescued women. Surely he'd not spot her, nor know they had the queen here either. Her Grace looked like a boy indeed, a half-dead one, though with eyes blazing.

"Fetch us horses and dry clothes," the queen ordered, sputtering and hacking. "You'll be well paid."

"A girl," someone said, sounding shocked. "All of them girls, one in boy's garb."

"Your men are gonna beat you black and blue for this stunt!" someone else—it was Ben Wilton—shouted before the crowd evidently caught a glimpse of Elizabeth's fierce expression. They hopped to obey, though they obviously didn't have a clue who she was.

"Hey, Wilton," another man said, making Meg startle, "you and your shooter lads couldna made it through that either this time o' tide."

"Stupid light skirts," Meg heard Ben mutter before he spat and moved away. Only then did she partly uncover her face.

Bett got shakily to her feet when the queen stood, and Meg scrambled up. The queen hugged her and Bett at the same time, crushing them together. At least that hid all their faces while people scrambled to obey royal commands they didn't know were royal at all.

"You saved me, both of you," she told them, her voice raspy.

"Laws, I owed you a life," Bett said. "I'm just glad swinging by that rope just now meant deliverance and not death."

"And I owe you everything, so we're even," Meg whispered.

"How did you...find me?" the queen asked, releasing them with a huge sneeze. "You should have been with Kat."

"Eh, she'll skin us sure," Bett said, wringing out her sodden skirts.

"Not now, she won't," Elizabeth promised.

Bett spoke up again. "Meg said you'd left her behind one too many times and took the

301

men. That's why we sneaked out on the old woman."

"Be-ett," Meg protested.

"So," Bett went on, "we took the other barge on down to Arundel. Meg knew how to handle it, just along the banks, and I planned to use their grappling pole for an angler if'n Gil couldn't get you in the gatehouse. When we climbed out on the public wharf so you wouldn't spot us and get all riled, that man set off with you. We were ahead of you on the tide but didn't reckon the current could get that fast to keep us there, and we couldn't get near you till we almost hit the bridge."

"Pray God there was no explosion at Arundel," the queen said. "Did you hear or see the men?"

"Explosion?" Bett cried, losing all her cockiness.

"Not—not that we heard," Meg put in. "When we set out, the men were fine. They ran out looking for their barge, Cecil too, and then we couldn't go back for them. Ned and Jenks were both shouting something, but it was hard to hear."

"Probably," Bett said, smiling though her teeth still chattered, "God save the queen."

"I do thank God we're all safe and that Jack St. Maur was a liar till the end," the queen said, and sucked in a big breath like a sob when Meg had never seen her cry.

Someone swirled capes around them. "Horses sent for," a man said.

Huddled in her cape, Meg dared glance at

the men's faces, but Ben was not in sight. Her cold, clammy skin felt branded where he'd held her all the way up that rope. She wished she could thank him without his seeing her. The brackish river water had burned her eyes, and tears began again.

She sniffed hard and straightened her shoulders, then sneezed in harmony with the queen. Ben Wilton be damned, she was not going back to her old life, no more than Her Majesty was going back to being a prisoner or a princess. How else could an herb girl get to lord it over Ned Topside by playing the choicest part in the whole kingdom, standing in for the queen of England? Still, the next time Her Majesty took a notion to go off to solve some crime, Meg Milligrew would just stay warm and safe in the royal bed, and that was that.

Afterword

The queen's ornate gold gown, ermine-edged cape, and crown weighed her down, but she held her head high. As she left her state apartments, she smiled at Kat, who fell in behind her with the rest of the ladies in her entourage. Her Majesty even nodded today at Lady Katherine Grey. She walked smoothly, carefully, down to mount the crimson cloth litter on which she would be carried through the streets to open her first Parliament.

Robin held her hand and helped her up into the litter. She told herself she would not trust him or any man again, but she matched his intense gaze before she looked away. Despite it all, she did not think about Tom or Jack today because she was only looking forward now. No more letting her heart rule her head.

Guards and horsemen fell in behind and before her, making a great, echoing clatter in the narrow streets. They traversed the Strand, but in the opposite direction her recognition parade had taken a dozen days ago. She smiled broadly to see Ned and Meg waiting in the crowd as they had that day, so proud to see her.

Just beyond, Bett and Nick cheered and waved, looking almost like country gentry in the new garb she had bought them. It had cost her a pretty penny, that and their two rooms near the court, and the purse of sovereigns she'd sent to their rescuers at London Bridge.

Suddenly she saw Gil hanging like a monkey from a tree, waving, signaling with both hands. She could not read all his signs yet, but he silently shouted something like *Great and beautiful queen! Wise and lovely queen!*

She laughed so loud Robin turned back in his saddle and beamed at her. But she sobered as she recalled the drawing Gil had finally done for her of Jack's distorted face at the window behind the firearm as he shot at her. At least that drawing also meant that Gil was healing. And she was too.

Yet when the first drumroll began, she startled as if she'd heard a shot. Or had that reminded her of the roaring river that cut through her city and her kingdom? Even that had not done her in, and she vowed nothing ever would.

She glanced up as the twin-towered Abbey came into view. Much of the land between Whitehall and Westminster was still open fields and sheep pasturage, but a few houses and a tavern stood along the way. Bella had said she and John would be somewhere here, and she skimmed the clumps of people for them.

Elizabeth wanted them to know all was forgiven, even though they were going into a temporary exile from court at their country home. She understood how John had thought he was protecting his wife and only son with lies and self-sacrifice. Yet however much she wanted Bella with her, she had to take a stand that if someone lied to the Queen of England, he or she would be banished—or worse. Besides, she did not approve of husbands and wives being separated, except for Robin because it was said his wife did not like living at court.

She caught sight of the Haringtons, nodded, and waved. John was shouting something more than huzzahs. From watching Gil lately—she intended for him to be a court painter someday—she was certain she could read John's lips.

"Saw Hester in the crowd!" That's what he was shouting, and he was pointing too. Did the man actually think she would deign to crane her neck and search this throng of people for a face she would not recognize? She frowned up at him. "But she disappeared before—" he went on.

" 'S blood," Elizabeth muttered to herself as she was carried past, "they don't dare ask me to help look for her. I am through with all sorts of mysteries and such untoward pursuits."

Awaiting her in their formal array before the arched doorways of Westminster Hall stood Parliament's peers and the commons of the realm. Her council waited too. Cousin Harry smiled proudly, and Cecil looked as if he had something up his sleeve.

Before Robin or anyone else could help her, she rose, took up her scepter, and stepped down into the cheering crowd.

Author's Note

I can never quite decide whether to add notes to books in this series. They can be enlightening and interesting, but perhaps they tend to detract from the illusion of reality I strive for. However, I am tempted too far this time and must make a few asides. I only hope these facts will not give away future plots.

John and Isabella Harington did have a son of their own in 1561, and the queen stood as godmother to him. Although the Haringtons named him John after his father, the queen insisted on calling him Jack or Boy Jack all the years she knew him. She treated him with great affection. Some of the most insightful records of her reign come from his pen. The Dowager Duchess of Suffolk died the year after the events that conclude this book. Much happened between Katherine Grey and Edward Seymour, but I *will* keep that for another mystery. Mary Grey was the third Grey girl to act rashly. She wed Thomas Keyes without permission, and they were separated. Her stepfather, Adrian, took her in until she died in the 1570s.

And Robert Dudley? Look for his future in the forthcoming book, *The Darke Tower*.

Karen Harper

LT
M

Harper, Karen (Karen
S.)

The tidal poole.

$27.95

DATE			